POWDER RIVER POISON

Maureen Anne Meehan

www.maureenannemeehan.com
info@maureenannemeehan.com

Table of Contents

SPRING

Opening Statement

"'This is your worst nightmare. It's like being married to me. I can do what I want, when I want and how I want.' The evidence in this case, Ladies and Gentlemen of the jury, will show that those words were said to my client, Beth Anderson, on March 19, 2004, by Ace Sanders, the president of a company called MethZap, a defendant in this case," I said, pointing to the short, skinny, red-haired man sitting at the defense table. I glared at Ace Sanders for a moment or two, making sure that the jurors' eyes took hold of him. Just as the uncomfortable stares defined him, I smiled and nodded at Beth, a tall, dark-haired, green-eyed, former Wyoming rodeo queen, as beautiful at fifty as she was at twenty. Beth had a self-assured air about her–almost regal–and as the jury altered their gaze toward her, Beth reached over and grabbed her husband's left hand. Butch Anderson, a fifty-six-year-old man of medium build with graying, brown hair and bright blue eyes, patted Beth's hand and nodded to the jury in a rancher's fashion. Not his customary tip of the cowboy hat, but a gentleman's nod. Several members of the jury nodded back.

"Before I tell you more about this case, let me introduce myself. My name is Mary MacIntosh and I'm one of Butch and Beth Anderson's attorneys. My senior partner over there," I said, pointing toward the plaintiffs' table, "is my law partner, Andrew Harrison. Everyone calls him 'Harry' and he'll be talking to you over the course of this trial also." Harry deftly grinned at the jury with his broad smile. He's tall and fit with twinkling hazel eyes and dark hair. A former Stanford football star prior to becoming a successful lawyer, Harry was handsomely dressed in one of his high-end Italian business suits, which fit right in with the venerable courtroom decorum of posh cherry wood paneling, fancy millwork and trim, and the elaborately carved judge's bench. Federal courtrooms were notoriously more grandiose than state courts, and this Federal Building was no exception. Listed on the National Registry of Historic Places, it consisted of as a massive three-story Classical Revival style office building brocaded with unique red pressed brick.

"During voir dire when we asked you questions about your past, some of you indicated that you'd never served on a federal jury before. You might be nervous about your role in deciding justice for the Andersons. Well, I have to share a secret with you. I'm a little nervous today too. This is the first time that Harry has allowed me to give the opening statement at trial. I've earned his respect after working for him for ten years, and I hope to earn your respect also. Respect is important, and it is an underlying theme to this case. You see, Butch and Beth Anderson are here because their land was not treated with respect, and no matter how hard they tried to get MethZap to respect their land, MethZap not only refused to oblige, but deliberately and callously defaced the Anderson's land, livestock and livelihood.

"But let me back up a bit and give you some history about the Andersons. Many of you may know of Butch, as he is world-famous on the rodeo circuit." Many of the jurors nodded in Butch's direction, acknowledging his fame. Dressed in a brand new pair of Wrangler jeans, boots and a light blue, pressed, button-down dress shirt, Butch looked the part of the modern-day born-in-the-saddle cowboy. His face was weathered from a lifetime of being outdoors, but it still held the glow of sunshine. His light brown hair matched his thick mustache and his light blue eyes sparkled under the courtroom fluorescent lights. He looked strange to me without his cowboy hat, but he understood that courtroom decorum disallowed it.

I continued describing Butch to the jury. "Now that he is in his fifties, he can no longer withstand the aches and pains of being thrown from a horse, as many of you can relate. Butch used to travel all over the United States giving seminars and training classes on barrel racing and other rodeo maneuvers and that sort of thing. He was raised by a foster family in Montana, and when he met Beth, he fell in love with her and married her. After years of saving money from Butch's rodeo circuit and Beth's teaching salary, the Andersons found the perfect ranch outside Sheridan, out on the Powder River, and they poured their own blood, sweat and tears into fixing up the ranch and calling it home. They raised their two sons, Wyatt and Greg, on that ranch and they even built a stadium-sized arena on the property so that Butch could hold rodeo seminars at home, instead of traveling all over the place. He wanted to be near the things he loves–his family and his ranch.

"Not long after the Andersons put the finishing touches on their brand new arena, they got a call from a 'landman' named Rowdy Rodiger who told them that he worked for MethZap. He said that MethZap had purchased the mineral rights underlying their ranch. Rowdy told them that there was methane gas under the ranch and that MethZap intended to mine the gas and that the Andersons would be entitled to receive large royalty checks from the gas mined from underneath their property. MethZap assured the Andersons that the ranch would be returned to its pristine condition after the initial wells were drilled, and that MethZap would only come on to the ranch occasionally to make sure that the wells were working properly.

Now, let's be honest. Butch and Beth were not happy that MethZap had purchased the mineral rights beneath their ranch, but they understood from talking to their neighbors who were going through similar mining operations that there wasn't much they could do about it. Their neighbors encouraged Butch and Beth to get along as best as possible with MethZap so that MethZap would keep its promises about respecting the ranch and Butch's rodeo business.

"Unfortunately, MethZap didn't keep its word to the Andersons. The evidence will show that MethZap built roads all over the ranch and drove big rigs and other heavy equipment in the pastureland, tore out fences, mutilated the grassland, and scattered unnecessary pipes and paraphernalia everywhere. Cows escaped, sheep got entangled, goats ate everything in sight and horses broke legs and had to be put down. Sludge oozed from the well sites, and the smell of sulfur permeated their home. It was the Andersons' worst nightmare. Or so they thought."

I walked to the plaintiffs' table and took a sip of bottled water. I turned the plastic water bottle around in my hand and read the label, hoping the jury would focus on the purified water for a second. I sat the water bottle down next to a pitcher of water on the table and continued. "As it turns out, loose livestock was only the beginning of the nightmare. What happened next will shock your conscience . . . and may even make you think twice before you drink the next glass of tap water flowing from your kitchen faucet."

I walked back to the plaintiffs' table and picked up a cake that I'd brought with me to the courtroom that morning. I'd made the cake the night before. It was a round, double-decker cake frosted in chocolate -- perfectly symmetrical. I held the cake in my right hand and paraded it before the twelve jurors and continued. "As I grew up as a little girl, my mother taught me how to make a cake from scratch. She was the Betty Crocker-type and she never used a box recipe for anything. The three drawers near her stove held tin canisters that fit perfectly in each drawer. One of them was full of flour; one was sugar; and one was salt. When she made a cake, she would take sugar from the sugar container and flour from the flour container and put them in the bowl. Then she would a pinch of salt from the salt container. Her cakes always turned out perfectly, just like this one in front of you.

"But suppose I played a trick on her. Suppose I took those canisters out of the drawers and mixed all the salt and sugar together so that it was one conglomeration and put them back in the drawers. Suppose that my mom came into the kitchen to bake a cake and when she dipped out what she thought was a few cups of sugar, she was really dumping in a bunch of salty sugar."

I walked my perfect chocolate cake back over to the plaintiffs' table and set it down. Harry leaned over and picked up a second cake, which had been sitting on the floor behind Butch's chair, and handed it to me. This cake was flat and sloped so that the icing clumped on the plate. "This is how my mother's salty cake would have turned out. Now, my mom would have been perplexed as to why her cake was sloping and ugly. She would have thought that she had mismeasured some ingredient or had forgotten to add an ingredient. She would never guess that her cake was loaded with salt. But once she tasted it, she would know for certain what had happened. It would taste awful. It might even make her sick.

"Well, this is essentially what has happened on the Anderson ranch. You will hear expert testimony in this case that thousands of years of soil segregation out there in the Powder River Basin left this fertile land with very low salinity. You may think to yourself, *What does salt have to do with the land?* We will prove to you that having a low quantity of salt in the soil helps plants grow. That is why ranchers have prospered in this area for centuries, because we have low salinity in our soil. You can think of it as a cake with just the right amount of salt in it," I said, pointing to my beautiful cake.

"The evidence will show that MethZap mixed up the sugar and the salt tins on the Anderson ranch when drilling for methane gas back in 2004. They sucked up all the salt from deep within the earth and mixed it with the Andersons' topsoil. Now, the Andersons have a lop-sided, salty cake to feed their livestock with. The wheat doesn't grow. The animals don't graze," I said, pointing to the ugly cake. "But this isn't the worst of the Andersons' problems. No. See, it is possible to haul in thousands of cubic yards of new topsoil to make the grazing land good again. The land will never be the same, but MethZap could do the right thing and pay for the topsoil to be repaired. We will certainly be asking you, the jury, to make them pay for that. But there is something far worse than the salty topsoil.

"Ladies and Gentlemen, the evidence will show that in dredging the methane gas out from the bedrock beneath the Andersons' soil, MethZap pumped hundreds of thousands of gallons of salty water onto the rangeland, which inevitably flowed into the Powder River and its tributaries, Clear Creek and Piney Creek. The ecosystem has suffered greatly because no longer do these creeks exhibit high levels of biological, chemical and physical integrity. The cottonwood trees are dying, encroached by noxious weeds and salt cedar that are taking their place. The increased salt loading from MethZap has and will continue to kill off bald eagles, western wood peewees, great blue herons, deer, wild turkey, sage grouse, and other species.

"Worse yet, the salty water that was left sitting in big pools on the Andersons' property attracted mosquitoes—the kind that carry the West Nile virus. The evidence will show that one of Butch Anderson's prize colts died of West Nile virus last summer.

"The evidence will show that MethZap tried to cover up the salty soil by dumping extra fertilizer all over the ranch in hopes that this would fix the problem and help the grass grow back. Well, the fertilizer just made things worse. MethZap still denies that they put extra fertilizer on the ground, but we will prove to you that they did," I said, walking over to the plaintiffs' table. "See this black box," I said, pointing to a shoebox sitting on the edge of the table near Beth. "This box contains two plants." I held them up. "This one in my right hand was planted in uncontaminated soil from the Anderson ranch. This one," I said, holding up the plant in my left hand, "was planted in soil flushed by methane runoff and then fertilized by MethZap. I'm going to leave these two plants in this black box with the lid off during the course of this trial. These plants will receive the same amount of sunlight and water and will be placed in the window of the judge's chambers. During the closing argument at the end of the trial, you will see with your own eyes what happens to the plants and that this excess fertilizer, mixed with the toxic salty topsoil, created a condition called fertilizer toxicosis, which, some of you may know, can cause 'mad cow' disease. We will conduct an additional experiment with this soil near the end of trial, which will prove to you what happens to plants that try to survive in contaminated soil."

I walked over to the white board near the judge's podium and wrote down these words: *Destruction of Topsoil: Mad Cow Disease: Toxicosis: West Nile Virus: Dead Livestock: Contaminated Water.*

"There are things that have happened out on the Anderson ranch and the other class action plaintiffs' land that money can't replace. MethZap's big city lawyers will tell you that there is a value for these items, but we all understand why this is wrong. We've all had a pet that meant nearly as much to us as a human. We all have things that we hold near and dear to us–sentimental things that money can't replace. Most of us Wyomingites hold our pristine land dear to our hearts. Once the land is destroyed, what will we have left?

"All of this has been caused by a few government entities–the Bureau of Land Management and the Army Corps of Engineers, who are also defendants in this case, because they jointly have violated the Clean Water Act by negligently and wantonly issuing permits for coalbed methane operations in Wyoming. These unlawful permits that the Army Corps and the Bureau of Land Management have issued allow operators like MethZap to dump millions of gallons of polluted water into the Powder River and its tributaries. These permits do not consider the impact on landowners, ranchers and Wyoming's natural environment. Due to these unlawful permits, ranchers like the Andersons and the other class action members have had their lands flooded, their water rights eliminated and their fields poisoned by MethZap. And you, ladies and gentlemen, will be asked to make the defendants pay. If you don't, the water, like the dinosaurs, will be gone from Wyoming forever.

"This case is about respect. Respecting the spirit of the law. Respecting other people's land. Respecting the environment. During the course of this case, I urge you to think about the theme of our case often and ask yourselves, have Butch and Beth Anderson been treated with respect by MethZap? I think that you will come to the same conclusion that I have. MethZap has not treated the Andersons or the rest of the class of plaintiffs with respect."

# PREVIOUS SUMMER

Chapter 1

I'd met Butch Anderson a year ago when his stepson, Greg, introduced us. I'd been dating Greg for nearly three years since the *O'Connor* trial, a famous case that Harry and I defended some years ago that put Harry's name on the globe of hot-to-trot lawyers. Greg was the cameraman from CNN assigned to cover the trial, and it was love at first sight. Two years ago, Greg accepted a free-lance investigative reporting position with *National Geographic*. About the same time that Greg switched jobs, he brought me to northern Wyoming on a camping trip, which is when I met Butch and Beth. Greg is Beth's son from a previous marriage, but since Butch was a foster child himself, he welcomed Greg into his home like he was his own kin. Beth and Butch later had a son together, Wyatt, whom I had not yet met. Greg hinted that he and Wyatt were "different" and that they didn't enjoy each other's company much. I understood sibling rivalry all too well, so I never pushed Greg much for information about Wyatt. I was perfectly happy in love with Greg—a man who understood what it was like to lose a father at a young age, as I did, as well as how difficult it was to integrate into a new family. Greg seemed to understand every nuance of my feelings, and his openness and generosity in listening told me that he was the man with whom I wanted to spend the rest of my life. We talked often of getting married, but with our hectic schedules, it seemed like we didn't have time to iron out the details. Greg was on assignment in South America and I was busy packing my apartment in Jackson.

For a year, in an effort to expand our law practice, Harry had wanted me to open a satellite office of the firm elsewhere in Wyoming, although we weren't quite certain that we had enough business to justify the expansion. Recently, Harry and I had agreed that I would relocate to a community skirting the Powder River Basin so that I could be lead counsel in a new case he'd agreed to take. As I carefully wrapped framed photographs of my family and friends, I thought about what it was going to be like to move to the town where Greg grew up. I also wondered what it would be like to be in charge of a law office. I'd never been anyone's boss before, and I contemplated the responsibility of managing others. I hoped to hire people that I respected and who respected me.

From the moment Harry first started describing the case, I felt an uneasy sensation growing in my stomach. He told me that he'd received a call from a lawyer in Sheridan whom he'd known for a long time. Chance Baker called Harry and explained that he'd been handling a legal matter for Butch and Beth, but that the situation was heating up and it was outside the reach of his lawyering expertise. Chance and Harry went to law school together at Stanford some decades back, and Chance mainly represented landowners with oil and gas lease issues. He also served as lead counsel to the Powder River Basin Resource Council, helping community members protect and preserve their most valuable asset–land. Chance told Harry that it was Butch's idea to hire us. I assumed that Greg recommended me, and I was flattered. Chance explained the vastness of the case and the complexity of the issues involved, and suggested that I move from Jackson Hole to Sheridan for the duration of the lawsuit. The recommendation fit in nicely with Harry's plan to open a satellite office within the state, so Harry willingly offered to relocate me. And I willingly accepted. In all truthfulness, I wanted to move from Jackson.

Jackson Hole is one of the most beautiful places on the planet, in my opinion, and I loved living there. I enjoyed exploring the Teton Mountains and had met many nice people. However, Lela, my legal secretary, had been murdered there last year and after Lela's death, I needed a change of atmosphere. Also, I'd been working for Harry for nearly a decade in Jackson and it would be a great challenge to head up my own office. So, I packed my bags and drove my new Chevy Equinox over several mountain passes east of Jackson Hole until I ended up in the beautifully quaint western town of Sheridan.

Sheridan reminded me a lot of Jackson–nestled close to the Rocky Mountains and surrounded by picturesque beauty only glossy postcards capture. The downtown Main Street has more original late-nineteenth century and early twentieth-century buildings than any other community in Wyoming. Flanked by historic brick buildings that have withstood a few centuries of old-west style gunfights, Main Street today sports new facades worthy of modern-day latte shops, bookstores and western wear. The old and the new blended well and the spirit of the friendly people exuded the warmth and openness one might expect from a small town. But, small towns have a way of operating under a thick microscope, and large personalities that might go unnoticed in the city were front-stage performances here. I would meet some of the saltier townsfolk soon.

I can thank Chance Baker for what would turn out to be a thrill-ride through the torrents of debased landscape.

* * *

Butch Anderson and Chance Baker thought that the best way to introduce me to the issues of coalbed methane gas production in northern Wyoming was to attend a Powder River Basin Resource Council meeting, so we agreed to meet at the local library where the meeting was held. Butch recognized me immediately as I stepped out of my Chevy Equinox and waved me over in his direction.

"Howdy, Miss MacIntosh," Butch said, extending his right hand. "You are a tall drink of water, aren't you? Last time we met I think you were sitting down. You must be near five foot ten." I nodded and shook his hand. "And your hair was pulled back in a pony tail, I think. It looked brown then."

"Auburn. You saw me after three days of camping in the Cloud Peak Wilderness. I'm sure it was dirty!" Butch chuckled, exposing his large, yellowed teeth. I'd forgotten that we met Greg's folks *after* our camping trip. I'm sure I looked a little earthy then.

"Well, you clean up real nice. Real nice." He looked me up and down and nodded again before he led me toward the library entrance, where he opened the door. "I can honestly say that Greg has good taste in the ladies. You're downright pretty. And smart too. Just like my wife." Butch introduced me to several ranch folk as we settled into the crowd. As he chit-chatted and made small talk, I listened in on the conversations around me. Ranchers complained of the drought. Their wives complained of the methane company semi trucks speeding along rural highways. Environmentalists discussed their regrets about the saline wastewater laden with mineral toxins that had been pumped into huge containment pits. I meshed the conversations in my head, thinking of the irony that in a time of drought, water could be worthless.

Irony intrigued me. Like watching people order Big Macs with large fries and a small Diet Coke. Or spanking a child for hitting his playmate. A larger paradox occurred to me as I daydreamed and eavesdropped: environmentalists were teaming up with ranchers who, in previous years, had probably supported energy development in Wyoming as the best way to make jobs in the bucolic landscape befit with the boon and bust of energy development from coal mines. Life was like that. As a survival tactic, creatures aligned themselves with causes that suited their current needs.

Butch mingled through the crowd and I followed. It was early in the evening, about seven o'clock, and the sun was just beginning its descent behind the Big Horn Mountains. I glanced out the window onto Brooks Street. The warm summer sun cast long blue shadows from neighboring two-story brick buildings. The light in the room was fading a bit, but the conversation was heating up.

"I want to introduce you to Greg's best friend. I'm sure he's told you all about Sherman Todd," Butch said. I nodded as I spotted his long, curly blond hair bouncing around as he spoke with emphatic zeal. Sherman, a bleeding-heart liberal who lived on granola and yogurt, had been Greg's best friend since the first grade. I'd met him before and recognized him amongst a crowd of fellow tree-huggers, ranting and raving at the damage the methane gas developers were doing to the splendor of Wyoming's landscape. We joined his group as Sherman pounded on the podium in front of him, screaming of the "landwhores sucking the life out of Wyoming soil like She were one big-milked tit. They'll suck her and suck her until she runs dry, then leave the excrements of their project for the ranchers to deal with. That Superfund that the federal government set aside for toxic waste will be long gone and we Wyomingites will be left with pollution, effluence, toxic waste, smog, greenhouse gasses, and every other kind of contaminant known to man. I'd like to nuke every last one of them sumabitches." Sherman stepped away from the podium with wet eyes and a dry conviction that no matter what he said, the big money from the mineral stealers like MethZap would continue to pave the pockets of politicians. He probably sensed that his efforts and speeches would simply add to the toxic waste around him.

After Sherman's outcry, the meeting was called to order. One rancher after another took to the podium like an actor to the stage, professing his or her quandaries with coalbed methane plays on their land. Their words were runny, like egg whites sliding from the shell, as tears filled their eyes with each phrase. Yet, none seemed to lose their sense of humor. One man told of his experience. "I started to get methane in my water after they started drilling. Is that a coincidence? I think that common sense says no. We're all on wells out here in the Basin. Most folks are on water wells, unless you're in the subdivisions of town. In my well, the methane got so bad that the hose that I used for filling the horse tank with water would blow out of the tank unless I held on tight to it. And I can tell you one thing: You never wanted to flush the toilet while you were sitting on it." The group chuckled as the cowboy grew serious. "I know it sounds funny, and we must keep our sense of humor in life, but when the state officials told my wife not to light a match near the faucet, somehow it didn't seem so comical anymore."

An overweight lady stood in the back of the room. She was wearing an apron over her smock, as if she dropped by in the middle of fixing supper to tell her story. "The dreadful noise generated by a compressor station near my kitchen window was so loud that Ginnie, our black Labrador, was too frightened to go outside to do her business without a lot of coaxing. Now I don't know about you, but there ain't nothin' sadder than a dog afraid of takin' care of her own business." The crowd laughed, while the dog lovers in the audience nodded their heads.

We listened to story after story of fourth and fifth generation ranchers whose land was being destroyed. Their down-home wholesomeness, coupled with their lack of arrogance, made them genuinely believable and honorable. Of course, I was viewing them as probable witnesses in our case.

Not all of the attendees were against the methane gas development, and some were equally venomous in their outcry favoring productive use of land and the need for economic growth. A studious-looking man in a business suit stood to make his point. His nametag read: *Gardner Fox, President, Sheridan Chamber of Commerce.* "You people just don't get it, do you? Don't you remember the '80's, when half the coalmines around here were layin' off people and half of the blue-collar population didn't have jobs or medical insurance? We have to balance!" This, of course, started yet another round of shouting from both sides. By the time the meeting was adjourned, Sherman Todd looked like the blood vessels in his face were about to burst.

But as we filed out of the meeting, I noticed that the ranchers drove off in their brand-spanking new Chevy or GMC or Ford or Dodge pickup trucks. I mentioned it to Butch and he responded. "All them folks complain about the damage to their land, but they're the first in line to cash their royalty checks at the end of the month. Natives are downright embarrassed by their newfound riches around these parts. New log cabin homes are replacing the ranch houses of the past. I just don't know how to weigh up the mess we're in, Mary."

"Call me Mac."

"Mac seems like a sandwich or something. I prefer Mary," Butch said. As I climbed into his aging Chevy Silverado crew cab, I wanted to tell him that my dad called me Mary and that he died in a car accident when I was four and that I preferred that men call me Mac. But out of respect for him as a client and my boyfriend's stepfather, I kept my mouth shut and just nodded. I fastened my seatbelt and brushed the lint off my navy jacket, unsure as to the direction this lawsuit would take and unsure of the comfort I felt in representing Butch and Beth. As if Butch sensed my trepidation, he started up a conversation.

"I was talking to some of the folks at the meeting and they're glad that I'm suing MethZap. They think it's about time that someone stood up to them. We all agree that we have to be good stewards of the land and our ability to earn a living in the ranching business is being threatened by irresponsible oil and gas development. Some of them would like to join in on our lawsuit. Is that possible?"

"You mean like a class action?" I asked.

"I don't know what that is, but what I'm thinking is that we can all sue together, share the costs. Chance Baker told me that it was going take a good bundle of money to fight MethZap. Some of the ranchers you met tonight get fifty thousand dollars a month in royalties from the gas. I haven't seen a dime yet. So, I'm thinking that it might be good to have some other money involved."

"I'll have to talk to Harry about a class action. That would change the dynamics of this case quite a bit. But it might make sense." I paused for a moment to gather my thoughts. "Why don't we drive out to your ranch and take a look. How long before it gets dark?"

"Stays light in the summer pretty late. We've got plenty of time. Besides, Beth is anxious to see you again. It's been awhile."

* * *

Some of the most gorgeous plains country in Wyoming lies along U.S. 14, east of Sheridan, on the quiet scenic road that curves through mile after mile of ranchland and amber waves of winter wheat. The road meandered alongside cottonwood-bordered Clear Creek as we passed through small towns called Ucross and Clearmont and Leiter. After Leiter, we parted ways with Clear Creek and I noticed that I missed the ebb and flow of a river directing us. Twilight was setting in and the sky was fading from a purple-pink to a dark shade of blue, making it more and more difficult to see the beautiful purple lupine flowers that clustered near the banks of the river. About eight miles down the road, we came to a bridge with a sign reading, "Powder River." Butch took a hard right after the bridge. I looked back at the sinuous flow of water as we climbed through rugged hills and down a long green valley filled with fine ranches and modern homes.

In the tiny town of Arvada, we came to the first stop sign I'd seen since we'd left Sheridan. Butch beckoned the truck to his right through the intersection by tipping his hat and giving a one-fingered wave. I watched the beat-up Dodge drift by, reading the mass of bumper stickers pasted to the tailgate. "Honk if you're Horny." "Vehicle Protected by Smith and Wesson." "Save Your Horse–Ride a Cowgirl."

I allowed my eyes to wander to the right, catching the rays of sun illuminating the peaks of the Big Horn Mountains. The purple mountains were majestic in their own right. To me, they looked like an old cowboy lying down on his back at the end of a hard day's work. The peaks formed what looked like a cowboy hat, followed by a forehead, sharp nose, and a chiseled chin. I could understand why the Sioux Indians fought so hard to keep this country out of white hands. Butch must have read my mind.

"The Big Horns are imposing, aren't they? The Indians called Cloud Peak 'Ahsahta,' meaning 'The Big Horns,' after the Rocky Mountain bighorn sheep." I nodded with interest.

I smiled as I thought about my camping trip with Greg. He told me many campfire stories about growing up in the area and how well his stepfather knew the history of the land. "Greg told me that you know more about this part of the country than anyone."

"I don't know about that, but I sure love this place." Butch looked around for a moment and paused in thought. He was a handsome cowboy–the kind that could have posed for one of those Marlboro ads in his younger days. He knew the road like it was the back of his hand, hardly looking ahead as he maneuvered around each turn. "It's getting too dark to see anything on the ranch tonight. What'd ya say we stop by the ranch, pick up Beth and head to Spotted Horse for a steak dinner?"

I hesitated before answering, which caught Butch midstream. "Well, assuming you don't have other plans tonight, that is." I didn't have any plans worth keeping. I planned on unpacking boxes and feeding my cat, Ted. Ted and the boxes could wait a few hours. I'd moved to Sheridan less than a week ago and had only unpacked some clothes. My kitchen was a disaster still and I hadn't planned on cooking. "You're not one of those vegetarians, are you? 'Cuz it wouldn't surprise me in the least if you were -- being that you're Greg's gal and all. He takes that physical fitness stuff to an extreme. That boy was raised on beef. Don't know why he don't eat it anymore."

"I eat red meat. So does Greg."

"He didn't used to. Wyatt, his brother, gave him a real hard time about that one."

"From the way Greg describes it," I said, "Wyatt and Greg give each other a real hard time about most things."

"They're . . . well, let's just say that the two of them are so doggone different. Black and white. Night and day. Wyatt's a chip off the old block, if you know what I mean. Greg, . . . well, Greg is more like his *real* father," Butch said in a beseeching fashion, as we drove over the cattle guard and passed his horse arena. "Don't get me wrong. I love Greg like he was my own. Always have. He's just hard for me to get sometimes."

Butch pointed out the improvements he'd made to the place since the last time I was here. In the dim light, the red barn looked dark brown. He honked the horn as we pulled up to the ranch house. His black and white sheep dog came running in our direction and I could see Beth waving at us through the kitchen window.

As I jerked the handle of the pickup door, my purse dropped to the floorboard of Butch's truck, and so I bent over to pick up my purse. Suddenly, I heard a loud crack as the window of the passenger door shattered. Shards of glass scattered in every direction and I could feel the rush of cold air warn my cheeks of the danger. I felt my heart stop–then it started to pound again, in my throat, my wrists, my knees. The hair at the nape of my neck stood on end.

"Get down!" a voice yelled from behind the arena. I couldn't see who yelled my way, but I ducked down nevertheless. I crawled up on the seat of the truck like a turtle into its shell and pulled my knees to my chest. Butch grabbed his rifle from the rack in his truck and jammed bullets into chamber.

"Don't move," Butch said as he pushed my head down lower onto the bench seat of the truck.

"What's going on?" I whispered. He motioned for me to be quiet and snuck around to the front of the truck. I couldn't see what he was doing, but I heard voices. Beth was yelling at Butch, and another man's voice was yelling at Beth to get inside. I heard another loud crack, like a bolt of lightning striking at close range.

"Don't shoot in that direction Butch! You're going to scare Mocha!" Beth yelled at Butch and he yelled back, and I knew from the tones of their voices that there was a great deal of tension between them.

I looked at the other rifle on the gun rack in the back window of Butch's truck. I studied the inscription: *Remington 870 SPS-T*. The rifle was camouflage color and had markings like that of an oak tree. I studied the contour and shape of the rifle, wondering whether I'd know what to do with it if I had to load and fire it. Before I became a lawyer, I attended the police academy in Boulder, Colorado. The reason I left the academy was guns. I hated guns. I could fire a handgun if I had to, but I didn't have experience with hunting rifles. Either way, guns frightened me.

"It's okay," Butch said. "You can come out now. But come out my side." Not sure whether it was safe to do so, I slid under the steering wheel and crawled out of the truck as gracefully as I could in a skirt. I ran to the front of the truck trying desperately to see from where the shot was fired. I was in the police academy long enough to have extensive training on bullet trajectory and casing analysis. In fact, my expertise in forensic crime investigation had been one of the reasons Harry had hired me fresh out of law school. I scrambled to the passenger door window and peered through the hole that had perforated the glass. Based on the shatter pattern, I hypothesized that the perpetrator had fired at a fairly close range–say three hundred yards away. The .357 Mag. slug was lodged in the carapace of the garage door.

I instinctively reached for my cell phone and started to dial. "What are you doing?" Butch snapped.

"I'm calling the police."

"No cops. I ain't havin' a bunch of cops snoopin' around my ranch. Put the phone down."

"Someone just tried to kill us. I'm calling the police."

"I mean it, Mary. Put the phone down. This is my ranch and I refuse to subject myself or my family to interrogation. That sheriff would just love an opportunity to snoop around this place without a warrant. You are my lawyer. I insist that you not call the cops."

I was surprised by Butch's paranoia, but I was even more perplexed by his lack of concern about the gunshots. My hands were shaking and my adrenaline was still pumping hard, yet he seemed unreasonably calm. I had ten years of criminal defense under my belt and had seen my fair share of cop-haters. Butch didn't fit the bill of the typical cop-hater. He was a law abiding citizen and a respected businessman. *What did he have to hide?* Before I could finish dialing 9-1-1, Butch stammered, "I . . . I guess I should have told you–"

"You didn't tell her?" Beth hollered. "Butch–"

"I was meaning to. We just never got to the topic."

"What topic?" I asked.

"The topic of why Chance Baker backed off from being our lawyer."

Chapter 2

There's nothing like cold silence to make you feel ill at ease. Beth, with her obsidian hair pulled back in a ponytail and her emerald-green eyes sharpened by anger, stared at Butch in disbelief. A young man walked out from behind the arena, breaking the chill between husband and wife. I figured that he was the person who yelled at me to get down when the gunshot blasted through the truck window. I guessed that he was a little over six feet tall, as I watched him walk toward us with the confidence of a steed. His hair matched that of his mother, but his eyes were Alexandrite—a mixture of emerald and amber. I understood in an instant the strife of sibling rivalry. He pulled the leather glove off his right hand and extended it to me. "The name's Wyatt. You must be Miss MacIntosh." He had a surprisingly lovely, deep voice.

"Mac. Nice to meet you." I held his glance a second too long and sensed the redness of embarrassment emerging, like a scab pulled off too soon. I turned toward Butch, who had flipped on the outside lights and had started pulling the shards of glass from the truck window. "Why did Chance Baker quit representing you? Is there something that I should know about?" This was not a rhetorical question, of course. I knew that he owed me an explanation. However, Butch kept his back to me and continued his clean-up duties.

"No. It's a normal greeting in these parts to shoot at you when getting out of a truck," Wyatt said. "Makes you feel real welcome."

"Stop it, Wyatt," Beth said.

"You should have told her, Dad." Butch didn't respond. Instead, he methodically picked the glass out of the window and fetched a large push broom from the garage. Beth followed, whispering to him while gesticulating wildly, leaving me staring uncomfortably at Wyatt's boots. I felt guilty–like I'd just caused a marital fight. But my guilt was overridden by the fact that I'd just been shot at–and no one seemed to give it a whole lot of thought. Wyatt motioned for me to follow him to his truck. While Butch and Beth continued their standoff in the garage, Wyatt yelled to them, "We'll be in Spotted Horse."

* * *

The drive was short, but the weather changed dramatically in that small space of time. Large raindrops splashed on the windshield, interrupted only by blinding flashes of lightning. I was mesmerized by the sound of the raindrops as they splashed violently against the windshield of Wyatt's truck. I didn't feel like making small talk, and I wasn't sure how to approach the subject of why Chance Baker quit being the Andersons' lawyer, so I just watched intently as each spherical drop collapsed upon itself upon impact. As the splattered raindrops quickly streamed together forming tributaries of water across the windshield, Wyatt reached down and flipped on the wipers. My focus quickly changed to the speed of the wipers swishing back and forth. They made a scraping sound each time they swayed back in Wyatt's direction. As if he felt the need to talk over the annoying noise, he finally spoke up. "Did you know that lightning kills more people on the east coast but starts more fires in the west?" I didn't know. Wyatt continued to bridge the gap of silence. "And a bolt of lightning reaches fifty thousand degrees–five times hotter than the sun?" As we drove, the wind picked up and soon the rain was blowing sideways and the thunder boomed loudly in perfect timing with each bolt of lightning. The storm gained strength suddenly.

"This storm is getting severe!" I said.

Wyatt shrugged his shoulders and said, "Not technically 'severe.' A severe thunderstorm must have wind gusts of at least fifty-seven miles per hour. You can see that the rain is falling pretty straight most of the time. But it is a good one, I'll admit. Looks like we'll get a good inch of rain out of this one–and boy, do we need it. Drought is killing us. Six years without snow pack. Did you know that one inch of rain is about the same as five inches of snow? We didn't accumulate five inches of snow the entire winter. Never seen it so dry before. Maybe God is getting us back for sucking all the water out of the earth with this coalbed methane gas operation."

"You know a lot about weather."

"A rancher has to know a lot about weather. Weather has its own personality in Wyoming." We pulled into the parking lot of the Spotted Horse Saloon, which was a bar, café and grocery store combined in what might have been a barn at one time. "Did you know that this place was named after a Cheyenne Indian chief?" I didn't. In fact, the more I played the "did you know" game with Wyatt, the more I realized that I didn't know a whole lot of the things he knew. He was quite a trivia conversationalist, which was kind of a fun way to pass the time. After several "Silver Bullets," which was what he called the Coors Light beer that he ordered for us, I walked around the place, amused by the collection of old junk and historic photos that cloaked the walls. One sign in particular caught my eye:

> *May your horse never stumble, Your spurs never rust, Your*
> *guts never grumble, Your cinch never bust; May your boots*
> *never pinch, Your crops never fail, While you eat lots of beans,*
> *And stay out of jail.*

"Do you think your parents will show?" I asked after three beers in two hours. I kept looking at the door whenever it opened, expecting Butch and Beth to join us.

"Doubt it at this point. Probably havin' a rip-roaring fight. They're behind the eight ball with this methane gas play. Most of their ranching friends have made a bundle from it and don't care about the land anymore. Dad has lost business from having them trucks running all over the pastures, and he's afraid to speak out. But the ranch is being destroyed and those MethZap people won't listen to reason. Hell, we've tried everything with them. They just don't give a damn about the land and the livestock and the water."

"I was reading Chance's notes yesterday. Tell me about this Rowdy Rodiger character? Do you know him?"

"Know him? Hell, I went to school with him since he was knee high. He's a sneaky, sly, skinny, creepy little son-of-a-gun. A good argument for natural selection, if you ask me. Calls himself a 'landman' and hires himself out to methane gas operations as a 'facilitator' to the ranching community. The only thing that bastard facilitates is his wallet."

"So, you and Rowdy aren't high school buddies, I take it." I smiled at Wyatt sideways, unwinding with the help of the beer. I hadn't eaten much all day and the booze was going to my head. Wyatt reminded me of Greg in that he was a great conversationalist. Greg was worldly and better traveled and perhaps more 'book smart,' but Wyatt was interesting and charming and knew a lot about the environment. I intentionally hadn't asked about his relationship with Greg. I knew that they didn't get along that well, and I didn't want to alienate him.

"No. Rowdy and me aren't buddies. I think the little sawed off shit is who has been shooting at us."

"Shooting at *us*?"

"It's not the first time we've taken fire at the ranch. Chance Baker got shot at and damn near lost his left ear. That's why he quit. Dad's been shot at twice. And now, you," Wyatt said, as he pulled out a circular canister of Copenhagen and took a pinch of tobacco between his index finger and thumb. He shoved the tobacco under his lower lip and slid the can back into his jean pocket. Wyatt must have noticed the disgust on my face. "Never seen a guy chew before?"

"Yeah, I've seen lots of people chew. I tried it once in high school and immediately threw up. That stuff is awful. And it gives you cancer of the mouth. Not to mention gum recession and -"

"All right, mother. I get it." He grabbed a napkin from under my beer glass and spit the wad of chew into it. He wiped his teeth clean and tossed the napkin over the bar and into the garbage can. "Better?" he asked. I nodded.

"Why didn't your dad tell me about Chance? I think that's a pretty important detail when deciding to take a case, don't you? I mean, most lawyers think about whether they can win the case, whether they'll get paid, whether they have the expertise to handle it, things of that nature. We usually don't contemplate whether we'll be shot down in broad daylight."

"I don't know nothin' about why lawyers take cases. What I do know is that my dad didn't tell you because he didn't think that it was important. He didn't think it would scare you off either way because he says that you have guts–and that's why he chose you. He knows you won't back down. Although I have no idea why a pretty thing like you would get mixed up in this big ugly mess. If I were you, I'd head back to Jackson Hole where all them celebrity-types hang out. This ain't no place for you."

"I'm not going anywhere. I'm not going to be intimidated," I said, probably half-heartedly.

"My dad says you remind him of himself when he was younger. He's not named after Butch Cassidy for nothing."

"He's named after Butch Cassidy?"

"Hell, yes. His real name is William. His foster dad started calling him 'Butch' when he was a kid because he was fearless and wouldn't back down from nothing."

"I hate to admit this," I said, "but I never saw that Butch Cassidy movie, so I don't know that much about him."

"See, Butch Cassidy was born Robert Parker, but in the late 1800's, he met up with a Utah cattle rustler named Mike Cassidy. A strict Mormon upbringing didn't set well with young Robert Parker a/k/a Butch Cassidy, so Parker picked up a few of Mike Cassidy's tricks. They called him 'Butch' because he worked at a butcher shop before he robbed a bank in Telluride. After that, he went back to horse stealing in Wyoming. Now, my dad isn't a horse thief or nothing like that, but Butch Cassidy was sort of revered as a Robin Hood of sorts around these parts. He made good with politicians so that he could go about his cattle rustling business and legend has it that he never shied away from a challenge. He was shot at and put in jail and all sorts of things. He even holed himself up in the rocks south of here for a long time to avoid being caught. My dad's kind of like that. He's a survivor. And he thinks you are too."

"Well, I may be a survivor, but I don't get paid enough by Harry to get shot at on the job. Believe me, it's happened before. I told Harry that I needed a nice, civilized case. No more criminal law for me. Harry told me that this would be a great case for me—relatively easy to prove that MethZap breached the Surface Damage Agreement and easy to prove damages. This is supposed to be one of those 'open and shut' deals that I could probably get a good settlement before trial. No gunshots. No broken bones. No car chases. Just plain and simple litigation."

"Nothing in life is 'open and shut.' There's always something else happening on the sideline. Especially in this town. There's so much gossip around here that I can hardly tell the truth from the bullshit. That's why I live out here on the ranch. Not much action out here, but at least I know what the cows are thinking."

"What does Greg think of all of this?"

"Greg? Hell if I know. I never talk to the guy. You know more about him than I do."

"Well, he must talk to your dad sometimes. He must have encouraged your dad to hire me, right?"

"Wrong."

"Wrong? Of course he did."

"When was the last time you talked with my brother?"

"A few weeks ago, before I moved here. He was on assignment in New Orleans—some Mardi Gras thing. Then he had to go back to South America to wrap up some other story he'd been working on."

"That's interesting," Wyatt said, as he escorted me out of the Spotted Horse Saloon. The rain had stopped and the air smelled fresh and damp.

"Why?" I asked as I crawled into the cab of his pickup truck.

As he started the engine and threw it in reverse, he said, "Because I've seen Greg in Sheridan a few times during the last month hanging around with Sherman Todd."

Wyatt glanced at me as he made his comment, like a tennis player putting a little extra spin on his backhand, just to see how I'd handle it. I thought about it for a second. Greg traveled all around the world with his job, and it wouldn't be unusual for him to have a few days off, but he swore to me that he'd been working like a dog for the past month and that is why he hadn't had time to visit me in Jackson.

"I'm sure it's nothin'," Wyatt said. "Anyway, we have bigger problems to think over. Was that crazy Mrs. Becker at the meeting tonight?" I shrugged my shoulders. I didn't know who she was. "She's the one who's threatening to sue us for killing her kid."

"For *what?*"

"Dad didn't tell you about that one either?" I shook my head. This was getting scarier by the moment. "This crazy lady named Louise Becker had a ten-year-old son who was loony in the head just like her. Everyone knows it. The kid always went to one of those 'special' schools. Well, she's claimin' that her son ate beef from one of my cows and that it gave him 'mad cow' disease and that is why he was nutty and that it killed him. I never fed my cattle meat-bone meal or nothin' of the sort. She's full of malarkey, that lady, but now she's rantin' and ravin' all over town about it, scaring half the folks around here to death. I'm sure the lawsuit is on its way. Dad said that you'd probably be able to handle that too. If my cows have any kind of disease, it is because of the crappy water all over the ranch that's poisoning everything in its path. If she sues me for the mad cow, I'll cross-sue MethZap. How's that for crazy?"

Unfortunately, in the world of litigation, it sounded quite sane.

Chapter 3

The rain had let up and the crescent moon shown brightly in the clear night sky. I held my head out of Wyatt's window and looked at the stars as they twinkled in delight. My long auburn hair flapped in the wind, feeling free from the confines of lies and half-truths. Mad cow disease. Gunshots. Greg. My past few conversations with Greg rose in my mind like the tide, and a wave of betrayal washed over me. It wasn't the first time that he'd lied to me during the course of our three-year relationship, but the other untruths seemed innocuous. Everyone told fibs. Right? And Greg's fibs were usually because he was on a top-secret assignment and was forbidden from disclosing his whereabouts. I understood. Maybe that was happening again. I was willing to give Greg the benefit of the doubt.

"Awfully quiet over there. Cat got your tongue?" I hadn't noticed the dead air space. The white noise of the tires on the wet pavement, coupled with my thoughts about Greg, tuned everything else out. Wyatt had his left arm dangling over the steering wheel and his right arm was palm down on the seat next to me. I studied the lines and veins of his hand–thinking that they looked like tree roots and knowing that they told his story of ranch work. Greg's hands were soft and smooth.

"No. Just thinking."

Wyatt fiddled with the radio, trying to tune in a station. "Don't get much out here in the hills. The stations come in pretty good at the ranch. Umm. Well, how about telling me a little about you? Can't say that I know much more than the fact that you're a lawyer and Greg's girlfriend. Where you from?"

"I was raised in Boulder, Colorado. Harry hired me after law school, and I've been working for him in Jackson for the past ten years. He's like the father I never had, but he's tough as nails to work for sometimes. He's trained me well, but he expects a lot out of me."

"That's good. To expect a lot. Then you deliver a lot. Umm. What happened to your father, if you don't mind the intrusion?"

"He died in a car accident when I was four. It was snowing and he lost control. My mom remarried a man with two kids of his own pretty soon after my dad died, so I have one brother and two half-sisters. I don't see them much though. I work a lot."

"What do you do for fun?" Wyatt asked, as he reached into his back pocket and pulled out his can of chew. With his knee on the steering wheel, he took a pinch with his left hand. Before shoving it deep in his gum, he looked my way. He put the chew back in the can and tossed it up on the dashboard. "I know. I need to quit." I nodded.

"For fun? I love to travel. I've been on a few great trips with Greg over the last few years. I also love to run–I jog four miles every morning, rain or shine. I have this adorable tabby cat named Ted. He keeps me company. I like to read and play basketball and ski and hike. Anything outdoors, really. And you?"

"I like being outdoors. I like to hunt and fish and ride horses or motorcycles or snowmobiles. I like going fast. Want me to show you?" he asked, glancing at me sideways while downshifting his truck as we rounded the corner quickly. I shook my head. My father's death had curbed any desire for dicey driving. I told Wyatt about the times in high school when kids would speed or drive crazy and how I would scream my head off until they let me out of their car. He understood.

As we rumbled over the cattle guard toward the Anderson ranch, I remembered that I drove out with Butch and that my SUV was parked at the library in town. As if he read my thoughts, Wyatt said, "After a few beers, it's best you stay at the ranch tonight. Too many antelope and deer shootin' across the road at night. Mom or Dad can drive you into town in the morning. Anyway, I'm sure that Dad will want to make amends." I didn't argue. The beer had made me drowsy and I wasn't familiar with the road. Wyatt showed me to a spare bedroom and set me up with a clean washcloth before saying good night.

"I live in the guest house out back in case you need anything." He smiled and gave me a cowboy nod, lowering his head a bit and tipping his hat, and then quietly he slipped out the back door.

* * *

The next morning, Beth greeted me at the breakfast table with coffee, biscuits and gravy, and scrambled eggs. She was dressed in jeans and a light blue sweater and looked like she'd already spent part of the morning outdoors. "You can borrow some jeans and boots if you want to take a look around the ranch," Beth said. I agreed, trying to figure out how I was going to choke down this huge breakfast of fat-laden food. Normally, I got up and went for a run, then had coffee and fruit for breakfast afterwards. The calories and cholesterol in this single meal would put me over my daily intake. Nevertheless, I smiled and nibbled the best I could. After breakfast, she set me up in horseback riding attire and then shooed me out to the barn.

Butch was in the barn tying fancy knots with his rope. Two horses were saddled. I asked him what he was doing. "Hobby," he answered. "My foster father must a taught me to tie a hundred kind of knots. Used to practice under my desk at school. See, a rope is a cowboy's friend and in order to get acquainted properly with this kind of friend, a cowboy has to try out lots of different ways to tie knots–to find out which one works best for him."

"Which one works for you?" I asked, slightly puzzled by the topic. I wasn't sure whether Butch was serious.

"Depends on what I'm up to. The hackamore is probably what I use most out here on the ranch, but it's not my favorite to tie. I like the double round turn hitched knot a lot. It's tied by first making a running loop in the middle of the line. Next, take one end and pass it through the loop twice, like this." He showed me his loop. "See, the loop makes a round turn. Now give the other end an additional turn, or in other words, double the loop. Now the knot is complete." He threw me a coiled rope and suggested that I try it, but I could never have repeated the steps and have it come out looking like his knot. It was sort of like a yo-yo trick. Some people were good at it–others couldn't even "walk the dog." He showed me his old-fashioned double bow knot and the sliding monkey fist in loop, and finished his demonstration with his sliding blood knot noose.

"Ride much?" he asked, nodding at a beautiful horse decorated in white and brown spots.

"Not much, but I love horses. Is she gentle?"

"If she wants to be."

"What's her name?"

"Well, you're not gonna believe this, but my wife named her Mocha Cappuccino. It's her favorite drink. My wife's favorite drink, that is. Beth goes to town nearly every day for one. I just call her Mocha for short. She's a real charmer if she's in the mood. Have to tell you though, she is a bit moody." I walked under Mocha's neck and scratched her near the ears. She quickly flicked her ears back at me once and then set them straight again. She stomped her front foot and whinnied."

"She's straight with you. That's Mocha's sign that she'll take you for a ride."

"Her sign? I didn't know that horses give signs."

"Of course they do. All living creatures give signs. You just have to know what to look for. Go ahead. Mount her." Carefully, I slid back under Mocha's neck and put my left leg in the stirrup. I hopped twice and then swung my right leg up and over into the saddle. I took a deep breath and grabbed the reins. "You look nervous. Don't let her on to that. She needs to think that you're in control."

"I love horses but I've been afraid of them for a long time. When I was a teenager I had several bad experiences with horses, including being thrown off when I went to a dude ranch for summer camp."

"That was then. This is now. Take her out of the barn and gently nudge her into that pasture over there. She'll take you for a nice ride. I won't take us too close to the wells or compressors. She doesn't like them much."

Mocha started into a canter the minute we left the barn. "Whoa. Whoa." I wanted to slow her down, but she had a mind of her own. She followed Butch's horse closely as we charged into the green pasture. The grass smelled sweet and fresh and it graciously bowed with each step Mocha took. She stopped on occasion to nibble a few blades but quickly picked up her pace with a gentle nudge. The mountains were glittering a sapphire blue and were crowned by a clear turquoise sky. A few peaks were still crested with white caps of snow, but for the most part, the snow had melted by this spectacular July day. The wind was picking up a bit, and I noticed a low, brownish haze moving in near the foothills of the mountains. I pointed toward it.

"Seems too early for forest fires. What's that brown haze over there?"

"Pollution. From methane gas development, of course. Half the people around here are coming down with asthma from it. Pneumonia even. Contaminating the land wasn't enough. They had to go for the air too."

I could see that Butch was fixated on the methane gas. Since I was hired to talk about it with him, I took the bait. "Tell me about your relationship with MethZap. How did it develop?" I nudged Mocha to catch up to Butch's horse so that I could ride alongside him.

"At first, it was okay, I guess. I wasn't happy about the fact that they were fixin' to pump the gas out of my property, but I understood that there was really nothing I could do about it. So, Chance Baker helped me negotiate the terms of the surface damage agreement so that when the drilling was done they'd put my ranch back the way it was before they started the drilling. I was concerned about my fences and the roads they wanted to put in. We had a number of issues about that. And I was very concerned about the water.

"We'd had some things go wrong in terms of trash and cigarette butts and the methane workers going to the restroom on our ranch. There was no Port-a-Jons up there at first. And the mud. The mud was horrible. Damn near drove Beth to her grave. There were quite a few places where my fence had been destroyed. I was upset, and I talked with Rowdy Rodiger about it first, before we ever talked to an attorney. I just said, 'Listen, I don't know how things are where your employers are from, but you know that in this country if you tear out a man's fence, you ought to be man enough to call him up and at least apologize and tell him you're going to make it right.' So, Rowdy called up his boss and got permission to mend some fences. Of course, Rowdy didn't know a thing about tamping a fence or Budd-Eaton barbed wire, but I schooled him on it real fast. Hell's rope."

I gave Butch a quizzical glance. "What's hell's rope?"

"Barbed wire. I call it hell's rope. If you've ever had it tangled around your ankles while building a fence, you'd know what I'm talkin' about." I nodded at Butch, understanding his point. Without prompting, he continued talking. "So once we got straight on the fact that the fences were there to keep the livestock in certain pastures, he seemed to catch on."

We rode up a steep hill and Mocha again started to canter. I held on tight and let her do what she wanted. What she wanted was to beat Butch's horse to the top of the hill. When she crested the top of the plateau, she put on her brakes and nearly threw me over her neck as she stopped a few yards short of some kind of a hut.

"What is *that*?" I asked. I felt like I had landed on the moon. The jade-green hillside had turned into a russet and barren plateau. Copper and plastic pipes were strewn in every direction. L-shaped pipes jutted into the ground, flanked by meters and gauges hissing mysterious tunes. A few feet away were tan cylindrical huts bordered by indicators and conduits of unknown function. Further down the horizon, I saw a house-like structure with two antennae that stretched from its roof, making it look like a giant ant crawling toward us. The giant bug-creature hissed and groaned like a jet engine preparing for take-off. The land smelled like rotten eggs and appeared infertile–the only living things I could see were weeds. Dust clouds billowed with each step Mocha took. She reared back.

"This, Miss MacIntosh, is why you are here."

Butch deftly swung his leg over his horse and dismounted. He reached down and pulled a handful of weeds out at their roots. "I'm a cowboy, Miss Macintosh. I'm not a farmer. But I do know all about noxious weeds. I come from Montana, and they're a huge problem in Montana. In fact, the western part of Montana is gone. We do have weed problems here in Sheridan County. There are leafy spurge, beggar's lice, cockleburs. It affects your livestock, especially horses, because of the fact that in the summertime horses will stand head to tail, and they'll sort of swat flies for each other. And when they have burrs in their tails, that ends up getting in their eyes and then you have ulcers and you have blind horses, the whole nine yards. Because of that we have to have a weed-spraying program on the ranch. And all of those things are, you know, the scourge of the west. You got to stay caught up with it. So, anytime you disturb the surface, you are going to have weeds. There's no question. If you're wheat farming and you disturb the surface, you have to take care of weeds."

As far as I understood the case, the weeds were not a huge issue. But Butch was a cowboy at heart and it seemed like he wanted to make sure I understood that the weeds affected his business a good deal. "I take it that you didn't have any weeds before MethZap arrived on your property?

"No. I'm not saying that. Weeds are everywhere. Like I was just telling you, where I came from, we had a knapweed problem in Montana. Well, here it's leafy spurge. And unless you want to run goats on your place–that's about the only thing that'll eat leafy spurge–you gotta spray. So, every year I called Abby Rodson up at the weed board and she issued me my weed spray for the year for the ranch. Now, typically that would be around twelve to fifteen hundred bucks a year to do the whole ranch. At first it was quite a bit more, because the prior owner of the ranch hadn't done it for a long time. They controlled the weeds before I bought the ranch by overgrazing to where there was nothing left to eat but cottonwoods, and the animals would eat the weeds. But since I wanted grass to grow, I had to spray weeds to give the grass a chance. So, that's kind of what my program was. It's sort of like having a race, you know, in terms of controlling weeds. It's competition between weeds and grass."

He walked with his horse for a few hundred feet and Mocha followed along without much coaxing. He bent down and pulled more weeds from the earth and held them up for me to see. "Now, obviously, when MethZap first started drilling, we understood that the surface was going to be disturbed in terms of the weed race and that meant that as long as the reclamation of the land hadn't done happened, the weeds got out of the blocks first and were on their greedy way towards winning the race. So even if a fellow wasn't going to immediately do proper reclamation of the ground, the weeds needed to be controlled in the meantime so that at least when the reseeding started we all got a fair start on the deal. I don't know if that makes sense."

"Makes sense. So you had some weeds before MethZap, but they were under control. Now that MethZap has destroyed your land, the weeds are winning the race, right?"

"Right. The weeds have won. But as you can see," he said, pointing to the wellhead which was ticking like a time bomb, "I suppose those weeds are not my biggest problem." Butch grabbed his horse by the reins and led him over toward the compressor station. Mocha and I followed, but as we got closer, she was clearly uneasy by the loud sounds spewing from the ground. Butch pointed to a reservoir of water over the hillside that was overflowing its banks with a muddy, sudsy liquid that smelled like sulfur. "That, Miss MacIntosh, is my biggest concern. See, as it overflows, which happens too often to account for, that spill-off traverses its way down my ditch to the Powder River. The sludge is poison, I tell you. And it's filling up the Powder River with poison. The Powder catches up to a number of tributaries along the way. I can only imagine what it looks like at the mouth of Cottonwood Creek. These rivers and cricks and streams feed our livestock and all of the animals that live in nature: deer, antelope, sage grouse, prairie dogs, fox, peregrine falcons, trumpeter swans, owls, frogs, sturgeon chub. Some species are endangered. Think of what them environmentalists will say someday when they figure out that half of the indigenous creatures are extinct. The methane gas companies will be long gone by then. The government will turn to us ranchers and tell us to clean up the water and fix the hillsides. How we gonna do that? The damage will be done. Can't bring something back from extinction, right? Remember the dinosaurs?"

Butch tied his horse to a tree and walked toward the first dam.

"Have you been cited for contamination yet?" I asked.

"Cited? No. But, the Oil and Gas Commission said, 'You have to get those fixed, because that's a heck of a liability holding up that much water,' because once those—let's say those dams were full and they started to wash, boy, that would turn loose a lot of water down for Martha Stevenson, who lives down the Powder River from us–close near where Cottonwood Creek intersects the Powder. See, I have two stock reservoirs below them in other pastures, and one is big. Once all of that water would let loose, that's millions of gallons. It would wipe her out. So, the Oil and Gas Commission said, 'You got to fix this.' Problem is–problem is that I don't know how to fix it. MethZap says that they have the right to discharge the crap. They say they have government permission from the Bureau of Land Management and the Army Corps of Engineers. They say that all the mining laws say that they can discharge whatever they need to. How can that be?"

Butch leaned down and scooped up some dam water into his hands. "Do you really think that my livestock should drink this?" I knew it was a rhetorical question, but I shook my head nevertheless. He continued. "Do you think they should graze on the grass that grows from this? If any grass grows, that is. Do you think that Wyatt's cows should eat and drink this sludge and then be sold at the County Fair and put on the butcher block for the good people of Sheridan to eat next winter?"

"So, do you think that lady might have a case against Wyatt for her son dying of mad cow disease?"

"Crazy Mrs. Becker? Hell no. That woman is just lookin' for someone to blame for her kid being crazier than her. But, I'm not ruling out the possibility down the road. I'm downright scared that the cows'll get contaminated and someone'll blame us for it. Mad cow disease is a misnomer in these parts, if you ask me. I don't think it exists around here, but I'm sure someone as loony as she is might be able to convince some folks otherwise."

Butch kept going on and on with his monologue as we walked back to the horses. As we approached, Mocha was rearing up and whinnying wildly. Butch's horse was prancing around like he was standing on hot coals. Butch held up his left hand at me. "DON'T TAKE ANOTHER STEP!"

I stopped dead in my tracks and looked around. Butch unsnapped the holster on his belt and pulled out a Ruger .22 pistol. He jerked back the chamber and took aim. I heard a noise that sounded like "hdddddddddddddt, hdddddddddt" but I had no idea what was going on. I thought that he was going to shoot his horse by the looks of his aim.

"Stop!" I yelled. Butch pulled the trigger and a crack as loud as thunder discharged from the gun. Both horses reared up in fright.

"Rattlesnake." A one-word explanation was all it took. He walked over to the dead snake and scooped its bleeding carcass up with the barrel of his gun and flung it away from the horses. "Practically the only living creature I hate," he said as he turned and calmed the horses. Butch whispered in his horse's ear for a few seconds and then into Mocha's ear. Both horses looked as if they understood him perfectly. They stood calmly as he removed the hatchet from his belt and found the snake corpse in the grass. Butch raised the hatchet high in the air and then hammered it to the ground, slamming it into the snake's neck, decapitating the quivering creature. He dug a hole in the earth with the blunt side of the hatchet and buried the head of the snake so that no one could step on the venomous fangs. "Nuisance. And there are hundreds around here. Watch your step, if you please." I trailed him closely on horseback all over the ranch, now mindful of every little hole in the ground.

"Do you always pack a gun?" I asked, thinking about being shot at the night before.

"Pretty damn much. Hell, people look at you sideways if you don't. I remember one time when I was on the professional rodeo circuit; I was boarding a plane in Casper. It was close to hunting season in the fall and the security lady asked if my weapon had been checked and I told her that I didn't have a weapon with me. She looked at me and then looked at her supervisor and then asked for me to step aside. They practically did a full-cavity search before they let me board. I swear she didn't believe me. *Everyone* has a weapon in Wyoming. Well . . . almost everyone."

* * *

Butch showed me the damage MethZap had done and was continuing to do. He told me how his business had suffered from having MethZap on his property. Then he told me about the "Well from Hell."

"That's what all the drillers called it. It was a mess up there and very dangerous for my horses. The compressor station, it was a jumble, I tell you. Pipes and rubbish everywhere. Those are the kind of things that looked pretty dangerous for people to be around. That ties right into why I was upset about not being able to use my property. My horses are broke and they were scared when I rode up there near that compressor. And for whatever reason, that compressor wasn't working right. In town, at Hardee's restaurant, Wyatt overheard Rowdy Rodiger talkin' that MethZap was fixin' to explore other opportunities elsewhere in the area because the 'Well from Hell' was causing them too much trouble. Game over. He said that if they found another viable coal seam somewhere down river, that they might move on. Well, considering this, I realized that they might not be paying me any royalties for the drilling they'd done on my property, and they might leave it looking like hell. If that was the case, then I'd be in a heap of trouble because I wouldn't be able to run my rodeo clinics with all that mess on my property, and I wouldn't be getting no income from the royalties they promised."

"So what did you do?"

"I did what any man would do. I confronted them."

"And what happened?"

"MethZap promised me that they were going hold up their end of the deal and get the gas out from under my property, pay me the royalties, clean up their mess and then move on."

"Did you believe them?"

Butch looked around his land and then gave his mustache a slight tug. "Would you?" I wouldn't either. After listening to Butch describe all of the ways he tried to work things out with MethZap, I realized that this case was not going to settle easily. And if it wasn't going to settle easily, I might as well consider putting together a class action. If enough ranchers joined us in our pursuit, we might just get MethZap's attention. But class action lawsuits were very expensive. *That* would get Harry's attention. I would have to call him when I got back to my office.

As we rounded the corner back toward the barn, Mocha picked up her pace. Her cantor had earnest, and this time, I didn't try to slow her down because my thighs were aching so much from the ride that I couldn't wait to dismount. After settling the horses back in the stalls, I turned to Butch and thanked him for hiring me. "I'm honored that Greg recommended me to you," I said.

"Sorry to be the bearer of bad news, but Greg didn't recommend you. In fact, he'll be downright mad when he hears that I switched lawyers," Butch said as he reached down and patted his black and white Border collie. "This is Cody. She's the best herding dog I've ever owned. Hell, she's the best friend a cowboy could ask for." Cody looked up at Butch with adoring eyes, as if she understood his every word. I reached out to pet Cody, but he backed away a few inches.

"Why would Greg be mad if you changed lawyers?" I asked.

"It's a long, complicated story. I couldn't begin to tell it all to you in a day. What I can tell you is that Greg was so doggone set on having Chance Baker as our lawyer that it made me apprehensive, to be perfectly open with you. But it was Chance who wanted out. He hates death threats, being a tree-hugger and all. And even the tree-huggers in Wyoming carry guns."

"But that doesn't explain why Greg would be mad if you hired *me*. He knows what a good reputation Harry has. He saw us in action during the *O'Connor* trial. I don't understand what—"

"When this all started heating up," Butch said, "I asked Greg if he'd call you and talk about it. I wanted him to ask you a few questions about the mining laws and whether we had to let the MethZap folks have ingress privileges to our land. It irked me to no end that they could just buy the mineral rights *under* our property, but also have the legal right to use the *surface* of our property to get to them. It didn't make any sense to me. Greg knows a lot about the environment and that sort of thing, so I asked him to ask you about it. Now, I don't mean to be putting you down or anything, but Greg said that environmental law wasn't your expertise. I think that's the word he used. So, I didn't call you. But when Chance Baker told me that Harry was one of the best lawyers he'd ever known, then I gave Harry a call."

I fiddled with the thoughts going through my mind, trying not to take offense to the fact that Greg hadn't recommended me to Butch. In all honesty, environmental law was not our forte, but it seemed unfair of Greg to discourage his father from consulting with us. Harry had handled a fair number of cases that had environmental issues involved, and I'd told Greg about a number of them during a recent trip that he and I took to Central America. I knew that it wasn't worth obsessing over, but my feelings were pinched, nevertheless.

Still, the more I learned about Butch and Beth's case, the more enthusiastic I was about it. I couldn't wait to go through the rest of Chance Baker's files and figure out who to sue for what claims. It was at that moment I realized that I had become a partner in Harry's firm. I no longer just accepted the cases that were shuffled in my direction. I now was in the unique position of evaluating the case and deciding whether it made sense to proceed. I very much liked that feeling. I embraced the litigation, accepting its burdens and benefits. I was ready to take on the challenge of a new area of legal expertise and I hoped to learn a great deal from the process.

* * *

When Butch dropped me off at my car later that evening, I found a note on the windshield. It read:

> *Wastewater is not the only poison around here. Watch what*
> *you drink lawyer woman.*

The Sheriff, an overweight nonchalant fellow, listened patiently when I told him about the shooting on the Anderson ranch, but the sheriff didn't seem to think much of it. He said that he'd look into the incident and make a report. Worse, when I showed him the note, he shrugged his shoulders and even went so far as to suggest that it was some silly prank. I insisted that he send the note to the crime lab in Cheyenne for analysis. In a tone laden with sarcasm, he assured me that he'd "get right on it." I drove from my office parking lot to my apartment in complete silence. I couldn't bear to listen to music. I needed to be alone with my thoughts.

As I climbed the steps to my second-story apartment, I constantly looked over my shoulders, making sure that no one was following me. I quickly jammed my key into the lock and thrust myself into the darkness of my apartment. I reached with my left hand and flicked on the lights. When I saw that everything was how I left it that morning, I slammed the door behind me and clicked the deadbolt. Ted, my orange tiger cat, came running in my direction, mewing loudly for food. I hadn't fed him his customary can of wet food in twenty-four hours and he was not shy about protesting. I followed him to the laundry area and pulled open a can of Feline Feast, shaking the contents of the meshed meal into his round, blue bowl. Ted lapped at the juices first, and then took his time biting into the brown lump of cat food. All the while, he purred loudly, letting me know that there was little else that he needed to complete his day.

I slipped into my pajamas and washed my face before getting into my un-made bed. I patted Ted on the head and scratched his cheeks and reminded him that he was the one boy in my life that I could count on to love me no matter what. He seemed to understand me as he cuddled in closer. I fell asleep within seconds and dreamed vividly of being trapped in a den of rattlesnakes with no way out.

Chapter 4

"Do you have any idea how much money it takes to fund a class action, Mac?" Harry was not wild about the idea, apparently. I called him from my new satellite office located on the second floor of the Hallmark store on Main Street. Ted came with me to the office and took perch on the windowsill overlooking Brundage Avenue. The building was old and historic and would probably cost an arm and a leg to heat in the winter, but it was close to the courthouse and had a great view of the small-town happenings on the main drag through town. Sheridan was home to around fifteen thousand people and, typical to most small towns, was governed by generations of families and the gossip that tagged along with them. People were friendly and helpful by nature, and also ready and willing to fill you in on the scandal of the day over a drink at the famous Mint Bar.

"I'm going to have to hire staff, Harry. Why not try out a pool of paralegals during the class action lawsuit? The ones that shine can stay on after we win a nice big verdict."

"Or, they can help you pack after we lose our shirts when the big-city firms kick our butts. Hell, Mac, you're talking about fighting the big guns here. From what you tell me, we'll need to sue the Army Corps of Engineers, the Bureau of Land Management and, perhaps, local and state officials. Do you have any idea how many firms they'll hire? They'll paper us to death. Discovery alone will cost *at least* one hundred thousand. And think about the expert witnesses. They'll hire an expert for every little environmental nuisance known to man. We'll have to depose all of them plus we–"

"Slow down, Harry. You'll have another heart attack if you're not careful."

"Experts will cost another fifty grand and that just gets us to the trial. The trial will cost another–"

"Harry, listen to me–"

"The trial will cost another fifty to one hundred grand in fees, depending on how long it takes, so we're looking at about a quarter of a million bucks, Mac. You have that kind of dough sitting in your bank account? Now that you're a junior partner of this firm, you have to put up or–"

"Harry," I said, trying to not to crack up laughing. He was so hysterical about the idea that it was hard not to find humor in it. Or get mad. "It's only money." I knew that this would put him over the edge, and it was wrong of me, but I couldn't control myself anymore. I could picture the adrenaline heating up his blood. Before I let him blow his top, I continued, "I already have the money."

"You *what?*"

"I have fifty people who are willing to sign on as plaintiffs and put up five grand a piece. That'll get us to the trial. They all understand that they might have to put up another thousand or two if it goes all the way. And, I've met with Earthrich and a few other groups that fund environmental causes around here and they've all agreed to penny up. They've even volunteered to help with manning phone lines and press coverage issues. You know that this will be the talk of the town."

"Are you serious, Mac? Because if you're just messing with me, I'm going to be furious. This isn't a game and the ramifications of a class action lawsuit are very serious because the downside is–"

"I am serious. I think it is the only thing that makes sense. You should see the mess these methane gas developers have made up here. The landscape looks like the moon with a serious case of acne. There are things poking out of the ground every which way you look. The groundwater is a mess. I can't imagine what the long-term implications are. This area has been desecrated with a capital 'D.' MethZap is not going to settle with Butch and Beth. They'll offer them a pittance to do a surface cleanup of the ranch, but they'll never offer them money to make up for Butch's lost business and they'll never fix the water problem. They think that they can haul in a shitload of topsoil to cover up the mess and move on. Topsoil isn't going to do the trick, Harry. And Butch and Beth don't have the money to take this to trial. They are one of the few ranches where the methane royalties haven't paid off. Everyone around them is cashing big royalty checks every month, but the wells on the Andersons' ranch haven't produced. They can't afford a trial. But they can afford to pitch in—and they really feel like they are stewards of the land. Butch and Beth want all of the Powder River valley cleaned up, not just their ranch. So, it is a win-win."

"That's only if we win. What happens if we lose?" There was a considerable pause on both ends of the phone line. I'm an optimist. I rarely think of losing anything. I lost my "fear of failure" when my dad died. Harry was a Gloomy Gus—overly concerned about the downside potential. But, he had more life experience than I did, and certainly knew more about running a law practice. He promoted me to junior partner not long after we won the *O'Connor* case, and had helped me finance my way into the partnership. He bought me the Equinox (his son works at the Chevy dealership and got me a good deal) and gave me a stipend for the move to Sheridan. He was not stingy with his money, just conservative. And there's nothing wrong with a financial purist.

"If we lose, we lose big, Harry. Not only the potential money—we lose for the entire state of Wyoming. I don't think most of the people here understand what's happening to their water. They've been in a drought for years—you'd think they'd be more concerned about it than ever, but it seems like most of them don't appreciate the severity of the long-term pollution happening here."

"Is Chance behind the class action? Because when I talked with him recently, he thought that Butch and Beth had a decent case against MethZap, but he didn't mention anything about any other people wanting to sue. And he certainly didn't push me to sue any governmental agencies."

"Absolutely. Of course he is behind the class action. In fact, he's pushing for it. He said that the Powder River Basin Resource Council was considering filing a lawsuit against the government agencies for violating the Clean Water Act anyway, so this saves him the trouble. He had been consulting with Earthrich and a few other environmental groups about suing the government, so he thinks that if we combine the allegations, we can get a whole lot of folks' attention. He's even promised us money and manpower if we need it." I failed to mention that Chance couldn't wait to drop the case because he'd been shot at. I figured that Chance should have told Harry himself, being that they were old friends. The fact that Chance neglected this pregnant detail made me question his motives, but I decided to let it go for now. Perhaps my ego had the best of me because the idea of commandeering a lawsuit of this magnitude overshadowed my concern for safety.

"I'll have to come up there and co-chair it with you–you know that, right? You can't expect to tackle the big boys alone. I'll let you do some direct and some cross-examination, but you'll have to leave the summation to me. Agreed?" I knew it would come to this. I would, as usual, do all the backbreaking work getting ready for the big trial and Harry would swoop in at the last second and take center stage. I wanted nothing more than to do the opening and closing statements in a trial. Harry had never let me do either of them before. He'd let me do just about everything else, but not the fun part. I wanted to tell him to shove it, but I couldn't. He was my boss. And I needed him on my side.

"Agreed," I said, crossing my fingers behind my back. I was not going to give up on talking him into letting me give the opening statement. For now, it could wait.

"Send me a draft of the complaint when it's done."

"I'm emailing it to you now. It's twenty-eight pages long–sleek and to the point."

"You already *drafted* the class action lawsuit?

"Never hurts to be prepared, right? That's what my boss always tells me." I heard him let out a big sigh, then a low grumble of a laugh. I hung up the phone and sent the draft through the fax. As the pages churned through the machine, I dialed Greg's cell. I didn't expect him to answer, assuming that he was in the middle of a jungle somewhere in South America. When I heard his voice I was surprised.

"Are you on your cell?" Greg asked, his voice hoarse. "Can I call you back in a few hours? I'm in the middle of something right now."

"Sorry to have interrupted," I said. "Sure, call me back." The line went dead.

He called back later in the evening, apologizing for his curtness earlier. He said that he could only talk for a minute, apologizing again for his brevity. He blamed his sour mood on deadlines and the pressures of work and being separated for such long periods of time. Of course, I took this as a compliment that he missed me and quickly forgave him. Let's face it–at thirty-five, my internal clock was ticking louder by the day and I didn't want to blow another relationship with constant hair-splitting over who's right and wrong. And he said that he would be in town over the weekend to visit, so I wanted to part on good terms. Greg knew that I'd moved to Sheridan to open the satellite office, but I hadn't told him yet that I was representing Butch and Beth. It had been too long since I'd seen him and we had a lot of catching up to do.

* * *

"I'm emailing the draft complaint back now with my corrections," Harry said early the next morning. His customary seven o'clock call started my day rolling. Harry was an early bird and took it upon himself to ensure that anyone who worked for him got the worm as well. I learned quickly to get up with the sun and get my jogging in before I dashed to the office. He expected his associates to work long, hard hours, but he did so in a way that made me want to be better, stronger, smarter, more prepared. He joked that the best way to motivate is by fear, but in reality, he motivated by example. "Most of the corrections are minor. You did a good job." This was a big compliment from Harry. "The main question I have is why you plan to file this lawsuit in the state court in Sheridan? We're suing federal agencies. This will be removed to a federal court."

"I know it will," I said, cradling the phone in my right ear as I opened a can of cat food for Ted. He sprang from the office windowsill and lapped the oil from the top of the wet food. "I am hoping that the federal agencies will ask me to stipulate to a change of venue. It puts me in the bargaining position right off the bat. We can either consent to the change of venue, but stipulate to the Casper federal court instead of the Cheyenne federal court, or we can force them to file a motion to change the venue."

"Why waste your time? Why not just file it where you want it?"

"Because I've done a fair amount of research on the federal judges in Casper and Cheyenne, and there's one judge in Casper, Judge Bruce Laird, who would be best for our case. He's been on the bench for quite a while and he is very levelheaded in his rulings. In fact, he recently ruled against the Bureau of Land Management for issuing too many coal mining permits in the Gillette area."

"Why not just file it in Casper then?"

"Because we're not guaranteed to get Judge Laird as our presiding judge if we do that. I want to play a little 'judge poker' with the defense counsel. I'll stipulate to remove the case to federal court so long as they stipulate to Judge Laird. What do you think?"

"I think it might be a waste of time, but I don't see the harm in it. Also, you are not guaranteed to get Judge Laird, but it sounds like you've done your homework. Fine. But let me see the re-drafted complaint one more time before you file it. When do you think you can have it done?"

"In an hour. I intend to file it today."

"What's the hurry?"

"It's Friday. And it's Rodeo Weekend so everyone who's anyone will be at the Mint Bar tonight. I've made a friend down at *The Sheridan Press* who promises that she'll get it in the evening paper headline if I can have it filed by noon. Mint Bar gossip is fundamental for our case. I want it filed today so that I can find out the local spin on things after the townsfolk have a few drinks tonight at the rodeo. I'm told that this town really puts on a party for rodeo weekend and I figure that this is the best time to crash the local gossip chain."

"Don't get too caught up in the launch. I know how fun it is to cast the first stone, but don't forget that these agencies have a staff of lawyers and you are going to be inundated next week with paperwork and phone calls. Get some rest this weekend, 'cuz you're going to be earning your keep for the next year with this one. By the way, did all of the plaintiffs sign the retainer agreements?"

"Yes. All fifty of the signed agreements are in their respective files. We're ready to take 'em on."

"That's what you think, Mac. This is going to be one hell of a fight. I hope you're ready for it. You think you worked hard during the *O'Connor* trial? You're going to work twice as hard on this one. You won't see the light of day for the rest of the summer. And you can forget about Greg."

"He's already forgotten about me, it seems." There was a pause on the other end of the phone. Harry wasn't wild about Greg. He never said as much, but he'd hinted from time to time that something about Greg didn't sit square with him. I didn't pay much attention to it because Harry didn't like the boyfriend I had before Greg. I figured that it was his fatherly role not to approve of my boyfriends. "He's coming to town tonight though. We're going to the rodeo with Butch and Beth."

Chapter 5

"The Sheridan Wyo Rodeo is the world's largest one go-round rodeo," Butch said as we drove around town together running errands. After I filed the lawsuit with the County Clerk, Butch, Beth and I dropped off a conformed copy of the complaint at *The Sheridan Press*. Norma Roberts interviewed Butch for the evening headline.

"Word around town is that you're filing this lawsuit because MethZap didn't pull any gas from your property and you are mad because you aren't getting any royalty checks. Is this some kind of revenge lawsuit?" Norma shoved the tape recorder in Butch's face, wincing a bit with the burden of blindsiding Butch with a question she promised she wouldn't ask.

"Norma, I learnt real young that character is everything. I am not filing this lawsuit because I haven't received any royalty checks. I'm filing it because MethZap destroyed my property and has severely damaged the water surrounding my land. They didn't abide by their word and where I come from, a man's word is his moral fiber. Failing to keep your word means you are roughly the equivalent of a pile of cow shit. Or worse. At least cow shit has its uses."

"Can I quote you on that?" Norma asked with a smirk.

"You betcha," Butch said with a wink. He and Norma were old friends and I could tell from their banter that they shared mutual respect. She patted him on the back and wished Butch and Beth good luck as we left her office.

After the interview, Butch and Beth accompanied me back to my office, where I prepared the instructions to have the government agencies as well as MethZap served with the complaint. I changed into my 501 blue jeans, boots and a light sweater, and then we drove up Fifth Street and parked near the north gate of the fairgrounds.

Rodeo weekend in Sheridan consisted of three nights of hard-core partying, beginning on Thursday. Many of the hung-over patrons of Thursday's party marched through downtown Main Street on Friday morning for the annual Rodeo Parade. Children and parents lined the sidewalks with their lawn chairs, anxiously awaiting the fire truck loaded with clowns throwing handfuls of candy. Local high school marching bands did their best to play and march at the same time, all the while searching the bystanders for a glimpse of friends and relatives who'd come to watch. The Drum and Bugle Corps (a/k/a the Drunk and Bugle Corps) looked like General Custer on his last stand as they drummed and marched their way back to the Mint Bar. A variety of locals rushed the street with bed races and other foolishly fun events that kept the kids laughing. It was small-town Mayberry R.F.D. at its finest—cornerstone Americana gathering for a community celebration.

In the early evening, the Big Horn Mountains formed an impressive backdrop to the huge, white grandstands where the crowds gathered and watched the live action of bucking broncos, barrel racing and other roping events. I had never been to a rodeo and was excited to attend with Butch. He had agreed to do some of the radio commentary that evening, and was even scheduled to perform one of the skits with the clowns and a bucking bronco.

When we arrived at the fairgrounds, the carnival was in full swing. Teenagers were running free, comparing notes on how dizzy they were from the Zipper or the Tilt-A-Whirl or any number of other flashing rides. Young children begged parents for cotton candy, and carnies yelled from every direction, trying to get someone to throw a dart at a balloon or toss a ping-pong ball into a fish bowl. Butch stopped at the target shoot and scored one hundred percent by nailing every plastic duck that flew by. I tried my luck throwing darts at balloons and walked away with a cheap stuffed toy for Ted to rip apart. I kept looking at my watch, wondering where Greg was. He was flying into town on a private plane and was unsure of his arrival time. He planned to meet us in the grandstands.

We watched the barrel racers practicing in the arena. "Why are they wearing different color socks?" I asked.

"You're observant," Butch said. "Cowboys and cowgirls tend to be very superstitious people. The cowgirls wear different colored socks when barrel racing for good luck."

"Oh, Mac, you don't know the half of it," Beth cut in. "When Butch was in his rodeo days, you wouldn't have believed what he would and wouldn't do before a competition. For instance, he would never set his cowboy hat on the bed."

"Why?"

"Says that it is too close a connection with sleep and death. And the dangerous lifestyle of a cowboy. And he would *never* wear yellow in the arena because it is a cowardly color. And he always had to shave right before the rodeo. Don't ask me why. And he would never compete with change in his pocket."

"Why?"

"Because legend has it that if I competed with change in my pocket, that's all I'd win," Butch said. "See, real cowboys don't earn a salary. The only money I made back in those days is when I won. Here's another superstition. For luck, we always put our right foot in the stirrups first." I shrugged my shoulders at him, beckoning a reason. "This one goes back to Medieval Europe, I'm told. The theory goes that knights would mount from stands during jousts and would stick their feet in the right side stirrups first because the left side was considered bad or evil." Butch continued telling stories about cowboy superstitions as if he belonged to some secret fraternity.

As I listened, I spotted Greg climbing the steps in our direction. I hadn't seen him in about four weeks, and his hair was longer and his face looked leaner, but I would recognize his polished gray eyes anywhere. His blond hair curled up at his neck, drawing attention to his chiseled, tanned chin. He wore khaki shorts revealing his muscular legs and a pale blue collared shirt. His face seemed red as he took the steps two at a time. I noticed that he had something rolled up in his right hand.

I stood to give him a hug and a kiss. I missed him so much. Over the last month, I realized how much I needed him in my life. He was so good about calling and emailing and sending thoughtful notes and flowers that I'd almost come to expect daily contact. But with his recent trips to remote areas of Central and South America, I'd hardly heard from him and my loneliness had made my bones ache. I reached for him, but he pulled back with a sense of bitterness only betrayal knows.

"What the hell is this?" he demanded, thrusting a newspaper in Butch's face. Before Butch could respond, Greg continued. "And why is *she* involved? I thought Chance Baker was representing you. This is not how I -"

I shuddered inwardly at his tone of voice and said to myself, "*Don't cry. Don't cry.*" I fought hard to blink back my tears.

"Nice to see you too, Greg." Butch stood and gestured for Greg to sit down next to me. "I'd like to introduce you to Mary MacIntosh, our new lawyer and your former girlfriend." Butch's sarcasm did nothing to calm down Greg. Beth looked like a deer staring into headlights. She scrambled to intervene.

"Greg, please calm down. This is not something we've taken lightly. MethZap has refused to cooperate with us -"

"Bullshit. They did the reclamation promised," Greg said.

"Watch your tongue, young man. That's your mother you're talking to. You treat her with respect." Greg bit his lower lip like a shamed schoolboy and lowered himself into the seat next to me. Butch continued explaining in his typical calm tone. "They recontoured, you know, smoothed some topsoil over the well sites and sort of tidied it up a bit. And while it looked pretty good on the surface, it wouldn't even grow grass. Well, even on the roadways–you know, all of those roads that were supposed to be temporary, those now permanent dirt roads won't even grow weeds. Now, if a weed won't grow, there's a problem. So, MethZap smoothed over the ranch with topsoil, but even *that* topsoil is just like clay. We all know that clay doesn't grow anything. And sure as shit that salt ain't going to grow even a weed. The reservoirs are a filthy mess. It smells like a sewer out there. Trees continue to die. I haven't seen a sage grouse all summer. And I don't have anywhere to put the cows and run my clinics. So what I'm tryin' to tell you, son, is that they haven't done the reclamation promised."

"They seeded the entire ranch, dad. Not that I should care. Now that you've decided to give the ranch to Wyatt."

Give the ranch to Wyatt? I didn't know what Greg was saying. He'd never mentioned that Wyatt would inherit the ranch. *Was it because he was Butch's stepson?*

"Greg, they used an aerial sprayer to blast the ranch with seed. Sure, there was grass seed all over the ranch. Generally speaking, you kind of need to bury the seeds to get them to grow. The birds, I'm sure, appreciated it. But, that's about as far as the seeds went. Nothin' has grown, son. We tried to plant some of our own seed in the mares' pasture, but it didn't grow at all and -"

"So you sued MethZap, the BLM *and* the Army Corps of Engineers? What kind of fight are you looking for? Are you trying to go bankrupt here? Why would you agree to do this to my parents?" Greg said, pointing the newspaper at me.

I was taken aback by Greg's tone and accusation. He'd been the nearly picture-perfect boyfriend for the past two years. He called often, took me with him on fun vacations, and, more importantly, supported me emotionally after my legal secretary's horrific murder. I'd seen his confrontational side at work—but he'd never brought it into our relationship. I could feel Beth's discomfort as she shifted in her seat next to me. I cleared my throat and dug deep to find words.

"First of all, I'm completely baffled by your reaction to this. You're the biggest environmentalist I know. You've spent half your life fighting for environmental causes and now, when one is right under your nose, you back away like a timid fox, which isn't like you. Second, I'm not trying to bankrupt your parents, Greg. In fact, one of the goals of having a class action lawsuit is so that your parents don't have to foot the entire bill. It is going to be expensive, but we're prepared, and third—"

"Prepared? You're a rookie lawyer taking on the corporate giant." His words sliced into me like shrapnel into flesh. All the compliments he'd given me for the *O'Connor* trial and Lela's case were stripped away like old paint. It was so important for me to have a partner in life who respected me and treated me as his equal. His words hurt so deeply that I couldn't fight back.

"That's quite enough, Greg," Beth said. "No wonder you're still single."

As Greg loaded his arsenal for another verbal exchange, Wyatt walked up the grandstand wearing faded Wrangler jeans, a red short-sleeved shirt tight to the chest and a tan Stetson cowboy hat. His sparkling hazel eyes glittered under the old-fashioned lights overhead. Greg stood and squared off with Wyatt. Wyatt, still standing two steps down from us, took a giant step and looked down on Greg. The silence was deafening. Greg opened his mouth first, but Wyatt beat him to words. "Don't bother introducing me to Mac. We've already met." Wyatt grinned a devilish smile and tipped his hat in my direction. I felt my pulse race faster and my cheeks flush. Greg pinched up his face and puffed out his chest.

"I'm sure you have. You've never met a girlfriend of mine that you haven't tried to steal."

"Truth is, big brother, they're ready to leave the minute you open your mouth."

"Okay, boys. Let's not do this again," Beth said. She looked at her watch and then down into the arena. "Butch, you'd better go down there. It's time to get things started." Butch nodded and patted me on the shoulder.

"What you don't understand, Greg, is that Chance Baker backed down from representing us after he was shot at a few times. I don't suppose you know anything about that, do you?" Greg looked sideways at Butch like a wolf sensing the movement of an unprotected lamb, and then quickly averted his eyes back to the arena.

"I have no clue what you're talking about."

"Mary was shot at a few days ago out at the ranch. Obviously, someone doesn't want us to go after MethZap. The message is loud and clear. But no one is going to intimidate me into not doing the right thing. And

Mary, here, has the courage to stand up to them, don't you?" I nodded half-heartedly in Butch's direction. I wasn't sure if I had the courage to see it through. I hadn't told Butch about the threatening note on my car and in all honestly, I hadn't had time to digest the gunshot. It was surreal to me still. But what wasn't surreal was the lack of concern on Greg's face when he learned that I'd been shot at. Greg just stared at Butch. He didn't say a word. And as if he'd said his peace, Butch turned in Beth's direction and said, "You ladies going to be okay up here or should I send a referee?"

"I'm coming with you, dad. I told Blake that I'd tend the bulls tonight," Wyatt said.

"You mean bullies, don't you?" Greg said.

"If I stay away from you, that job will be taken care of. The bulls have better manners," Wyatt said as he started down the grandstand steps. "Hope to see you at the Mint later, Mac." With a wink and a shit-eating grin, as they say in Wyoming, he walked away.

Flanked by Greg's mom on my left and Greg on my right, I averted me eyes to the clowns in the arena. They were juggling bowling pins and teasing the bulls in their pens. One clown would unlatch the lock on a bull's pen and then tease it before jumping over to the safety of the grandstand. The unsuspecting clown, still juggling, turned around in time to see a bull charging at him at full speed. The children yelled to the clown to run, which he did, in time to escape being gouged. The analogy struck me. I was the clown in the arena juggling a boss, a client and a boyfriend, and I knew that I was about to be wounded. I was prepared for a fight with the MethZap lawyers and I expected the government lawyers would paper me to death. What I wasn't prepared for was Wyatt Anderson versus Greg Fisher. Two brothers with different fathers and different temperaments—but similar taste in women.

I heard Butch's voice bellowing over the loud speaker, announcing that the Indian Relay Race was about to begin. Each Indian had to race three separate horses three laps around the horse track while riding bareback. After each lap, each rider would have to switch to a new horse by jumping off one horse and on to the next horse. Many riders were bucked off during the transition and dragged around the track. The crowd roared with excitement as Butch whooped into the microphone. Wyatt was busy corralling the horses back into the chutes after they'd been ridden. Greg, all the while, sat with a scowl on his face, gleaming at his little brother. I thought about the exchange that had just taken place among Wyatt, Greg and Butch and wondered what Greg meant when he said that Butch and Beth had decided to give their ranch to Wyatt. I decided that it wasn't a good time to ask for clarification.

"Look out!" Beth yelled down to the arena. The crowd rose to its feet, screaming at Wyatt. In the noise and confusion, Wyatt turned toward the grandstands, trying to determine what the crowd was so excited about. What he couldn't see was a runaway horse which was barreling down on him. Wyatt had his back turned to the uncontrolled horse and had no idea what was about to hit him. The crowd made a collective yell as the horse grew closer, and then a collective grunt as Wyatt's body was hurled to the ground and trampled. Beth bolted from her seat and ran down the grandstand steps toward her son. Butch yanked his headset off his ears and sprang from the viewing tower. Greg, however, sat with a smirk, glaring at his half-brother who lay lifeless in the dirt in the center of the arena. I looked at Greg, ashamed of him for hating his brother–wondering what could have happened in their lives that could have created such disdain.

Chapter 6

Structure is what I know best. So much so, that chaos felt scratchy–like a wool sweater. When I was young, not long after my father died, my mom introduced structure into my life. We got up at the same time every day, ate breakfast and headed off to parochial school, where the nuns made sure that structure was a virtue not to be overlooked. We got home from school in time to have a light snack before doing homework, ate dinner and took a bath before bed. This routine never wavered–until my mother remarried a man with two daughters. Then chaos became the wool sweater I wore until I went to college. And now, settled in the mob of partying folks swaying in the middle of Main Street in front of the Mint Bar, my wool sweater was choking me off at the throat. Country music was blaring–folks singing ballads of love lost and times gone bad. People were dancing and singing and drinking more than their bladders could hold.

The Mint Bar was a narrow strip of property in mid-town Main Street. It was flanked on one side with an alley and on the other side with a retail store. It was a taxidermist's dream come true in that elk heads and moose heads and a number of other mammals were plastered to the walls, all bearing marbled eyes and fierce expressions as if the rest of their bodies would soon be bursting through the parapet. Patrons sat on burl wood benches and the fifty-foot, C-shaped bar looked weathered and worn. A rattlesnake skin that seemed to be a foot wide and about six feet long overlooked the bartender's cash register, which was ringing like a teenager's cell phone all night. The pool tables at the back end of the narrow bar were crowded with forty-year-old former high school friends who'd come back to their hometown on their annual drunken pilgrimage to reminisce. People laughed and drank to the good 'ol days and told stories full of half-truths.

Wyatt was among the patrons, sitting on a barstool with one arm in a sling and the other cradling a beer. Wyatt was lucky that he only received a glancing blow from the horse. His x-rays were negative for a brake, and the emergency room doctor confirmed that he's only suffered a sprain. Wyatt repeated his version of the rodeo accident with the horse, claiming that the animal was in worse shape than he was. He didn't seem to mind the attention that he was getting from the pretty ladies. Greg was visibly annoyed with Wyatt, and directed me outside.

I was surprised by how many people seemed to know me, despite the fact that I'd only been in town a few weeks. Many folks seemed genuinely concerned about the effect of methane gas extraction poisoning their land and were happy to see that someone was willing to do something about it. Perfect strangers approached me as I stood in the alleyway, flopping their arm around my shoulder in a sloppy drunk fashion and told me their life-long stories of growing up in Sheridan. I heard about branding cattle in the spring, water skiing in the summer, hunting in the fall, and snowmobiling in the winter. As the golden amber of beer and whiskey was sloshed down, the stories grew incessantly harder to follow, but what I understood from these people is that they loved where they lived and they didn't want the methane gas industry to wreck their hometown.

Greg and I watched the legendary butt-dart contest for a few minutes. Contestants had to hold a dart in their buttocks and navigate through an obstacle course. At the end of the obstacle course, they had to position their bottoms over a tiny shot glass and try to drop the dart into the shot glass. It was quite comical.

We danced to the country western band playing in the middle of Main Street in front of the bar, and quickly learned a few swing steps from Butch and Beth. Butch made the rounds, talking to the locals about his problem, and most of them agreed with him and showed support. However, there were a number of slurred-speaking numb knuckles that told me to mind my own business and get the hell out of town. Or else. After a number of what I considered idle threats, I convinced Greg that it was time to go home. Since we'd been apart for over a month, he readily agreed.

With soft music playing in the background, I lit a few candles in my apartment and asked Greg to sit and talk with me. I was upset by how he had treated me at the rodeo and I expected honest dialogue and an apology. He did apologize, claiming that Wyatt somehow got the best of him. He said that he was tired from long travel days and did not mean to be rude. I accepted his apology over a slow dance.

Patiently, Greg undressed me and with our arms around each other, we explored each other's bodies, until finally, when we could stand it no longer, got into bed.

* * *

The next morning, while wrapped in the softness of my comforter, Greg asked for aspirin with a coffee chaser. I set both on the nightstand before leaving for my morning run. While jogging through the streets of this sleepy town, I thought about the previous evening and what had happened between Wyatt and Greg at the rodeo.

To me, abusive behavior was as inevitable as a hole in an old pair of sweatpants. My stepfather was verbally abusive to my mother in an amazingly subtle way. His backhanded compliments were common. I remember my mother hosting a dinner party for some neighbor couples. One of the men complimented my mother on her cooking. And then another woman at the table complimented her on the décor of her home. My stepfather quickly chimed in with slurred speech, "Oh yes. Everyone *loves* Elizabeth MacIntosh . . . until they get to know her." The table grew quiet for a moment, and then my mother changed the subject—telling the guests about my stepfather's great accomplishments as an architect. As long as he was in the spotlight, our world orbed. If he wasn't the center of attention, the orbit of abuse resumed.

I decided years back to change from my mother's orbit and take on a new flight path: a nice boyfriend who would make a nice husband and a nice father to my children. Until last night, Greg had been my new astronaut—on a mission with a new flight plan that seemed to be taking me on a positive trajectory. But I'd never seen him in the company of his parents or his brother, and family, it seems, can either bring out the best or worst in a person. The scars of the past can run deep and I was afraid that the fissure between Greg, Wyatt and Butch might affect the lawsuit, which is what Harry had warned me about. "Don't represent family or friends in legal matters. It forces you to take a field trip from your head to your heart. And we all know what happens when a lawyer thinks with her heart," Harry said, half jokingly. I assured Harry that my relationship with Greg would not affect the lawsuit in any way. I was starting to second-guess myself.

"Wyatt said that he's seen you around town a few times in the last month with Sherman Todd," I said to Greg when I got back to my apartment.

"In the last month?" Greg asked, surprised. "I've been in New Orleans or South America. Can't be in two places at the same time." He slipped out of bed and put on his boxer shorts. "Wyatt probably just misspoke. He doesn't know what day it is most of the time. He lives on rancher's time. The day is as long as it needs to be to get the work done. Or maybe Wyatt was trying to stir the pot and make you think that I've been lying. I wouldn't put it past him."

I decided to drop it. Even thoughtful people have lapses in judgment, and I figured that Wyatt probably said it to bother me or to get back at Greg for something. There seemed to be a lot under the surface of their relationship and Greg had never seemed comfortable talking about it. I decided to make the most of the short time that I had with Greg and focus on us. With that simple attitude adjustment, the rest of the weekend with Greg was perfect in every other way—well, almost perfect. We had a great time hiking in the mountains and catching up. He was over-the-top apologetic about his behavior at the rodeo and he reassured me one hundred times that he was very proud of my lawyering skills and knew that I could successfully represent his parents. He reiterated several times that he didn't think that a class action lawsuit was a good idea and he was afraid of the money it would cost to see the case to trial. He was worried about the stress it would cause his parents. But he didn't want to dwell on it all weekend so he charmed me with his wit and his recent adventures on assignment in New Orleans with *National Geographic*. But despite the charm and the wit and the compliments, something felt different between us. I sensed distance along with a certain pull of caution, which I knew I would overanalyze.

* * *

Monday at my new office was unlike any other Monday morning I'd known. The phone was ringing off the hook and the new staff provided by the Powder River Basin Resource Council was eagerly fielding calls. The fax machine was churning out paper like water flowing over a dam. Megan, my new, perky, twenty-year-old assistant, handed me a stack of phone messages. One call, in particular, caught my attention. It was from Davis Dunne, MethZap's lead counsel, known throughout the state as a first-class bully of a lawyer. Courtroom dramatics were his stock-in-trade. I'd never met him in person, but had seen him interviewed on the courthouse steps after a big trial he had won. He was short and had a large balding spot that made his dark hair look like a clown's wig. He wore round frameless glasses that illuminated his beady eyes and he walked down the courthouse steps with his bubble butt sticking out. That was how I remembered him. I expected his call, and while I was prepared for his ritualistic animosity, I wasn't prepared for his profanity and threats, especially at eight in the morning.

"You are out of your fucking tree, Miss MacIntosh, filing this bullshit case against my client. And let me tell you something, my dear, you've picked a battle with the wrong guy. I've been working with Chance Baker for months trying to settle this dispute with Mr. and Mrs. Anderson. And how am I repaid? I'm blindsided with a class action. I've–"

"Mr. Dunne, I called your office last week to set up a last-ditch effort toward settlement and your associate told me to -"

"That's fucking irrelevant what my associate told you. For all I care, he told you he wanted to screw you. The point is that you filed a lawsuit alleging all sorts of ridiculous causes of action against my client and you are going to learn a little lawyering lesson from a pro. You don't even have ten years under your belt–or should I say, pantyhose–and experience is what it takes in federal court. Which is where this case is heading. Shows your ignorance right off the bat–filing this motherfucker in state court.

You're wet, Miss MacIntosh, and I'm going to use it to my full advantage. Are we clear?"

Before I could respond, the dial tone buzzed, so I slammed the phone down in protest. Davis Dunne was known as a Hummer-driving, abusive, recovering alcoholic. He had the feral instinct of a lion stalking prey. But I had instincts of my own. I thought of myself as a clever spider, spinning a web that could entrap him. Maybe it was time to use my experience with abusive behavior to my advantage. One thing that seemed to frustrate abusive people was extreme kindness. The other was extreme mockery. I'd have to pick my battles carefully. Just like my mother taught me to do.

* * *

After I hung up with Davis Dunne, Megan popped into my office full of vigor. Her bright blue eyes bulged with excitement as she tucked her shabby-chic hair behind her ears. "Guess what!" she said, waiting for me to respond. "The Sheriff is holding on line three. Should I tell him that you'll take the call?" I nodded, and then I picked up the line and made brief small talk.

"I'm calling you to tell you that I got the results back from the crime lab."

I had no idea what he was talking about. I figured that he had dialed an incorrect number. "Crime lab? For what?"

"That note that was on your car. You said that you wanted me to have it analyzed. Well, I did. And I got the results back."

I assumed that he'd tell me the results without prompting, but apparently I was wrong. After sufficient dead air space, I asked, "So, what are the results?"

"Whoever left you the note used a pencil to write it," the Sheriff said. Great. That meant our list of suspected included every elementary school kid in the county. "And he or she appears to be left handed." Okay, we were making slow progress narrowing down the suspects. "The person was wearing leather gloves and there's trace evidence of rope fibers on the paper."

"Rope? What kind of rope?"

"Sisal rope."

"Never heard of it. What kind of rope is it?

"It's a specialized type of rope used for roping a calf in a rodeo."

Chapter 7

The Sheriff agreed to send me a copy of the fiber analysis from the crime lab. I wanted to do some research of my own about sisal rope when I had the chance. It wouldn't happen anytime soon because Harry wanted me to do a videotaped interview of Butch–similar to a deposition–so that he could help me with the structure of the discovery phase of the lawsuit. Harry was stuck in Jackson in a medical malpractice trial and would not be able to be in Sheridan for a month. So I had my new paralegal, Pamela, purchase a tripod and digital recorder and we set up a mock deposition in our new conference room. Pamela, a single mom with short mousy-brown hair and stocky build, didn't seem to take much pride in her appearance, but she did seem to take a great deal of pride in her work. She was exactly what I needed.

As I prepared for Butch's mock deposition, I gave Pamela a research assignment on sisal rope. I told her it might be like trying to find a needle in a haystack. "Don't worry, Ms. MacIntosh," she said. "I have a five-year-old daughter who wanted a pink poodle piñata for her birthday party. I don't even know if they make pink poodle piñatas, and I'm sure that I couldn't afford one, but I was able to figure it out." I nodded, as if I understood what she was talking about. "After Butch's deposition, I'll go down to King's Saddlery where her daddy works and ask him about it. If anyone knows about ropes, it'd be my ex's boss." Again, I nodded, clueless but hopeful. Megan poked her head in my office and told me that we were ready to begin.

Butch sat across from me at our conference table and Beth sat by his side. My office budget only afforded me eight folding chairs and two card tables, so Megan purchased attractive floral lawn chair seat cushions at Wal-Mart so that we could withstand the rigors of sitting for a few hours of depositions. My mother, the interior decorator, would not have been impressed with the office décor. But she wasn't here, and I had more important things to worry about. In the remaining seats, I sequestered a few of the staff members to sit in on the interview so that Butch could get the feel of what it would be like when four or five other lawyers would be lying in wait to drill him with questions. We started with his childhood and how he became interested in horses.

"Well, I've been riding horses since I was a kid, going back to when my brother and I used to sneak into the pasture at night and ride the ponies bareback. But as far as the teaching of horsemanship and rodeo technique, I've been doing that since the 1980's."

"What was it that led you to get involved with horses in the first place?"

"Well, I went into a foster home when I was a teenager with a family that lived in Montana. And they didn't have much money, so my foster dad told me, he said, 'You need to learn two things if you're going to survive in these parts. You need to learn how to shoe a horse and how to ride a colt. If you learn that, you're at least going to be able to eat if you live in this part of the country. So that's kind of what got me started. And he was a cowboy, and really, a pretty good cowboy at that. He was kind of my hero, if you will. He was kind of what I wished my dad had been. I wanted to be just like him, so I started riding colts and young horses and trying to be a cowboy." Butch fiddled with his moustache through most of his answer. Before I asked him the next question, I motioned for him to put his right hand down on the table. He blushed a bit at this gesture—as if he'd been scolded before.

"Once you moved away from your foster parents as a young man, did you start right off the bat on the rodeo circuit?"

"No. I–I worked for some small cow outfits, and then I cowboyed for a while on a ranch near Bozeman—up there in the Gallatin River area. That's where I got to spend some time around my mentors. That really got me going with this kind of horsemanship and rodeoesque, if you will. I was there at that ranch for four or five years. With my foster dad, we worked with lots of horses. And in those days it was kind of–I don't know. I think you are probably more of a horse fighter than anything.

You just kind of tried to get by the best you could. We always loved the horses, but it was pretty rough. Kind of the old west way of doing it. And that's all anybody knew how to do in those days. And then, of course, that changed when I went to the Gallatin Ranch and started working with a horseman named Hunter Ray, and that's kind of where I really got my start in terms of what I do today."

"What's the difference between the things that you do today from the old west ways of dealing with a horse?"

"Well, it's—by now, twenty years later, and it's really quite a phenomenon. But the approach to working with horses is really a willing communication. Instead of punishing them, I set them up. I arrange for things to happen and allow my idea to become the horse's idea. So, it's kinda like raising kids. You create a learning and loving and safe environment for them to explore, and when they stack the blocks up just so, or they learn to trace their name in the dirt, you applaud them and make them think that they are the only one in the world who could have done it on their own like that. Well, that's how I train the horses and the rodeo cowboys who ride them. I set them up in an environment that presents a positive approach to learning. I don't whip them into obedience. I praise them for their proficiency."

"Sounds a little like horse voodoo." I wasn't trying to offend Butch, but I wanted to prepare him for what might be coming down the pike.

"I know you must think I'm a gasbag or bragger, but, honestly, it works. It's been working for decades. All living beings respond better to praise than criticism. You should try it." Pamela, my new paralegal chucked at this. Apparently, I'd been barking at her most of the morning as we were setting up. I nodded and winked at Butch, acknowledging his fatherly advice.

Without prompting, he continued. "I want you to understand that my life wasn't an instant success. After I left the Gallatin, I didn't have much money. I think I had only a roll of dimes in my pocket. And right outside my apartment was a pay phone on the wall besides a bar. So I got on the telephone, started calling, and before I ran out of dimes, I got a couple of colts to ride. But it was going to be—that meant at best it was going to be at least thirty days before I got any money at all. And for about two months, I lived on pancake mix, without syrup, I might add, and carrots from an old lady's garden. So, no, it wasn't an instant success. In fact, building up my business has been doggone slow. There were plenty of times where it was kinda looking like I was going to have to go back to cowboying for four hundred bucks a month. But gradually it built and grew into something to where I was busy and I was finally getting some work doing clinics for the rodeo circuit. But that meant that I was on the road most of the year following the circuit."

It was a warm July day and the air conditioner wasn't keeping up with the thermometer reading on the bank across the street. Megan had the great idea of making sun tea early in the morning and she entered the room with a pitcher of tea and eight plastic cups filled with ice. She offered Beth a drink first and then proceeded to pass the iced tea around. The coolness splashed against my throat and I immediately felt like the room had cooled off.

"Was that a difficult thing to manage as a young, single fellow?"

"Well, no. When I was single, well, I was on the road pretty much all the time, even when I wasn't doing rodeo clinics. If I wasn't on the road, I was hanging out at a ranch somewhere, somebody that I knew, kind of riding the grub line, because I didn't really have a whole lot. There wasn't nowhere to go home to except my foster mother, and I didn't want to wear out my welcome there riding the grub line at home."

"Did something change in your personal life at some point?"

"Yes. I got married in—'82." Butch looked over at Beth and she smiled, happy that he remembered. Beth looked beautiful, as always, with her dark hair pulled back with a colorful scarf that matched the pattern of her colorful skirt. Her white cotton blouse was unbuttoned in the shape of a 'v' deep enough to reveal a large turquoise pendant necklace. Her green eyes sparkled from the hue of the pendant as she gave Butch a sideways glance. She had the grace to appear cool even in the warmest of weather.

"She thought I was gonna mess up the date. I got married in '82 and Beth had a son already. Greg. So, immediately it seemed pretty important to come home. Then not long after that she got pregnant with Wyatt. My ranchman. And after that, I hated being gone. But backing it up a bit, before I got married to Beth, I had bought me a house up in the Bozeman area, or I guess I should say that me and the bank bought that little house. And I felt like I had a place of my own–some land. And after I married Beth right here in Sheridan, I took her and Greg back up there to Bozeman. They needed stability. They couldn't be traipsing all over Tarnation. You don't just drag your family all over with you. It don't work. So, we bought a little place."

"Did Beth help you out with the business?"

"Heck yes. It's no secret that she was Miss Wyo Rodeo. She's a hell of a horsewoman. And after the boys got up in years a bit, and when she got them in a saddle of their own, she started working with me on starting a ranch-based clinic. You know, one where people would come to me for rodeo training. So that I didn't have to go to them. We talked about doing a 30-day clinic–we thought that would be unique. We wanted to have them come to the ranch and give 'em a month of teachin' and working with the cattle in an arena and in the country–a more inclusive training experience. That was our dream. We wanted a big ranch and a big arena so that I could be home with the family and do what I'm best at. And she could help. That was our dream. See, being on the road is not very doggone glamorous. So the appeal to me was to still be able to teach and then be able to be on the ranch in that environment again. I missed that part of my cowboy living, you know."

"So why did you move to Wyoming? Why didn't you stay in Montana, where you were?"

"That's a very good question. The short answer is Hollywood."

Chapter 8

"Hollywood?"

"Hollywood. See, a few years back I had a bad horsing accident and I was nearly paralyzed. So, I decided that I had to make some changes. Beth and I decided to make good on our dream. But in the Bozeman area, all the movie stars moved in there and made the land to where it was so doggone expensive you couldn't afford to buy a piece of ground unless you really had a lot of money. So, the Powder River Basin was to me what the Bozeman area was when I was a kid. And Beth and I had done a few clinics in this area, since she had some good connections from her rodeo days. We had friends here, so it wasn't like we were moving to a totally strange place. So, we bought our current ranch in Arvada with the intention of doing the clinics on the ranch, once we built the arena and fixed the place up a bit."

"Was the ranch in good shape when you bought it?"

"The Crazy Woman? Heck no -"

"By 'The Crazy Woman,' you mean the name of your ranch, right? So the jury will understand what you are talking about." We obviously didn't have a jury around, but I wanted Butch to get used to what it would be like in court.

"Oh, yeah. That's the name of our ranch. Beth don't like it much, but that's the name it already had, and I guess it stuck. People like things to stay the same around here, and we sort of get that. So, we decided that if we told people that we bought The Crazy Woman, people from around these parts would know exactly what we were talking about. So, the name stuck."

"What did the ranch look like when you and Beth bought it?"

"The place was a dump when we bought it. That's why we could afford it. If you could see the pictures Beth took, you would be amazed how run down the place was. There were fences that had been broken down and were lying all over the place. Half of the posts were broken off. So, Wyatt and I took to tearing out old fences, which took a good part of a month just to get the old fences torn down. Some of them were just falling down. They wouldn't hold anything, which I suppose allowed them to run a few more head of livestock, since they were on the neighbors' all the time. The only fence I didn't replace was the one between me and Beatrice Betts' over near Wild Horse Creek. There were so many things to do, I knew I was years away from being able to start my clinic; but I got started anyway, with the building of the arena."

"Did you have to reconfigure the ranch when you installed new fencing for your clinics?

"You bet. I had to have certain pastures set off from one another, so Beth and I designed the ranch in a way that we thought would best suit my clinic needs. Then Wyatt and I did the building. It was a lot of work, I tell you. Have you ever tamped a fence post into the ground?" I shook my head, understanding that I would have to tell Butch that it wasn't customary to ask questions when being deposed. "Well, Wyatt and I tamped fence posts until our arms ached and–"

"What made your clinics unique?" I made a note to myself that I'd have to work on honing Butch's answers. He'd talk for hours about weeds and fences if we let him, and the jury would be lost. The case was about contamination. I knew that he was equally upset about the fences and the weeds and the pastureland, but he needed to be able to convey to the jury that the most crucial issue of the case was the groundwater pollution.

"We could work in the arena in the morning, get some basic skills established. Then in the afternoon, we'd go climbing up and down hills chasing cows, crashing through the brush and jumping the creek doing all the things that make a decent horse into a phenomenal horse. You can't expose your horses in your backyard to what I can out on the ranch. The real world to a horse. The horse needs to work the arena for sharp skills, but needs to work the countryside for the well-roundedness that my clinic uniquely provides. I work cattle out in the pasture; being able to move cattle; sort cattle; teaching how to rope and doctor cattle; getting the horse to watch a cow. You have to think of it this way; most people don't make a living riding horses. Doggone hard making a living riding horses, even if you are handy.

"And remember. To some of the people who attend my clinics–this was their vacation. I didn't want it to be boot camp. They come to Wyoming because Wyoming is a heck of a lot more appealing than some of the places they live. So it was about coming and seeing pretty country and being in Powder River country. And, after the clinic, some of the folks would head on over to Yellowstone, you know, and make a nice trip of it."

It wasn't the first time I'd noticed Butch putting the end of a key in his ear. He kept his keys on a ring attached to his right belt loop. He often unsnapped the keys and poked the short gold one into his right ear to scratch it. He was doing this now. On video. I motioned for him to put down his keys. As with his mustache twirling, he blushed at my gesture and set the keys down on the conference table. I resumed my line of questioning.

"Couldn't you just have done your clinics in the arena? Did the condition of the ranch really matter to your livelihood as far as the clinics went?"

"Well, you see, if you're educating a young horse and you spend all your time just asking them to turn and stop and change directions and back up and go forward, that can be a little bit like, well, you're drilling a horse; and they can get to hating you pretty quick just training them like that. Whereas when you're on a horse working cows, you're doing all of those athletic things but there's a purpose and a meaning and you're in that environment working a cow. You are teaching a horse how to control a cow and do all of these accurate movements that you would try to get them to do. But there's a reason for doing it, it becomes something that's not drudgery to the horse; in fact, it's real pleasing to the horse.

"But you just got to understand something about cows. Cows are not like the ones you ride on out front of Wal-Mart, where you just keep putting in quarters. There's a point to where a cow can get pretty savvy to what's going on. So, I talk a lot in my clinics about fresh cattle. See, now the general rule of thumb that I've formulated through my years of working cows is that for a ten-day clinic of around fifteen to seventeen students, you're going to need fifty to seventy-five head of cattle. If you were going to put on horse show and a cutting with the cows, you have to have three head of cattle per cutter per day. And that's the minimum. And to have cattle, you need land to pasture them. And to pasture them, you need grass to grow on your land–not weeds. Not soil filled up with salt. Not water full of sludge and saline runoff. See my problem here? It all works together. And if I tried to keep my cows in the area where there was no drilling, I'd run clean out of grass. If I tried fewer cattle, the clients weren't going to get a whole lot out of it once the cattle get gentle. They are done. They are sure nice to handle then, because you're not going to run any weight off them in the fall. But as far as to be able to effectively work your horse on them, well, that's all done then."

"What's 'cutting'?" I asked.

"When you teach a horse how to round up cattle, you teach the horse to cut the cow off, to redirect them."

I accepted Butch's answer. I was certain that there were a number of things that happen on a ranch that I wouldn't understand unless I saw them with my own eyes. Cutting could probably be included on this list. I decided to move forward. "Where did you keep your horses?

"Well, that was another problem. Can't keep 'em with the cows, for the love of Dixie. And you gotta keep the stud alone. Away from the mares. The colts have to be separate from the mares. That's the last place you want a young horse–with the mares. The stud is going to protect his territory. And, you know, the people are riding pretty fractious kind of horses. They are not well-broke horses, by any means, when they come to my clinic. That's why they are there. To learn to ride *their* horse.

"The other pasture had some of my geldings in it. When you ride out there with a group of young horses, a lot of times the loose horse gets to bucking and running and playing and kind of the pack mentality kicks in. The colts want to join in on the fun–but their new owners don't know how to keep 'em from the frolic. It wouldn't be so bad if everybody on the horses was really calm. They could probably support their horses enough to where they could ride out through that big group of horses. But due to their inexperience with their horse, they get afraid and kind of clamp down with their hands and legs and then the other horses tear off with their tails over their backs. There's just no way that you're going to ride in those pastures with those horses, especially in the stud pasture. So we needed to use the highway pasture to work out.

"I know I'm a long-winded fellow, in fact, Beth says that for a cowboy I sure talk a lot, but that's me. I like to explain things so folks understand. Maybe that's why horses get me. I'm patient. But to help you understand why I'm so upset with MethZap, I need you to see that they were using up half of my ranch with their drilling, and messing up the other half with their pipes and dams and salty soil, to the point where my horses couldn't pasture properly and my clinics couldn't run smoothly and it was just a big stinking mess. That's all. I don't know how else to explain it. Other than it was screwing up my dream."

"Explain what MethZap did to your land that was so objectionable." I had some of Butch's photographs blown up to the size of a poster. We would use these during deposition and trial, so I thought it might be good for Butch to get comfortable using diagrams when he talked.

"Well," Butch said, using his left hand to point at the blown-up diagram of his ranch. I noticed that his pinky finger was missing and I couldn't help but stare. "In this particular picture, I'm pointing here to the well sites that were pretty upsetting to me because of the fact that some of the wellheads were in terrible places; there were two pieces of barbed wire to protect the wellheads. That's what MethZap considered a fence. Two pieces of barbed wire. Now I don't care how good the barb is—it could be Budd-Eaton for all I know, it ain't strong enough to keep cattle out. And there were trenches, literally holes in the ground all over the damn place. Break a horse's leg in a half-minute. And the roads! The network of roads all over my property, making it scarred up like the roots of a tree. The beauty of a ranch is that there aren't roads clogging up the hillsides. But MethZap put roads wherever they damn well pleased. Right in the middle of my pastures. Those roads were so slick with that smelly, sulfur-laden sludge that you could hardly stand up on them, let alone be on a horse.

So with all of these obstacles that were out there and the garbage and the pipe laying all over the place, I don't know how you could have planned to ride to where you could have avoided it. Seriously. It was another link in the long chain of disappointments I had with MethZap."

"Couldn't you have avoided the areas where MethZap was operating?"

"Well, even if you didn't ride right up to the wellhead, the object itself is such a foreign thing for a horse to see, it looks so out of place. And a horse's only means of survival is flight, so they are very suspicious of things they are not familiar with. Just the sight of that wellhead from a distance could get somebody in a heck of a lot of trouble on a horse. Especially a young horse that they were trying to train. That was the purpose of my clinics, you know. To allow folks to learn their horses. Pastures and methane gas wellheads are not a good match for learning a horse. There was sludge leaking everywhere, which was slippery as snot. Couldn't let a horse step in that crap. Hell, it looked like my ranch had a terrible case of diarrhea."

"Why couldn't you downsize your operation enough to make it all work with the land that you had and the arena?"

"Oh, I tried all right. I tried real hard. But I know how things on a ranch work. See, yearlings are like kids. They see a hillside of disturbed dirt, and that's the first place they run off to. Every time. I couldn't cram the cattle in with the yearlings. And if I put the yearlings in my stallion pasture with my mares, those stallions can get real tough on yearlings. They're protective you know. They get downright aggressive, those old stallions. So, you couldn't possibly do that. I had no home for the cattle. I even tried to put 'em with the geldings in the big reservoir pasture. But we had a real prairie dog problem out there and MethZap had just flooded it with whatever sludgy water from the wells. In no time at all, the grass was dead. And so were a few geldings. A prized one at that." Butch's eyes welled up with tears. He grabbed Beth's hand and looked up for a moment. I asked him if he wanted to take a break, but he declined. He had a story to tell and the rest of us in the room were hanging on his words like a cat on a rope. "See, a gelding is like a child to me. It's a chance at life. And because of that putrid water and the mess out there, I let one die. I let one die."

Butch's tears turned into a flood rolling down his cheeks. I would have given anything for a jury to have seen this tender moment. This was a real man who truly loved his horses and nature. He could not have told a more heart-felt story. He would make a great witness, I decided. He was long-winded, but thoughtful, and his genuineness made it clear that he loved the land. But I knew that one great witness wasn't enough to prove our case. We needed good experts to prove the damages the Andersons suffered as a result of MethZap's mess. I continued to tape Butch, assuming the mock-nature of this deposition.

"Very shortly, Mr. Anderson, we're going to be putting on evidence through an expert witness regarding the damage done to the soil on the ranch. Are you going to be asking this jury to award you money for the damage they've caused to your ranch and your business?"

Butch looked quizzically at me, as if he wasn't sure that he was entitled to anything but the chance to tell his side of the story. I liked that about him. "Really, Miss MacIntosh, all I want is—I want my home back the way—maybe it can't be the way it was, but I want it restored as close as I can. I bought this ranch for a reason, or I'd have stayed on my measly little five acres in Montana. I want a place to be able to carry on my business, and it's—it seems like it's asking quite a bit now this late in the game. But this is my home; and this, this ranch—and it may not mean anything to the MethZap folks or to anyone else, but this ranch represents every dirty, rotten, bucking, running off, son-of-a-gun horse in the world that I've been on over the last twenty years. And I'm half what I was physically when I started doing this for a living. This is everything. It's what I have to leave to my boys. This is my entire working life wrapped up in this piece of property. Hell, it's all that my youngest son thinks about. Wyatt—Wyatt loves this ranch as much or more than I do. It's all he's ever known. It's all he wants. And twenty years ago, it didn't even look like I'd get this far, so this ranch, and all it represents, is something I'm real proud of. I want it back. That's it. That's all."

Chapter 9

Tsunamis had been on my mind quite a bit lately. I'd had a few dreams about giant, earth-swallowing waves after a big one hit Thailand and Indonesia, and although I didn't have much to worry about living in Wyoming, they still seemed to be haunting my thoughts. Like, exactly how deep must an earthquake hit in order to cause a tsunami? And if a huge earthquake hit deep under Alaska, could a tidal wave gain enough strength to wipe out the West Coast? Would it be possible for Wyoming to be a coastal state some day? Perhaps the deeper meaning of the dreams had something to do with the three-foot high stack of paper on my desk. Was it going to come crashing down on me at any moment? It was certainly sucking the air out of my lungs–choking me like blotting paper on a spill. Natural disasters fascinated me.

The *un*natural disaster that was about to re-enter my life did not fascinate me in the slightest, however. I am referring to Davis Dunne, of course. And the day I had been dreading for some time had come–the day of Butch Anderson's deposition. My law partner, Harry, couldn't wait for the deposition. In fact, he drove all night from Jackson to Casper to get here. Since Casper is located in the middle of the state, Harry had to drive over two mountain ranges and cross the Continental Divide for this sacred event. He didn't dare miss Davis Dunne's deposition of Butch Anderson.

For Butch and me, it was a mere two-hour drive south. Butch picked me up long before dawn, and with the verge of the rising sun, Butch and I talked about the future of his ranch once the trial was over. He was hopeful and that was good. He didn't seem nervous or anxious, despite my warnings that Davis Dunne was going to try to chew him up and spit him out.

It was early September and the warmth of fall was closing in. Normally, this time of year brings peace and solace and a sense of tranquility in my life. The days are still warm, but the evenings cool off. The afternoon rain showers of summer taper with the crispness of dusk, and it seems as if Monet traipses across the landscape turning green leaves from golden to auburn to crimson to chocolate in a sort of slow-motion photography. Normally, this is a diplomatic season in my life. However, the provocation this fall would prove to be similar to a festering boil.

* * *

"You didn't want MethZap on the ranch at all, did you? You didn't think they had a right to be there, mineral lease or not?" Davis Dunne wore a navy suit and a navy tie and sat across his marble conference table from me with his beady eyes reflecting the stone's glare. Dunne's law offices were near the railroad track in downtown Casper—not terribly far from the federal courthouse where the trial was set to take place. Dunne's bright yellow Hummer occupied two parking spaces in the adjacent lot, leaving no place for Butch's truck. We parked across the street under a large maple tree.

My initial plan had worked as far as filing the lawsuit in the state court. I accommodated the change in venue so long as they stipulated to Judge Bruce Laird. I was surprised by opposing counsels' willingness to agree to Judge Laird, especially in light of his recent ruling against BLM permits in the Gillette area. All the lawyers in the case agreed that Judge Laird was fair and impartial and sufficiently experienced to handle the class action litigation. Harry was pleased that my strategy worked.

"I understood their rights," Butch said to Dunne. "That didn't mean that I liked it."

"You tried to stop MethZap right away by going to a lawyer, right? Didn't you hire Chance Baker the minute you learned about MethZap's proposed operations on your ranch?"

"The first time I heard about MethZap was when Rowdy Rodiger, a MethZap landman, showed up on my land one day. He shoved a surface damage agreement in my face and told me I had to sign it. I didn't want to sign it without having a lawyer look at it. I trust Chance Baker. He's been a friend for a long time. So I asked him to look the agreement over. Chance worked with the Powder River Basin Resource Council, so I knew he'd be familiar with the goings-on of methane gas. I knew it was coming my way. Hell, damn near every ranch around here has wellheads littering up the hillsides. I just wanted to make sure everything with MethZap was on the up and up, that's all. I may be a dumb ol' cowboy, but I'm a businessman too. I have property to protect and a family's future to keep in mind before I go signing it all away to some strange out-of-state mineral outfit."

"But eventually, you signed the agreement, correct?"

"Yes. I did. I felt like I had no–"

"A yes or no will do."

"Yes."

"And you were told where the wells would be placed, correct?"

"Yes."

"But you immediately objected and told MethZap where to put their wellheads, didn't you?"

"I wouldn't say that's an accurate–"

"Objection. Move to strike. Please advise your witness to answer the question with a yes or a no." Harry's fists stiffened with Dunne's demands. The sinews on his neck looked like tree roots exposed in the dead of winter. He turned and whispered in Butch's ear, and Butch nodded back and continued his answer.

"I made recommendations on where wellheads would be less likely to interfere with my business."

"So, that's a 'yes,' correct."

Butch shrugged his shoulders a bit and reached up with his left hand and started twirling his mustache. "Correct."

"You were happy with well site Number 8, correct?"

"Happy may be strong."

"I understand. But you were satisfied with its location?"

"Yes, I guess so, if you could call it that. I wasn't satisfied with–"

"A yes or a no!"

"Some answers are not accurate with a 'yes' or a 'no'," Butch said. "I am trying to answer correctly."

The expletives flowing from Davis Dunne's mouth following this answer caused us to take a short recess from the deposition. He was obviously displeased with Butch's desire to explain his side of the story. Harry thought that it was so funny that he privately told Butch to keep it up. "Remember, Butch," Harry said. "Jewels are just rocks under enormous pressure. Let's keep the heat on Davis Dunne and see what he turns into by the end of the day."

The next phase of the deposition concerned where MethZap placed roads on the Crazy Woman Ranch. Butch had made it clear to Rowdy Rodiger that he didn't want his ranch marred with roads, but as things go in litigation, Rowdy didn't recall such conversations.

"And you don't have a single piece of paper, or email or anything else that you can produce that shows where you said, 'I don't consent to this road being here.'"

"I didn't think I had any power whatsoever, because I made suggestions early on to Rowdy Rodiger, and they were ignored. When Beth complained, Ace Sanders showed up in our kitchen and told her, 'Pretend we're married. I can do whatever I want, wherever I want, whenever I want.' I figured that the battle was lost."

Ace had been seated next to Davis Dunne throughout the deposition, and had, from time to time, whispered in Dunne's ear. Otherwise, he had been fairly quiet. However, hearing the statement about pretending to be married made his face turn a shade of crimson–close to the color of his red hair. This reaction told me all that I needed to know about Ace.

Dunne carried on with his line of questioning, lifting a giant aerial photograph of the Anderson ranch from the floor and placing it gingerly on an easel near the court reporter. "This is one of our trial exhibits," he said for the record. He took a pointer from the ledge of the easel and said, "Looks like that's a road there, right. Isn't that a road?"

"That's a cow trail, partner."

"A what?"

"A cow trail. You know. A trail that cows walk on, side by side."

"Two-by-two? You're pulling my leg, right?"

"No. Two-by-two–right next to each other. Like little kids holding hands on a field trip. We walk cows that way in these parts. Suppose you might not know that, being a city kind of guy."

"Objection. Move to strike. Harry, your client is argumentative and demeaning. One more comment like that and I'll . . . I'll make a motion before the court requesting sanctions."

"For what? Educating you in ranch life? Be my guest."

"Keep it up Harry and I'll ask the court to sanction you too."

"On what grounds?"

"For impeding the discovery process."

At this point, Harry was hiding behind his legal pad, chuckling silently. I couldn't help but join in. We had to take another break. This time, we headed out the door for a bite to eat.

"Mac, I'm in the mood for a good bowl of spicy chili," Harry said, as we left Dunne's office building.

"Sounds good to me," Butch chimed in.

Chili made me nervous due to Harry's long and disturbing history of confusing heartburn with heart attacks. But under the circumstances, I joined them.

When we resumed the afternoon session of the deposition, I noticed that Dunne had changed his shirt and tie. I didn't know the meaning behind his madness, but assumed that the heat of the morning session had made him sweat. Whatever the reason, a change in clothing did nothing to squelch the heat of the bridges he burned with Butch that afternoon.

"Isn't it true that you were never paid royalties on the project and that's what this lawsuit is all about? You're disgruntled because your land didn't produce methane gas royalties."

"Truth be told, sir, I was disappointed that we didn't get royalties. Hell, half of the ranching folks we know are living high off the hog around here from their royalties. So, yes, it is a setback for us, especially since our land was practically destroyed in the process. But that's not what this is all about. This is about being a steward of the land. Beth and I are here because our land was destroyed. Sure, those royalty checks would have been a nice supplement for our retirement, and it would have been nice to leave some money behind for our sons and grandkids someday. But I ain't here for the royalties. I'm here for my ranch and for every other piece of beautiful land in Wyoming."

"But didn't MethZap pay you a big check just for allowing them out on your land after you signed the surface damage agreement? I mean, regardless of royalties or any other money, you received a big chunk of change just for letting MethZap scope out your property, correct?"

"That's a matter of record. I'm not sure exactly how much we received. I wouldn't say it was a 'big chunk of change' as you say. It was somewhere in the range of twelve thousand or so. Now, that might seem like a bunch of money to come snooping around someone's land, but in the grand scheme of the damage done to my property–"

"Objection. Just answer the question. Now, Mr. Anderson, earlier in the deposition, when we were looking at one of the roads, you testified, 'You see that white stuff? That's salt.'"

"Yes, I recall telling you that the white residue all over the place on my ranch is salt."

"You have no reason to believe, other than what your expert witness has told you, that the white stuff is in fact salt. You've never tested it, correct?"

"Basically, everybody has science classes. In high school, it's practical experience. In Montana, when you grow up, there's always a portion of the biology class in high school that deals with saline seep, which is a big problem in the farming country. My old high school was the same. Based on my layman's opinion, that's what it was. Salt."

"But you're not an expert in soils management, are you?"

"I don't know how you define expert, Mr. Dunne. If you're asking me whether I have some fancy college degree in salt identification, then my answer is 'no.' If you're asking me whether I have been home-schooled about soil and land and ranching–"

"Mr. Anderson, please answer my questions with a 'yes' or a 'no!'"

Butch nodded at Davis Dunne, acknowledging him, but not agreeing to oblige.

"Mr. Anderson, I'm showing you another exhibit that we plan to use in the trial. I submit to you that this is aerial photograph shows the spring-fed draw on your property. It has white stuff all around it. Is it your testimony that this is salt too?"

"That's clay."

"Didn't you just testify that it was salt? Now you say it's clay?"

"I didn't say that everything that is white is salt, because there's snow up on the side of that hill, and it's white, but it's not salt."

"So, now you're testifying that the spring-fed draw is not contaminated with salt?"

"I wouldn't say that. In this part of the country, each layer of soil is a little bit different. From what I understand about the minerals in the ground, they leach whenever water runs over them or through them. The soil that may be right on the bank of the reservoir where there's standing water is quite different because of the salt than what you're going to have out on dry rangeland that water isn't running over. So, I don't think you can generalize about that kind of thing."

I could tell by the look on Davis Dunne's face that he didn't understand what Butch was saying. Out of frustration, Dunne moved on.

"Mr. Anderson, MethZap did not, in fact, pull methane on your property, did they?"

"They drilled for it, but they didn't find it. They still could."

"But they didn't, did they?"

"The agreement says '. . . drilling or production . . . ' and there's a difference for sure."

"So MethZap could still go out there and drill and try to produce gas?"

"You got 1870's mining laws on your side. I think you could, partner. The mining laws in this part of the country allow someone to buy the mineral rights underneath your property and come out on to your land, without much in the way of permission, and start digging holes and extracting minerals. It's one-sided, if you ask me. And the agreement I signed with MethZap allows them to keep coming out to my ranch to try different well sites."

"MethZap has never notified you that their drilling activities are complete, have they?"

"No. But that would coincide with the fact that they've never notified me when they intend to drill, when they intend to finish, when they intend to reseed, when they intend to–"

"Objection! Harrrrrrrry! Pleeeeaaaaassse, please instruct your witness to answer the question, 'yes' or 'no.'" Harry could hardly contain himself, and when he asked Dunne if he wanted some cheese with his whine, we had to take another break.

* * *

After our break, Harry switched positions with me so that I sat next to Butch. He said that Dunne was getting on his nerves and he needed a little more personal space from him.

"Mr. Anderson, it appears from the complaint that you are claiming that my client committed waste on your property. Can you explain that?"

"Objection. Calls for a legal conclusion," I said. "Butch, if you can answer that question in layman's terms, go ahead. For the record, Mr. Anderson is not answering the question with the presumption that he knows the legal definition of waste. He's only answering from the common-sense definition that a rancher would have." I nodded to Butch to continue.

"Waste. Well, there was a lot of waste goin' on at the ranch when MethZap was there. They left garbage all over the place. Fast food wrappers and cups and all kinds of junk was left in piles. Like the pile of wood they left out in the middle of my pasture next to the arena. Of course, at that time I was recovering from back surgery, so hauling wood wasn't my deal. It wasn't really recommended by the doc. But I couldn't have it snow over the pipe MethZap had left all over the place and then have someone drive over the top of it. A lot of it was laziness. But it's sort of like if someone plucked one hair out of your head you wouldn't mind that so much, but if they keep doing it, eventually it is going to become a problem; you're going to become uncomfortable. They keeping plucking hair out of my head. Like I say, that's not a big issue to haul all the garbage and wood from my arena to the dump. It was more because I forgot to cover it up with tarp, 'cuz the police fined me for that. So, here I am hauling their garbage off my land and I get fined at the dump for not covering it. I was starting to feel like I was balding. You know, one hair at a time being plucked."

And as if poetic justice was on our side, with the sun setting, a ray of light suddenly shone through the window onto Davis Dunne's bald head. Dunne didn't notice, I don't think. But Butch, Harry and I did. And possibly the court reporter noticed too. Dunne looked at us quizzically as we all let out a muffled giggle.

"What other types of reclamation did MethZap do on your ranch?" Dunne continued. "You've admitted that they hauled in some new topsoil and they put down some seed for grass and even fertilized. Didn't MethZap clean up the reservoirs also?"

"They made some attempts with the reservoirs. They brought the reservoirs up to a standard that looks like they might be safe for now. But I wouldn't recommend drinking any water from there if I were you. And certainly don't let your livestock drink it. Especially -"

"Thank you, Mr. Anderson. You've answered the question."

Chapter 10

Pamela was waiting for me at the office when I got back to Sheridan after Butch's deposition. It was nearly eight o'clock in the evening and she had her five-year-old daughter set up in the corner of my office with a TV dinner, a box of crayons, a coloring book and a few of Ted's stuffed toys. I appreciated the fact that Pamela was working hard and couldn't begin to imagine the difficulties of trying to raise a child without help. I smiled at the cute little girl's ketchup-smeared face, and watched as she colored with one hand and patted Ted with the other. Ted stood watch over her, probably sensing that she might not finish her chicken fingers.

"Sisal is a type of grass grown in Africa. It is a natural fiber that was used to make ropes before nylon was invented. It isn't used much today—only in calf roping."

"Who sells them?"

"In Sheridan? Only King's. But you can buy them over the Internet and in lots of other equine supply shops." Pamela didn't seem knowledgeable enough about horses to refer to a saddle store as an equine supply shop. I figured that she was repeating what had been told to her.

"Do you think we can find out from King's who has purchased sisal rope from them?" I asked. Pamela took a deep breath and then looked over at her daughter, who was tugging on Ted's whiskers and sucking her thumb. "Pam, I didn't mean for you to do it tonight. I meant in the next few days."

"Sure. I can do that. Maybe over the weekend. She goes to her daddy's sometimes. Not that I'm happy about it. He hardly feeds her and when he does, it's Twinkies and doughnuts. But, I need the break and it's his duty, you know. Judge told him if he didn't take her, he'd up the child support and if he didn't pay the support, they throw his skinny ass in jail. He's got himself this new girlfriend and she . . . ."

I suppose we all need someone to listen sometimes–maybe someone who doesn't say a word–who just listens and that's all. As I listened, I couldn't help but wonder whether her little five-year-old was listening too, and to what extent she could understand what her mother was saying. But I'd heard the words before, dozens of times and it didn't help persuade me about marriage. I wanted to belong. I wanted to get married and have children and have the happily ever after.

But some people need to belong to something bigger so that they can lose themselves in the belonging. I didn't want that. I didn't want to get married just to belong to the group of married people. I wanted to marry so that one day, when the career wasn't as important and the kids were off in college, I would wake up with the person I loved to spend my days with.

I listened to Pamela for a long time that night. Not because she was telling me something I didn't already know or surmise. But because sometimes we all need to feel heard.

* * *

I helped Pam carry her drowsy daughter to the car and thanked her for the time and dedication she gave to the law firm. We talked about how much I depended on her tenacity and motivation. I reminded Pamela that she was our office leader–she seemed to like hearing that very much. And as I buckled her sleepy-eyed daughter into her car seat, I felt the tug on my heartstrings as the little girl held on to my fingers. I leaned in and gave her a light peck on the forehead, wishing her sweet dreams. She quickly fell back asleep, in the peaceful way children do.

As Pamela drove away, I realized the pang of loneliness in my heart. There is so much under the surface of a person's life. I didn't know much about Pamela or her daughter or why she divorced her ex-husband. But the one common thread I felt at that moment was loneliness. I hated to admit it because I didn't really expect to be so morose. That, to me, was a feeling residing in people with nothing better going on in their lives. Perhaps I'd become one of those pitiful people. As I waded in my pool of self-pity, I decided that I'd been working too hard. It was time for a day off from the ugly world of litigation. Instead of consuming my thoughts with contamination and waste and defilement, I needed to fill my head, heart and lungs with fresh air and open space. If only I had Greg around to share it with.

Chapter 11

To some, fishing was spiritual. To Harry, it was sacred. After weeks of a calendar jam-packed with expert depositions and dreadfully boring written discovery, Harry, who'd been in Sheridan for a week to help me with the lawsuit, was desperate for a day of fishing. I'd only accompanied Harry on a fishing expedition once, in Jackson Hole. Perhaps I was not invited again due to my lackluster effort in catching the poor little, scaly, gill-breathing creature before gingerly removing the hook from his throat and quickly releasing him back to his natural environment. Not that I'm against fishing. It's just not for me. So, imagine my surprise when Harry informed me that he'd arranged for Wyatt to take us to Willow Park Lake for a day of trolling for rainbow trout.

After looking at a topographical map, I was more enthusiastic when I learned that the lake was situated near the border of the Cloud Peak Wilderness in the Bighorn National Forest. I spotted one hiking trail after another and knew that I could sneak away for a wonderful hike and enjoy some desperately needed fresh air. I was told to be ready by four thirty in the morning on Saturday. Harry assured me that I heard the time correctly. I was to meet him and Wyatt in the lobby of the Holiday Inn (where Harry had taken up residence) at four thirty sharp. I was to bring long pants, shorts, varying layers of shirts and jackets, mosquito spray, sunscreen, a hat, food and water.

So, at four thirty in the morning, I found myself slouched in a cushioned chair in the hotel lobby with a triple espresso in my hand and a bursting backpack by my side.

When I saw what Harry was wearing as he walked through the lobby, I almost spit out my coffee. To his credit, Harry was a very handsome man in his early sixties. He exercised regularly and still had a full head of hair. I was sure that he had his hair dyed, but I'd never had the guts to ask. Today, it wouldn't have mattered. He wore a tan fishing hat that was plastered with every kind of hook and fly known to the anglers of America. His goggle-like sunglasses hung from a string around his neck. He sported multiple shirts with zippered sleeves, so that he could convert them from long sleeve to short sleeve at a moment's notice. His pants were similar, with zippers at his calves, knees, and thighs. But what caused my sudden burst of laughter was watching him pull our trial transporter, which was like a suitcase on wheels, stacked high with a cooler, multiple tackle boxes, wader boots and other gear. Harry was ready to go fishing. Apparently so was Greg.

I hadn't seen Greg much since rodeo weekend two months ago. He had an assignment that took him out of town and I had been buried with work. When he walked in the lobby with Wyatt, I was genuinely shocked. Wyatt looked somewhat shocked also. "Guess we've got a fourth wheel," Wyatt said to Harry.

"Great," Harry said, extending his hand to Greg. "I haven't seen you in a long time. Glad to have you along." Since I knew that Harry wasn't crazy about Greg, I wasn't convinced of the sincerity of the exchange, but Harry seemed genuine enough as he and Greg traded small talk.

We threw our gear in the back of Wyatt's truck and headed south on the I-90 until we reached Buffalo. In Buffalo, we stopped for more coffee. Wyatt suggested a potty break too, as the road to Willow Park was, according to him, "a bladder buster." I thought he was exaggerating as we headed west on Highway 16, but I understood him perfectly when we redirected north on a tiny makeshift road just shy of Boulder Park. The road should have been called Boulder Park because all we did for the next forty-five minutes was bounce from one boulder to the next. I thought my neck was going to slip off its axis with each jolt, and for the first time I envisioned what a bucking bronco ride must feel like. It wasn't pleasant.

What was even more unpleasant was listening to Harry grunt "Ohhh" with each impact. He complained bitterly about the problems of growing older and his shrinking prostate and other bodily functions that, in my opinion, are best kept confidential. Wyatt and Greg listened intently, wincing every now and then at the excruciating details.

We drove for what seemed like an eternity through thick alpine territory. The tall pines made the road dark and the potholes hard to see. Wyatt seemed oblivious, as if four-wheeling was a way of life, as he sang along to a country-western song twanging from his stereo. Harry sat up front with him, while Greg and I cuddled in the back. His hands had the coldness of a stranger, though, as I hadn't heard from him much in the last few weeks. Still, I could feel my heartstrings pull with each soft word he whispered in my ear.

"Why didn't you tell me you were in town? Where'd you stay last night?" I asked.

"Got in real, real late so I crashed at Sherman Todd's pad. My assignment ended ahead of schedule. I tried to call you at home, but no answer."

"Why didn't you call my office? I've practically been living there for months. Or my cell? You could have left a -"

"Didn't want to bother you. I know you've been working like a mad woman."

I couldn't argue about the hours I'd been putting in, but it seemed strange to me that he wouldn't call and at least leave a message that he was coming to town. "You are usually so good about calling me."

"I can't win with you. You tell me that you're buried with work and that I shouldn't expect to see you for a few months. And then when I pay you a surprise visit, you chastise me. What's worse is that you're off playing hooky instead of working. So, you're too busy to see me, yet you have time to go fishing. I'm the one who should be put out here. Not you."

I decided to let it rest. He had a point. But the truth was that I'd been putting in eighteen hour days, seven days a week for two months, and this was the first time I'd come up for air. Still, it didn't make sense to defend myself further. I didn't want our discussion to escalate into a fight, especially not in front of Harry and Wyatt, so I bit my tongue and looked out the window, pretending to be in my own world. I listened to the conversations among the men and realized more than ever that

Greg bore little resemblance to his brother. Wyatt was altruistic and self-effacing. Greg was more of an extrovert and ambitious. Wyatt was happy with himself and the path he'd chosen in becoming a rancher. Although he would not admit it, Greg was not satisfied with his job and probably would not be until he was rich and powerful. This notion caught me by surprise. I hadn't really given it much thought before.

* * *

After two hours of driving, we finally emerged from the thicket into what I can only describe as the crisp beauty of heaven. Willow Park Lake shimmered in the early morning sun as the smooth-as-glass water was occasionally interrupted by the splash of a fish, leaving an orbital ripple of water emerging from its epicenter. The mountain peak west of the lake was still dotted with remnants of winter's snow and the cotton ball fluffs of clouds in the lapis-blue sky mimicked the snow clusters, almost like nature playing a joke on itself. The lake was encircled by a thick forest in every direction and I couldn't wait to get out of Wyatt's truck and smell the crisp, clean mountain air.

Wyatt's silver fishing boat was resting bottom side up at the edge of the lake. He and Greg deftly flipped it over and slid it into the muddy banks of the lake.

"You leave your boat here unattended?" I asked, showing my naïve, city-girl spirit.

"My dad's boat. And yes, we've been leaving it up here for twenty-some years. Folks borrow it from time to time, I'm sure. But what's the harm in that?" Wyatt slipped his pocket-lined, tan fishing vest over his flannel shirt and reached in the back of his truck for the outboard motor for the boat. He clamped the motor on the boat, filled the tank with gas from a can in the truck, and loaded the boat with a cooler, tackle boxes and some nets. "All aboard," he shouted.

Greg scurried through his gear, loading a bulging backpack, and then waded knee deep into the water, giving the small boat a push before heaving himself in. Wyatt cranked on the motor for a few minutes before it gave way. As we slowly motored to the middle of the lake, Greg busied himself with his backpack full of gear. Wyatt looked on with disgust when Greg pulled out his black shiny "Fishfinder"–a sonar gadget that sensed where the fish were schooling. Wyatt leaned toward Harry, and in a voice projected for eavesdropping, said, "It's not that he fishes with a Browning that is irritating. It's that he uses a digital Fishfinder that bugs the hell out of me. And it's not just the Fishfinder; it's all the other gadgets he brings along for the trip. Navigational gadgets. Cell phone. Two-ways. Whatever happened to the fishing pole, the buddy, a six-pack and a compass, just to be on the safe side? I guess I'm an old-fashioned angler, like my dad."

Greg shot him a disdainful look and, with a brotherly lack of ceremony, cast his baited hook in the direction of the sonar signal. Within a few minutes, his Browning rod curved in the shape of his fishhook. Greg gave his line a quick tug and then gingerly lowered his pole horizontal to the water. He gently reeled in the fish, careful not to tug too hard. As his bobber approached the boat, Harry reached over the side with a large net and helped Greg bag a twenty-four inch speckled rainbow trout. Harry yanked the hook from the fish's gills and carefully threaded it on the dragline so that the scaly critter could remain in the cool lake water for the duration of our expedition. "My Fishfinder says that we're in the right spot," Greg said, winking at Wyatt. Wyatt shook his head and motored in the opposite direction.

Harry handed me a pole and a plastic container. "Get bait on your hook and show me some wrist when you cast." The wrist part I could handle. It was the bait part that was holding me up. When I peeled back the lid of the plastic container, several of the earthworms squirmed back down into the chocolate brown soil. It was if they were taunting me. I would have to dig down to get them, and then pull their slimy, squirming bodies out as they wriggled and twisted and tangled themselves before being pierced with a sharp hook and thrown to the depths of certain death. I truly despised baiting a hook, which visibly annoyed Harry. Wyatt was amused. Greg was somewhere in the middle, and, probably because he wanted post-fishing cuddling, was willing to lend a hand to help me through my misery.

"Being a good fisherman is the essence of being a good lawyer," Harry said. He tossed out his line and leaned back against the edge of the boat. He grabbed a beer from the cooler and popped the top. I knew what Harry was saying. When he first hired me, he used to tell me frequently that a good lawyer is just like a patient fisherman, tossing out a line until a gullible witness takes the bait. He reminded me often that great lawyers know when it is time to yank the hook.

I watched my fishing line bob in the water for a bit, then closed my eyes and let my thoughts drift back to the time when Greg and I went camping in this wilderness area a few years ago. We hiked up a steep trail and came upon a pristine lake. Spontaneously, we undressed and took a dip in the cool water, splashing, laughing and kissing . . . and not thinking much about the fish swimming nearby.

* * *

After several hours of pulling in fish, we headed back to the bank for a lunch/potty break. A potty break for the fishermen was simple: walk a few feet into the trees and take care of business. My female plumbing required a bit longer journey into the forest. As I ventured toward the tree line, I listened to the whir of the wind as it started to pick up its afternoon beat. The smell of sap and pine wafted through the air and roused my urge for an alpine hike. I'd had enough fishing for the day, and was tired of being a pincushion for giant mosquitoes. I informed the guys that I was going to take the Meadowlark Trail for a few miles and would be back in two hours.

Harry stood from his perch on the log where he was eating his turkey and cheese sandwich. "You are *not* going for a hike alone in the wilderness, Mac. If you don't want to fish anymore, fine. Take a walk around the lake. Read a book. It is not safe to hike alone."

"Oh, Harry! I'll stay on the trail. I brought a topo map. I know where I'm going. I'll take plenty of water and I'll turn back after an hour. There's nothing to worry -"

"Take my gun," Wyatt said, reaching for the holster attached to his thick leather belt. "It's not safe to hike up here alone without at least a firearm." I stared at Wyatt's shiny black pistol, knowing that it was smart to take it with me, but fighting my urge to explain my deep fear of guns. When I didn't reach for it willingly, he continued, "There are bear and mountain lions up here. You need a gun to protect yourself. I'm afraid if you don't take the gun, I can't let you wander off by yourself."

"What kind of gun is this?" I asked, thrashing my knowledge of weaponry.

Wyatt puffed up his chest a bit. "Ruger Blackhawk .357 Mag. Do you know much about guns?" I shrugged my shoulders and shook my head in a noncommittal gesture.

"You shouldn't go alone anyway," Greg chimed in. "Here, take this two-way. If you have any problems, call me."

"It's okay, guys. I'll be back before you know it." Nevertheless, I was forced to take the two-way and the gun and granola bars and two bottles of water. I needed a pack dog to carry everything that they had loaded on me.

I hit the trailhead feeling exhilarating freedom. My brisk walk soon turned into a gallop, and then a run. I was nervous about running with a loaded gun strapped to my belt, so I stopped several times to make sure that the safety was still on. The ruddy trail felt great under my feet and the smell of nature cleared my head. As the sound of the revving motorboat echoed across the lake, I slipped deeper into the forest, hearing only birds and the whisper of the wind through the boughs of the trees. I was startled by the occasional pinecone dropping from a high branch and the scuttle of a small creature (probably a squirrel) rustling into the brush. But after awhile, the small sounds of nature became part of me and I settled into them like a bird cozying into her nest. Perhaps I let my guard down.

* * *

I didn't hear her. I didn't see her. Nor did I smell her. But she saw me. Not only did she see me, but she tracked me like a hunter stalks his prey.

I had picked up my pace a bit, enjoying a trail run in the pristine beauty of the backwoods. Growing up in Boulder, Colorado, I'd competed in many trail runs, including the Pike's Peak race. I loved the strain of running at altitude–listening to my heart accept the lack of oxygen and gradually calm itself, like a baby finding its pacifier. My heart's steady rhythm drowned out the sounds of nature and perhaps that is why I didn't hear her approaching. She must have been slinking through the trees for a time and then, when she felt that the moment was right, she joined me on the hiking trail and picked up speed.

When her claws slashed through the flesh on my back, I had no idea what had hit me. I heard the bellow of her attack and felt my flesh ripping, but could not place her as the predator and me as the prey. The speed of her impact sent me crashing to the ground. I rolled end over end once before skidding to a stop on my back. Before I had time to reflect on what had happened, she pounced on top of me, her yellow eyes wild with excitement, as she wrapped her front paws around my neck and scrambled to disembowel me with her hind legs.

She was a powerful mountain lion, for sure, and I knew that my only defense was Wyatt's gun. If I hesitated, her hind claws would rip through my intestines and within seconds, her fangs would encase my jugular vein. That was how nature worked. I pulled my knees to my chest and thrashed side to side, doing anything possible to keep her from a steady grip. I reached down to my belt and tried desperately to rip the gun from its holster. I could feel the cold metal on my fingertips, but I could not find the clasp that held Wyatt's gun in the holster. I was thrashing back and forth, using my right hand to keep her mouth away from my face. But this forced me to reach across my body with my left hand for the gun.

My life was flashing in slow motion, yet I felt like I was riding on a speed train. I felt her fangs sink deep into my arm, although I hadn't assimilated the sensation of pain—as if my brain needed to hold off for a moment—to slow down the synapses long enough for my body to do what it needed to do to save my life.

I felt the overwhelming presence of my father—as if he were a ghost in the trees—egging me on in the fight. I could hear his voice saying, "Don't give up. Don't give up. You are stronger than you know." I could smell the scent of my dad's Allspice aftershave. I could sense his loving nudge.

I thought to myself: *Grab the gun. Grab the gun. Grab the gun.*

And as if following my dad's advice, I jerked the gun from the holster and wrenched the hammer back. The cold metal of the gun was a stark contrast to the hot breath of the lion on my shoulder. I squeezed the trigger with the speed of adrenaline-based fear, yet in the slow motion that allows sound to travel at a snail's pace. The shot that rang through the alpine fir reverberated in my ears for what seemed like minutes. The lion unleashed a howl like that of a child in pain. Her jaws released momentarily, and then settled back into my flesh. She wasn't going to quit. I was her prey.

Chapter 12

She thrashed her head back and forth, tearing violently at my left arm. The pain raced up my shoulder and down my spine, as if my body was trying to evenly disperse it so that I wouldn't be hammered with it all at once. My father's ghost-like voice whispered through the trees, chanting at me not to give up. The gun was still in my left hand, pinned slightly against my body and the pain from the flesh wounds was throbbing through my fingertips. I tried to pull back on the hammer, but my thumb strength had disappeared. I needed to transfer the gun to my right hand, but I was afraid to leave my head unprotected from the gnawing beast. I had no choice but to attempt to reach down with my right hand, exposing my face to her, grab the gun and fire again. If I didn't, I was certain that I would die.

Her rear claws were digging into my legs. She was hoping to wear me down so that I'd relax out of the fetal position enough that she could rip apart my midsection with her hind legs. She was still winning our match. I was growing weary and I couldn't hold her off much longer. I was lucky that I had very long legs to protect my torso, but my legs were fatigued and they needed rest. I reached down with my right hand, under the lion's chest, and grabbed the gun from the clenches of my left hand. I pulled back the hammer and squeezed the trigger again, sending an echo through the forest that made the blue jays fly.

I knew I had her. She stopped trying to pry my legs free. She loosened her grip on my left arm and slowly relinquished control of me. I rolled off to the side, pushed her hot body away from mine and stared at her bloody tongue as it hung out the side of her mouth.

My white cotton sleeve was saturated with a scarlet stain that seemed to be changing by the moment like the clouds overhead. Dark clouds. A storm was forming and the wind was gaining strength. I scooted away from the beast and pulled my knees to my chest, studying the .357 in my hand, and thinking to myself, *I hate guns. I've always hated guns. But I don't hate this one.*

* * *

My breathing started to taper off and the adrenaline evaporated somewhat, but I couldn't quite manage the strength to stand. My senses were keener now, and I sensed the pulses of nature–heard the gusts of wind swaying the tops of the trees and watched as the birds took shelter. I felt the first raindrop as it splashed on my right hand, sending droplets of water onto the shiny metal of the gun. I studied the raindrops as they fell freely wherever they pleased, making speckles on the trail in a haphazard fashion. She didn't feel the raindrops on her flaxen fur–would never again enjoy the refreshing air after a hard mountain storm. The air was getting colder and as the temperature continued to drop, I felt for her–felt sorry that I'd taken her life, and that was the last thing I remember before I gave myself up to the waiting darkness.

* * *

When I awoke, I felt my head dangling back, bouncing in a rhythmic cadence. He was carrying me in his arms and his body felt warm. The pouring rain had turned into snow and I could see the large, swollen flakes settle on his shirt. I could hear the squishing of his shoes splashing through the muddy earth. It was Greg. He had found me on the trail and was carrying me back toward the lake. The trees were no longer swaying in the wind, I noticed. They were still, absorbing the moisture of the first snowstorm of the season like soldiers poised for battle. They were protecting us from the storm. But as we came out of the protection of the trees and as we neared the lake, the snow pelted my face. I didn't have the strength to keep my head up, and Greg sensed that. He pulled me in closer to his body, his arm muscles flexed like steel.

"Do you want me to carry her for a while?" Harry's voice boomed from behind.

"No. We're almost there," Greg responded, out of breath.

* * *

I slept through the rough ride down the mountain, awakened only by the bright lights of the emergency room. As the doctors and nurses scurried to cut off my shirt, panic rose through my veins. The nurse shoved an IV into my vein. I heard the pulsating sound of the oxygen mask over my face and felt the claustrophobia of people hovering.

"Mr. Fisher, I must ask you to leave the room," a nurse said to Greg, who was pacing the floor.

I winced each time they rinsed my wounds before sliding the needle and thread to reunite my flesh. The doctor shoved a tetanus shot into my shoulder and explained that the puncture wounds in my arm and back would have to heal naturally and were bandaged without stitches. Otherwise, I was lucky. I thought about how I could have been killed had I not taken Wyatt's gun with me. Silver linings are what I strived for–and the silver lining to this experience was that I expected never again to be asked to accompany Harry on a fishing expedition.

I thought that the bandages around my arm might engender some sympathy from Davis Dunne, but apparently I was sorely mistaken. In fact, as the case was heating up and the defendants continued to point the finger at one another for responsibility, Dunne started taking on the demeanor of the mountain lion that had attacked me.

The Sheridan Press editor showed up to my office early Monday following the mountain lion attack with a camera crew and a tape recorder, anxious to get the gory details before the evening edition went to print. I recounted the story, and told him that they could get a photograph of the beast at the Game and Fish Department. Wyatt had hauled the lion back to town and had dropped it off for tagging purposes. After the Game and Fish people were finished with the carcass, they told me that I could keep it if I wanted. Naturally, I declined, citing that the lion would clash with my apartment décor. Harry, however, claimed the lion, planning to mount it in his cabin near Grand Targhee.

When the *Press* article ran that evening, half of the story concerned the mountain lion attack. The other half described the class action lawsuit and applauded our efforts in getting the methane gas companies and the permit-issuing agencies to take responsibility for the toxic waste they were allowing to clog the waterways of Wyoming. It was great coverage for us, not only as advertising for our new firm, but also for public spin about the case. Dunne knew this and called from Casper the minute he found out about the article.

"Just a damn publicity stunt. That's all that was. Probably was a lion from one of those sanctuaries. You probably staged the whole thing. Well, you're going to need more than a dog and pony show to win this trial. Don't think that you can parade your pretty face all over the papers and win the hearts of the jury. I'm going to make sure that the jury we empanel sees that you're as green as the grass in early spring. A mountain lion attack. What a crock of shit."

When I told Harry about the conversation with Dunne, he was furious. He drove directly to the Game and Fish office, claimed his prize, and took her to a taxidermist who promptly prepared her for mounting, removing all bones and tissue, including the cat's skull. Harry carefully packaged the skull in bubble wrap and sent it to a certain law office in Casper to the attention of the "High and Mighty Davis Dunne." The return address on the package was intentionally left blank.

When the Ethics Committee of the State Bar telephoned Harry a few days later, he laughed hysterically with the caller on the other line. Apparently, one of his colleagues sat on the committee and, although he was required to place the call and chastise Harry for such unethical conduct, he was not forced to take corrective action. Harry knew he went a bit over the line, but he would have done it again if given the chance. His only concern was whether the federal judge would get wind of it. But even so, he figured it to be a mere bug on the windshield of life. It takes more than one bug splatter to dirty the image.

* * *

Greg was on assignment in Guatemala last year when *National Geographic* helped subsidize an expedition to uncover Mayan ruins in a remote part of the jungle. The expedition would take years, but Greg's involvement would only last a month or so. Shortly after the *O'Connor* trial, when I wasn't knee-deep in work, he invited me to join him during the last week of the expedition. Since I'd never visited Central America, I readily agreed to join him. As we swam and snorkeled in the Gulf of Honduras, I fell in love with the turquoise beauty of the Caribbean coastline. But the focus of the journey was the dense jungle that housed hundreds of ruins from an ancient civilization that stemmed as far back as 750 B.C.

Tikal ("The Place of Voices") was the largest and most famous ruin site that we visited. So that I could get a better understanding of Greg's work, he took me to the Temple of the Giant Jaguar, a one hundred and seventy foot pyramid built from ancient stone. The temple had secret stairways and terraces, and is thought to have been constructed for a Mayan king around 700 A.D. The massiveness of the structure was impressive, especially in light of the fact that these primitive people did not have bulldozers or other machinery to help them build such a complex edifice. The symmetry of the construction was a geometric masterpiece, seemingly built for tracking the celestial calendar. Climbing to the top of this temple was a workout not suited for anyone with a fear of heights, but once at the top, it was startling and incredible to view the dozens of other temples built by these highly evolved and industrial Indians.

Greg's focus for his magazine piece was on newly discovered ruins that housed complex carvings of hieroglyphics that perhaps told a more inclusive story of the rise and fall of this empire. His team of archaeologists was unearthing mounds of jungle by tunneling through the tops of what looked like hills covered with a dense growth of trees and vines. The mounds were actually ruins that had been overgrown by jungle after they had been abandoned over a thousand years ago. Through these new hieroglyphs, the archaeologists found evidence that linked the various Mayan tribes to the ruins in Belize and Mexico, suggesting a causal link in the demise of these nations was largely due to tribal warfare over water. The ruins located on fresh waterways were eventually sought after as the landlocked tribes labored to keep fresh water in their communities. Polluted water or drought choked off tribes.

As I sat in dozens of depositions of expert witnesses in the MethZap case over the next few months, I often thought of this Guatemalan adventure. What happened to the Mayans? Did they perish because they didn't have access to fresh water?

In our case, some experts agreed with Butch's belief–that the methane gas industry was poisoning the water in Wyoming. The defense experts disagreed. Either way, I decided that the Mayans probably had experts in their community that disagreed over the importance of the water. And look what happened to them. They vanished without any explanation.

Chapter 13

Early on in a federal court lawsuit, the trial judge typically appoints a magistrate to conduct a settlement conference among all parties in an effort to resolve the litigation before the discovery phase causes the case to be astronomically expensive. At the settlement conference, the magistrate meets independently with each side and listens to their version of the facts, and then tries to strong-arm the parties into settlement by pointing out the respective strengths and weaknesses of the adversaries' case. It is sort of a cat and mouse game of shuttle diplomacy, where CEOs meet outside the courthouse steps with their respective insurance carriers and do risk management analyses to determine whether it is beneficial to settle the case. Often times, the magistrate talks out of both sides of his or her mouth, pacifying in one breath and scaring with the other.

On our way to the settlement conference at the federal courthouse in Casper, I rode shotgun in Butch's crew cab, while Beth sat in the back with her knitting needles nervously clicking as she repeated, "knit one, pearled two." She completed two scarves in less than two hours. At the same time, Butch and I strategized about the weaknesses of our case while listening to his favorite country music: Vince Gill, Faith Hill, Clint Black. The trip took longer than normal because we had to stop a number of times for road construction. As we encountered each bright orange road construction sign, Butch complained about the delay. I ignored his complaints and focused on the signs. "Danger: Blasting Ahead." "Expect Delays." "Watch for Obstacles in Road." I felt like the signs paralleled the warning signs of our lawsuit.

"Dunne is slamming me with discovery, Butch. Nearly every question deals with the damages you've suffered as a result of MethZap drilling on your land. We've been going back and forth on this, and he claims that you weren't happy no matter what kind of grass they planted for you. He said that you were just being picky–and were trying to get better pastureland than you had before MethZap stepped foot on your ranch.

"Utter bullshit," Butch said, bearing down on the accelerator. "All I said to MethZap is that I don't want to see that sorry grass they put along the highway, because that's quack grass. So I wanted to make sure they had gone to the Soil Conservation Service and they were putting in grass that was going to be legitimate. That's all I was concerned about."

"Okay. But in your deposition, you went on and on about range management, saying the words over and over, but never giving a good explanation. Now all of the follow-up interrogatories imply that your theory of range management eliminated any need for them to replant your pastures."

"I guess it's up to me to educate everyone around here from point A to point Z. I swear, the simplest notions are the hardest to explain to you lawyers. Let me see if I can whittle it down to the kindergarten level. See, there's a whole science nowadays that's basically called holistic range management. And that's based on using the impact of the livestock to preserve a certain amount of grass so you have a certain amount of seed going in the ground every year. You rotate the cattle from one pasture to another so that you harvest the right amount of the grass and you've left the right amount of grass behind so as to provide cover for the new seed coming up the next year. By having the cattle in there at certain times of the year, the grass is seeded by the hooves of the cattle, so you don't have to use machinery to get grass to grow. You let the cattle be your farm equipment. And you probably don't want to go any deeper into that."

"This is Dunne's point. Based on your explanation, you haven't spent a lot of money doing that, right. The cattle do it for you?"

"For the love of God! You lawyers just don't understand ranching. They don't give those cattle away. They cost a load of money, those cattle. And in order for the holistic range management to work, you have to have fences. That's what I've been trying to fix on you. See, Wyatt and I've been working on fences since the minute we bought the place. That's what we've been investing our blood, sweat, tears and money in—having fences that would keep the cattle home, keep them off the highway. Half the fences were torn down by MethZap. As I told you before, other pastures were occupied by compressor stations, wellheads and other gear. So, basically, my holistic range management system was shot to hell by MethZap."

"Ace Sanders testified in his deposition that MethZap replaced the fences. Did they?"

"Well, they eventually did replace some gate posts. They fixed some of the electric fence. They wired it wrong. I had to go back and do that. But they made an attempt. I don't know if the judge is going to know much about building fences. There were no brace posts in the fences that MethZap put up; and by spring 2005 they were certainly going to be falling down, like every other fence they put up. There's no braces whatsoever, just wires strung to posts that weren't even tamped down deep. And if you think that's going to keep out a yearling when he sees that new seeding, if there was any new seeding that would grow, that is. When they see that grass, that's the first thing they hunt in the spring. You better have a good fence if you're going to turn them."

"So, basically your testimony is that you wanted to run your ranch with holistic management in mind and you needed good pastureland, good fences and good cows to do so. MethZap ruined your fences and your pastures. So what's your beef, if you'll pardon my pun about the cows?"

"The cows are an important part of my equation because I ran as many as I needed in order to do my clinics. Wyatt, on the other hand, runs herds of 'em. I run cattle for my horse training. I'm smart enough to know you're not going to get rich running cows. I'm not cutting at Wyatt for doing it, mind you. I'm downright proud of him. It's just that he runs 'em out of a sense of obligation to his cowboy spirit. He don't know any different. I run 'em 'cuz I need 'em. But I can't feed 'em if I can't run 'em. And like I said, they aren't cheap. No, those cows aren't cheap. Especially when you have bad pastures."

"What's the price tag for the ranch to replace bad pastures?"

"I'm not going to buy a replacement pasture. This is where I do business. This is not a matter of grazing. That ranch is my office, so all of the value of my property is not derived from grazing cattle. Thank the Lord. The value of my property is derived from me being able to do business on my ranch, so–

"The question was–"

"-- Put a price on that, and that's how you value a company is how much money can be generated from that company." I looked over at the speedometer and noticed that we'd climbed from seventy-five to ninety in the last minute. Beth had set down her knitting to tighten her lap belt. It was early in the morning and the sun was peeking through the driver's side of the pickup. It was November, and there was a trace of snow covering the grasslands. The antelope were herded together near the snow fences, deciding which side of the highway would have better pasture to fatten up with. Flocks of birds formed their "V's" in the sky, heading south to escape the winter frost. Isolation was setting in. Outside in nature. And inside Butch's truck.

"But you're claiming that your land has been damaged. You have to prove it. We need specific numbers."

"Damn straight," Butch said, twirling his mustache with his left hand while idly groping the steering wheel with his right. A blast of wind pushed the truck a few inches sideways. Tumbleweeds bounced up the culvert and across the lonely stretch of highway. He took the wheel with both hands, fighting the current of air. "I'm *claiming* that my land has been *damaged* . . . because it has. And if the son a bitches don't want to settle up square, then I'll settle it with 'em the old fashioned way."

Chapter 14

Magistrate Raiza Kineski might have been cheated on height (she stood less than five feet tall), but she made up for her petite nature with her booming voice and presence. A native of Poland during extreme famine and war, she didn't waste food, effort or time. I'd never met her before, but her reputation was short on compliments. It was rumored that her male counterparts on the bench did not care for her gender, politics or sexual preference. Of course, as protected classes, those biases usually weren't mentioned outside certain circles.

Harry was friendly with nearly every judge on the bench in the State of Wyoming. He'd been practicing for thirty-some odd years, and he'd always made it a priority to schmooze with the judges at State Bar conferences or other perfunctory meetings. Harry liked Raiza Kineski because she was very prepared for each hearing. She read every brief carefully and, in the toughest of cases, even had her questions pre-printed and sent to the lawyers so that they could adequately prepare for oral argument. Being a victim of war and a first-generation survivor of immigration, she was not interested in toying with the lawyers during oral argument to see how quickly they could think on their feet. Intimidating others was clearly not her style. But the flip side of her generosity was her overwhelming demand for perfection, accuracy and preparedness. I sensed that Butch was not ready to respond to Magistrate Kineski's rueful probing and for once, after working under his wing for ten years, I wished that Harry was with me to bridge the gap between lawyer, client and judge.

"You signed an agreement saying that MethZap had permission to discharge water onto your property, didn't you, Mr. Anderson?" Magistrate Kineski didn't dance around the subject for long. Her sugarcoating consisted of a handshake and a seating-chart before her settlement discussions got under way. Butch seemed undaunted by her insolent nature and answered without hesitation.

"The agreement with them stated that if the water met the standards put forth by the federal and the state and the county, whatever it took to keep the government happy, that if it was totally acceptable, then I would in the spirit of cooperation, allow water to be discharged on my property. Basically, I agreed that I wouldn't stand in their way if it was legal and within, you know, Department of Environmental Quality or whoever was the governing body–"

"So, you have no basis for your opinion that the water discharged by MethZap was contaminated in any way?" It was more of a statement than a question. Magistrate Kineski didn't know Butch. She didn't understand that his rambling answers eventually produced a profound truth. I feared that Butch would be shut down and that she wouldn't get to know the value of the wholesome, honest cowboy that he was.

"You obviously weren't around when I testified in my deposition about the salt."

Magistrate Kineski was seemingly amused by Butch's straightforwardness. He didn't linger for a moment before going into one of his ten-minute dissertations about the salt discharged on his property and the short-term and long-term ramifications. Instead of interrupting this time, the judge listened intently, taking copious notes, as Butch gave Magistrate Kineski an education about holistic range management, rodeo technique, rangelands, fences, water, West Nile Virus, Mad Cow disease, dead livestock, and the rancher's duty to be a steward of the land to protect nature for the future of America.

She bought it.

However, she wasn't able to convince Davis Dunne or any of the other lawyers to cut a check big enough to settle the class action lawsuit. So, it seemed, we were going to trial.

I watched Davis Dunne and his methane gas cronies zoom away from the Ewing T. Kerr Federal Building in his big yellow Hummer.

When I called Harry to tell him that the case did not settle, he didn't sound the least bit surprised. "If I thought we were near the settlement stage, Mac, I'd been there myself. These cases don't settle early on. We'll need to spend another hundred grand before either side starts feeling the pinch."

* * *

I got the sense on the way home from the settlement conference that Butch and Beth had something heavy on their minds. Like Harry, I didn't expect the case to settle this early in the game, and I had told them as much, but somehow they both looked defeated and afraid. Neither of them talked much. Beth sat in the back of the crew cab and knitted while Butch drove along at a leisurely pace. We talked of weather and geological formations and Indian culture and nearly everything else other than the case. I imagined that Butch somehow felt responsible to get a good settlement for the rest of the folks who'd joined us in the class action. I wanted to reassure him that it would be all right, but I was afraid to open the can of worms. I didn't feel like making promises today. I wasn't sure how the case would turn out. We had a heavy legal burden to prove contamination of groundwater, and I knew that Davis Dunne was busy hiring every expert that money could buy. Harry had warned me not to shoot the moon with experts because they were expensive and often overkill. "The biggest mistake," Harry had said, "is that lawyers think they need to refute every expert with another expert. Don't fall for it. An expert is an expert only if he or she has something worthwhile to say. You can discredit an unworthy expert without calling a counter-expert."

Harry's motto had always been, "KISS." Keep It Simple Stupid. He liked simplicity and common sense. Jurors understood his ways. But I'm not Harry. I'm not as confident and casual and full of bravado. He can pull it off. I was beginning to wonder whether I could.

Butch broke the silence of my inner thoughts. "See that over there," he said, pointing out the truck window at a monument sign reading "Fort Phil Kearny Next Exit." I nodded. "Somewhere around 1865, Fort Phil Kearny was built near the Bozeman Trail. It had one of the shortest and bloodiest histories of any outpost in the West. It was constructed in open violation of the treaty between the U.S. government and the Sioux Indians. See, this was prime buffalo hunting territory for the Sioux, and Red Cloud and Crazy Horse swore to drive the white men out. During the first few months of occupation, the Sioux killed two-thirds of the garrison—half of which were killed in the Fetterman Fight." I nodded as he spoke, interested in the history of the area. "There were other battles. Bloody battles. The Sioux lost. But they won the war a year later when the government decided to abandon the Powder River Basin and the Bozeman Trail. And as soon as the soldiers left, the Indians burned down Fort Kearny. Ain't nothin' left of it. Nowadays, they have a museum there. You should go see it sometime. It's a good history lesson. And the movie they show at the museum tells an important lesson. It's okay to lose a battle or two. Just don't lose the war."

Chapter 15

When Butch dropped me off at the office, I was relieved to see that the lights were still on and, presumably, someone was still working at nine o'clock in the evening. I didn't like being in the office alone because I'd been attacked at gunpoint in our Jackson Hole office a few years back. An intruder had broken in before I arrived to work in the early morning and forced me to strip. Harry arrived before the intruder inflicted any physical harm, but the emotional scars were still very fresh.

Pamela, my new paralegal, met me at the door. Her breath smelled of stale coffee and her eyes were burdened with dark circles, but her mouth motored along with four hundred horsepower speed as she filled me in on her Lexis computer research. She rattled on and on as she followed me to my office. I picked up Ted from my office chair and set him on the ground. He slowly arched his back downward, stretching out his paws in front of him. Then he brought his paws together and arched upward so that his spine made the shape of a "C." Content with his stretching and his desire for a light snack, he sauntered over to his cat dish and munched on kernels of dry food. I watched my cat, vaguely listening as Pamela droned on and on about class action lawsuits and the timeline in which we needed to file certain documents. I'd already performed this research before I filed the case, and was well aware of what needed to be done.

Ted, in the middle of a bite, glanced sideways, honing in on an object under the hissing radiator in the corner of my office. With the instincts of a predator, he crouched down and slowly but repetitively flicked his tail to the right and then to the left. Patience was a virtue, and he was enjoying the splendor of the moment. I watched as he slowly crept in the direction of the radiator. Then, without a moment's notice, Ted sprung, lunged, trapped and gutted a small gray mouse in the middle of the floor. He was not apologetic about the bloodstain on the carpet, nor was he concerned about the remnants that he was disinterested in consuming. He was completely content with himself and his prey, and even had the audacity to rub against my leg, seeking a pat on the head for a job well done.

Pamela, who'd watched this entire episode in horror, continued with her monologue about civil procedure in the class action courtroom. "I printed the deadlines for you and downloaded them onto our system," she said. I nodded reassuringly, noting a large stain of dried up something on the thigh of her black stretch rayon pants. I looked around to see what she'd been eating. Her workbench was littered with soda cans and empty chip bags and a half-eaten can of bean dip.

"And get this!" she said, ruffling through a stack of papers, eventually pulling out MethZap's response to the form interrogatories we had propounded on them. "We asked for the name of the owners and executives of MethZap and they responded by listing a guy by the name of Everett Fisher as the CEO. Normally, I wouldn't think much of it, but Megan told me that your boyfriend's last name is Fisher. So I went online to check this Everett guy out and here is what my Google search found on him."

She handed me a manila file filled with computer printouts concerning Everett Fisher. I thumbed through several pages of information detailing how much stock he owned in the company and his various stock option plans and retirement funds. Usual corporate stuff. Then I focused on an article with a photograph of him shaking hands with the former governor of Wyoming. His profile was hauntingly familiar.

I quickly leafed through the rest of the papers. Everett Fisher was born in Montana and worked for years as a coal miner at Spring Creek Coal Mine as a rig operator. During the 1990's, he quit his job and started MethZap. In an article from *Miner's Log Magazine*, he was quoted, "I don't have much experience running a business, but I know the ins and outs of mining. I brought on a partner in the deal who knows the money stuff and so far, we're doin' all right."

"Did you do a public records search on him?" I asked Pam. She sprang out of her chair to help me find it in the file. Her large bosom fell forward toward me with the force of gravity and I felt compelled to back up in my chair. Oblivious to my personal space boundaries, she moved in closer, found the piece of paper and hurled it my way. I perused the information, noting his date of birth, which put him at fifty-nine years old, and his marital information. He was presently single, but had been married three times in the past: once to Winona Scott; once to Lori Webb; and once to Mary Beth Keller (now Mary Beth Anderson). My suspicions were confirmed. Everett Fisher was Beth Anderson's first husband. Greg was their son.

"Do you think Greg knows that his dad's company is wrecking his mom's ranch? Do you think Butch knows? Oooooooweee, if they don't know yet, boy are they in for a surprise."

"I have no idea," I finally said out loud. I sat there for a few seconds and pondered the problems this discovery created. The "what-ifs" were mind-boggling. *What if Everett deliberately caused mayhem on the ranch just to get revenge against Beth? What if Greg knew that his real father was drilling on his stepfather's ranch? What if Beth was caught in the middle of some horrible power struggle between her former husband and her present husband?* The thoughts swirled in my head, besmirching my theory that there weren't any conflicts-of-interest in the case. The fact of the matter was that I was suing my boyfriend's father while representing my boyfriend's mother.

I looked down at Ted, who was rubbing his cheek against my ankle, waiting for me to acknowledge his accomplished kill. Irony struck again. Somehow, I felt like I was in the middle of a "cat and mouse" game. The problem was that I wasn't sure who was the cat or the mouse.

FALL - WINTER

Chapter 16

Fall had a certain feel to it, unlike any other season of the year. But what made fall unique in the western part of America was elk hunting season. Sheridan was no exception to this rule, and I could sense a certain chill in the morning air as the men in bright orange and camouflage masqueraded through town, loading their trucks with their ATVs and enough beer to get them through the four-day weekend.

Harry, who was not a hunter, always joked about hunting season with his gun-toting pals. Every year, he circulated a fake Wyoming Penal Code section about hunting attorneys, which read something like:

Any person with a valid state rodent, snake, elk or deer-hunting license may also hunt and harvest attorneys for recreational and sport (non-commercial) purposes. The taking of attorneys with traps or deadfalls is permitted. The use of United States currency as bait, however, is prohibited. It is unlawful to hunt attorneys within two hundred yards of courtrooms, law libraries, health clubs, country clubs, hospitals, or brothels, except on Wednesday afternoons. It is further unlawful to chase, herd or harvest attorneys from power boats, helicopters or other aircraft.

He changed the penal code section every year to keep his cronies laughing. It had become so popular over the years that the *Bar Journal* even ran it in the "Public Notices" section. I thought of it now as I drove to work, watching the hunters prepare for their kill.

Sherman Todd, Greg's friend, had been conspicuously absent since I'd moved to town. I'd seen him during the first week I'd moved here, when I attended the Powder River Basin Resource Council meeting with Butch, but I hadn't seen him since. I knew that he was busy with his engineering job and he often went away to the mountains on the weekends, but I'd expected him to drop in at the office for a quick hello or something. But I had been so bogged down in the quicksand of litigation, I probably wouldn't have had much time for him anyway. I thought of him as I drove–how committed he was to the environment. I envied his conviction.

A minute later, as if my mind was seasoned with intuition, I spotted him driving toward me in his Subaru. He was awash in orange–like a pumpkin ripened for harvest–his hunting rife affixed to the side window. The irony struck me cold. I called Greg on my cell and asked if Sherman was a hunter.

"Of course," Greg said. "All environmentalists understand the importance and value of ecological balance. Hunters pay fees, which, in turn, employ wardens to enforce game management. Hunting forms the basis for animal population control." *So much for natural selection.* "Every year Sherman goes to the One Shot Antelope Hunt in Lander. The hunters are permitted only a single cartridge in pursuit of Wyoming's fastest animal. It's quite a party, I'm told."

"I see. Sherman just doesn't seem the type to jam a bullet into a gun and go running after antelope," I said.

"Was Rowdy Rodiger with him?" Greg asked.

"Rowdy Rodiger? The landman for MethZap? Why would he be with Sherman?"

"Nevermind. Forget I asked. I don't know why I said that."

* * *

Sure You Can Trust the Government! Just Ask an Indian. I studied the bumper sticker on the pickup in front of me on the way to work, which made me think about the depositions I was going to be taking that day–more testimony from government employees who'd issued permits for methane gas drilling in the Powder River Basin. It would be a rather boring day, to be sure. I passed the pickup that I'd been following with the bumper sticker. The man driving it looked like a skinhead. Bumper stickers told me a lot about the owner of the car. I looked for more on my ten-minute drive through town. *Horse Power is Like Sex! You Never Get*

Enough. The driver of this jacked-up pickup looked like he was heading to his construction site. *I Got This Truck For My Wife! Good Trade, Huh?* The driver of this beat up old Ford was a balding fat guy without his front teeth. *Bad Ass Girls Drive Bad Ass Toys.* The gal driving this souped-up Jeep had big hair and big boobs.

My cell phone rang as I passed the gal with the big hair. It was Pamela on the line. There seemed to be a problem at the office, and she suggested that I park in back and take the stairs instead of the elevator. When I rounded Coffeen Avenue, I saw a group of protesters with big signs marching in front of my office on Main Street. I quickly turned on Loucks Street and headed for the back entrance to my building. I could tell from the tenor and demeanor of the crowd that these were not people supportive of our cause.

Since the lawsuit was filed, we'd had a hundred of phone calls voicing their dissent about the case. Some people distrusted the judicial system and didn't feel that it should be allowed to dictate what happens on private land. Others were concerned that the lawsuit would squelch job growth and industry in the area. Yet another group felt that we were out-of-towners, just like the methane gas people, and that we were in town just to make a quick buck. I expected this sort of dissent in the community and respected people's free speech.

Today's group of protesters were an unusual breed and the basis for griping was unexpected. They were all men–or I should say, a specific type of men commonly referred to in certain parts of the country as "rednecks." It didn't seem like they were bothered by the lawsuit itself or job growth or groundwater. They were bothered that the lawyer commanding this lawsuit was a woman. A woman! Their signs were rude and demoralizing to females in general, explaining how we were inferior and stupid and should be doing what God intended for us to do: make babies and cook meals.

Pam and I peeked out my office window at the protestors holding their signs: *Women Belong in the Kichen. Women Don't Make Good Lawers.* I could only imagine the bumper stickers on their trucks. They certainly weren't winners of the Spelling Bee.

* * *

"Now that you've heard all the admonitions regarding depositions, please state your name for the record." Davis Dunne was taking our soil expert's deposition. He had walked through the line of redneck protesters and got down to business without remark or small talk. I was almost hoping that he'd say something about the protesters. Maybe we could joke a bit together. Break the ice. Actually communicate like humans. But, like the many other days I'd spent with Davis Dunne over the past few months, this too would be a long, tedious day. "Dr. Roderick, what is your profession?"

"For the past twenty-eight years, I've been a professor of soil science and land reclamation at the University of Montana. Over the years, I've probably worked with twenty-five or so mine companies, but currently I do most of my research for the Environmental Protection Agency, or as we call it, the EPA. We determine who is responsible for groundwater contamination and create what we believe to be the best design for clean-up of toxic soils and waterways."

"How did you become involved in this case?"

"Miss MacIntosh contacted me and asked me for my professional opinion on the soil remediation at the Anderson ranch. Specifically, I was asked to analyze the drill pads and whether the soil had been dealt with properly. Subsequently, I was asked to evaluate the groundwater."

"Dr. Roderick, what is your professional opinion regarding the soil and water on the Anderson Ranch?"

"In my opinion, MethZap did not preserve the good soil at the ranch. In addition, I found a problem with the chemistry of the fill material in that the soil has a very high electrical conductivity, which means that the soil has an extremely high salt content. This high salt content has caused a loss in plant productivity. And let me be precise in my definition of salt. For simplicity purposes, it does contain table salt, like the kind we put on our food. But it also contains calcium sulfate, potassium sulfate and magnesium sulfate, along with table salt."

Dr. Roderick talked for hours about soil horizons and geologic stratrum. He testified about his laboratory analytical data, as well as the in-the-field chemical testing. He used a document entitled "Soil Survey of Sheridan

County," prepared by the National Resource Conservation Service, to compare the soils on the Andersons' ranch some twenty years ago to the soils now. Dr. Roderick noted significant differences.

"Compaction is a major concern as the soil today near the coalbed methane sites on the Anderson ranch has the consistency of concrete and electrical conductivity at eleven mmhos per centimeter, which is exceptionally high."

Davis Dunne took copious notes, conferring regularly with his own expert, who also attended the deposition.

"Are you testifying that the soil near the well heads will *never* grow grass, Dr. Roderick?" Dunne looked up over his thick glasses, his upper lip curled back like a snake sensing his prey.

"No. I think it's appropriate to say that the plant growth is going to be permanently impaired for–I'll put a time limit–for at least a century."

"But you haven't tested all the soil on the Anderson ranch, have you?"

"No, that would take -"

"You just took one sample in the control area, but you took a bunch of samples on the well head sites and averaged them together to compare to the control area, correct?"

"Well, we–what we did in the control area was I made a professional judgment as to where the best location was to get a representative sample from the adjacent undisturbed rangeland. So, it was one sample from the rangeland."

"And it's important to have a control test, isn't it?"

"It is useful in this line of work, yes," Dr. Roderick said.

"But in science it is important to have your subject test and a control test, isn't it?"

"In most studies it is, yes."

"It's basically standard procedure, isn't it?" Dunne was pinning him down for a reason. Dr. Roderick sensed persecution.

"It's–control is often very important."

"So, now that we've established the importance of control testing, Dr. Roderick, let's get back to electrical conductivity of the soil. Your reports show an increase in electrical conductivity, don't they? And electrical conductivity is a measure of salt in the soil?"

"Yes."

"Salt could come from good things, correct? It's minerals in the soil that produce salt, right? An increase in electrical conductivity doesn't necessarily mean a bad thing, does it?"

I could have objected to Dunne's compound questions, but Dr. Roderick seemed savvy enough to answer whichever question suited him best.

"No. In soil materials, increasing electrical conductivity is a problem for plant growth."

"Put fertilizer on the ground and that's going to increase the electrical conductivity, is it not?"

"It does."

"So then using your analogy, you put fertilizer on the ground, that's going to be bad for plant growth?"

"No. That's not what I intended to say."

"That's what I want to know because we're searching for the truth, doctor. You're saying that the increase in electrical conductivity is indicative of something that's bad for the soil, yet I tell you that MethZap put fertilizer on the ground and you say, yes, that's going to increase the electrical conductivity. How can that be bad?"

"Well, fertilizer provides plants with nutrients—nitrogen, phosphorus, potassium. But, when we apply fertilizer to a lawn, the salt content increases. The plants can actually be greatly impaired by the high salt content, which is why we must water more often after fertilizing."

"As a matter of fact, doctor --"

"Therefore, if you over-fertilize, you can kill the grass."

Finally, common sense prevailed over antagonism. One of our contentions was that MethZap over-fertilized the soil on the Andersons' ranch after the land had been flooded with the salty methane discharge water. Therefore, the soil got a double-whammy of salt and it killed the grass. Normally, fertilizer is good for plant growth, provided that there is sufficient water to help the plants absorb the new nutrients. But when the soil is already saturated with salt, the additional fertilizer nutrients counter-act and kill what plant life exists. Davis Dunne's face pinched in frustration. It was time to take a break.

* * *

Our next expert that Davis Dunne deposed was Dr. Donaldson, Dean of Environment and Health Sciences at the University of Wyoming. He testified that the Bureau of Land Management had failed miserably in its evaluation of concentrations of salts and toxic elements such as arsenic, barium and selenium in groundwater reservoirs used in methane gas production. Dr. Donaldson also testified that the Bureau of Land Management did not consider the sodium absorption ratio, electrical conductivity or the pH of the water discharged. Neither Dunne nor the Bureau of Land Management attorneys were able to get Dr. Donaldson to waver on any of his opinions regarding groundwater contamination and the Bureau's irresponsibility in issuing permits without proper data.

Our last expert, Dr. John Dewey, was a professor of Ecosystem Management at the University of Wisconsin. He had extensive background and training on freshwater systems, with particular emphasis on streams and rivers. Dr. Dewey was prepared to testify at trial that the "Powder River, which was once a very healthy unspoiled river in a semi-arid region, was now endangering the ecosystems of flora and fauna for hundreds of miles." He went so far as to say during deposition that the methane water threatened the cottonwood trees, which are a crucial habitat to mammals and birds. He continued by opining that the standing bodies of run-off water were unnatural and likely to develop their own biota, as well as non-native fauna. When he suggested that West Nile virus was a real threat, Dunne nearly blew his top.

"On what basis do you form this opinion, Dr. Dewey? Are you now a self-proclaimed expert in entomology?"

Dr. Dewey wasn't intimidated. Instead, he showed Davis Dunne a number of field studies conducted by his research staff, several of whom had entomology degrees, confirming the existence of infected mosquitoes and identifying some sage grouse that had been stricken with the virus.

After listening to our experts testify during their depositions, I felt considerably better about our case. All three were professional and trustworthy, and were able to speak in terms that a jury could understand. Dunne and the government lawyers didn't pick our experts apart much and I felt confident that we had hired a good team.

Chapter 17

Davis Dunne did not want to end his week on a low note, so he made sure to notice Beth Anderson's deposition for Friday afternoon. She was as nervous as a child on the first day of school, but she tried hard not to show it. She wore a long black skirt, black high-heeled boots and a long-sleeved red knit sweater. The diamond horseshoe necklace that she claimed was her lucky charm shimmered in the sunlight. Her dark hair was pulled back off her face and fixed in a chignon at the nape of her neck. Her hands shook as she and I rehearsed her testimony behind closed doors in my office. Pam poked her head in several times to inform me that Dunne was ready to begin. I wanted to make him wait a bit—let him soak in the defiled pool of our conference room, which had seen more take-out orders in the past month than McDonalds.

Dunne stood when Beth entered the room, exchanging pleasantries as if she were his long-lost relative. She relaxed a bit as he went through the preliminary questions with her about how she met Butch and how they decided to buy the Crazy Woman Ranch. It was as if they were catching up on life. She explained that Greg was her son from a prior marriage and that Wyatt was her son with Butch, but that they'd raised both boys equally and they loved them both the same. She told how she helped develop Butch's business and her involvement with life on the ranch.

"Okay. Well, let's talk a little bit now about MethZap and your involvement with them. When was the first time you heard of MethZap?"

"When a man was snooping around on the ranch one day, surveying the land and placing stakes for well sites for methane gas. I asked him who gave him permission to come onto our property to do that. He said, 'Well, you have to call MethZap. That's all I know.' He gave me the number."

"So what did you do first? Did you call MethZap or did you get in touch with somebody else?"

"Well, naturally, I called Butch first."

"And then who'd you call?"

"My attorney. Chance Baker."

"Why did you call your attorney? Did you think you could scare MethZap off?"

"Well . . . I was hoping we could get them to find another property to drill on or something of that nature. I didn't want them on my property, that's for sure."

"You wanted to intimidate MethZap into going away, right? It's no secret around town that you are an anti-methane person. You've been quite vocal about it, correct?"

"Well, I don't know if I'd go that far. But, I'd agree with you that I haven't been fond of the fact that these outfits come into town with their noisy trucks and their foul-mouthed employees, and they think that they can just walk onto anybody's land and start drilling and wrecking the place. They leave their trucks parked wherever they darn well please and have no qualms about smoking cigarettes and tossing their butts on the ground where my cows and horses and chickens graze. They urinate wherever they want, as if my ranch was their outhouse. I could go on and on."

"Obviously. But the question posed to you was that you wanted to intimidate MethZap with your lawyer's letters so that they wouldn't drill on your property, right?"

"I didn't want them on my property."

"So, you were willing to do whatever you could to keep MethZap off your property, right?"

"I didn't say that."

"But you did try to, didn't you, Mrs. Anderson?" Beth was fidgeting with her wedding band and growing increasingly anxious and edgy. I walked over to the table near the window and poured her a glass of water. She took a quick sip, but it didn't seem to calm her nerves.

"Isn't it true, Mrs. Anderson, that you had Chance Baker place a telephone call to the CEO of MethZap, threatening him if he pursued drilling on your ranch?" Beth's silence was deafening. She'd never mentioned this to me before. Nor had Butch. "Answer the question, Mrs. Anderson." Davis Dunne was leaning halfway across the table, bearing down on her like a hungry cheetah.

"I didn't want them drilling on my ranch."

"So, you had Chance Baker call your ex-husband, who happens to be the CEO of MethZap, and threaten to blackmail him if he started drilling operations on your ranch, correct?"

"Blackmail is a strong word, Mr. Dunne."

"I call 'em like I see 'em, Mrs. Anderson. Now answer the question."

Chapter 18

"Everett Fisher was a terrible husband and a terrible father and whatever was said to him, he deserved tenfold. Do you have children, Mr. Dunne?"

"That's not the point of -"

"Well, it's the point I'm making right now, if you please. Children deserve a father who loves them and won't walk out on them the minute things get tough. Do you walk out on your clients when things aren't going your way, Mr. Dunne?" It looked like Davis Dunne was contemplating answering her. "Because if you did, I'd call you a quitter. Just like Everett Fisher is. He's a lowlife and a quitter and he walked out of my son's life. If it weren't for Butch, I don't know what would have happened to me and Greg, and before I forget to mention–"

"Did you threaten to expose Mr. Fisher to the local press if he didn't leave you and your ranch alone?"

"Threaten him with what, Mr. Dunne? I think the time for collecting child support has long passed, don't you? Greg is closing in on forty years old. This is an old score to settle. And I can tell anyone I want about what a no-good husband he was."

"But you threatened to damage his reputation as a businessman, didn't you? Like you said, this is an 'old score to settle.'"

"Businessman? Is that what he calls himself? He's nothing more than a flunky coal miner, if you ask me. He was always a shark, in his own sneaky little way. I have no idea how he got a company up and running, but I'm sure as the sun will come up tomorrow that he sweet-talked or swindled his way into it, like he's done everything else in his life. Anyway, it makes no difference as we sit here today. I had to sign the surface damage agreement and he got what he wanted—he got to destroy my life once again."

"That's what this is all about, isn't it? Your ex-husband got the better of you once again and now you've filed a lawsuit for revenge?"

"Objection. This has gone far enough," I said. I instructed Beth not to answer the question and demanded that we take a fifteen-minute break.

* * *

"Butch warned me that you were as feisty as Mocha, your horse," I said after closing the door to my office. Beth looked at me with fire in her eyes. "Why didn't you tell me about threatening Everett?"

"Butch and I talked about it and we didn't think it would ever come up. I know it looks bad. But it's not as if we threatened him like that attorney suggests. I just wanted Chance to put a little pressure on him and I hoped he'd back down and go away." *You hoped it would go away? Was she naïve or was I?*

"This is not going to go away, Beth. It's going to come up over and over and you'll be asked to testify about it in front of the jury. Davis Dunne is going to make this case out to be a case of vengeance. He's going to try to make it look like you went after MethZap to settle an old score with your ex-husband."

"Well, that's not what this is about."

"I know that, Beth." I looked into her eyes and saw frustration and fear and anger all wrapped up into a single package. "I know that this is about the ranch and your family and Butch and the life you deserve to lead. But you have to understand that as your lawyer, I need to know all of the reasons that you are here. I need to know about the past and the present and the future and how all of this affects you, because I can't represent you if you are not truthful and forthcoming with me. I can only be a good lawyer to you if I know what I'm up against. Do you understand? If I get sandbagged in court, I lose my credibility with the jury and if that happens, we lose. And I'm not just talking about you and Butch and Harry and me. I'm talking about the other forty-eight plaintiffs that we talked into joining us on the crusade. They've put up good money and good time to help us stop these gas hogs from sucking the life out of the Basin. If we lose, they lose, and that's not fair to them. You need to be straight with me about your agenda. Why are you here, Beth?"

She looked at me for a second and then looked down at her tightly clinched hands. She opened her mouth, about to say something, and then she closed it again. She sucked on her lower lip, stripping off a layer of lipstick with her teeth.

"I'm here because I feel like I'm a steward of the land and because I want to teach that son-of-a-bitch a lesson." It sounded rehearsed.

"Okay. That's perfectly okay. We can do both. As long as we're honest with each other about our motives." Her upper lip pulled back a bit, revealing the pleasure of a woman understood. She reached into her purse and pulled out a tube of lipstick and a small mirror, reapplying the red sheen with great vigilance. "So long as we're not here to nurse a grudge. I've found that many people are quite fond of their resentments. In fact, I know a few people who hold their resentments near and dear to their heart. I want to make sure that we're not spending hundreds of thousands of dollars for the sole purpose of doting on your past bitterness."

Beth considered my remarks for a moment before responding with a wink. "This case is primarily about the ranch and the environment. But we all have different motives, Mac. All fifty of us class-action plaintiffs have different ideas about this case. One of mine has to do the jerk who walked out the door and left me with a small child."

"I understand that you want to see Everett Fisher burn in hell for what he did to you, but that's not going to happen as a result of this lawsuit."

"I know."

"So?" I asked. "Is there more to this story?"

Beth took a deep sigh as she reached over and embraced me, like we were girlfriends confiding in each other. She took another deep breath and looked me in the eye. "I suppose there are some things you should know." And with that, she told me a long story about her past with Everett. I knew that Dunne was waiting for us in the conference room, but I sat patiently and listened. After she was finished, she gave me another hug, as if she finally had some closure. As she released our embrace she said, "Just don't tell Butch about the son-of-a-bitch part. He thinks I'm long over Everett Fisher."

Chapter 19

"At some point in the course of your meetings with the MethZap people, did you meet with Ace Sanders, the president of the company?"

"Oh, sure. I'll never forget that meeting," Beth said, resuming her deposition testimony.

"Why?" Davis Dunne acted conversational. He removed his thick, round glasses and set them on the table, as if he was genuinely in the mood to listen.

"He came out to the ranch one day, inspecting the pipes and the roads that they were going to use to drill the wells. This was before they started drilling. See, Butch and I were making a fuss about the big rigs hauling pipes all over the place and scaring the living daylights out of the horses. We raised quite a ruckus with Rowdy Rodiger, so he finally sent the big boss out. That Ace Sanders is a crafty man. He came out to the ranch and spent a good hour touring the arena and the ranch house, complimenting us on all the improvements we'd made to the place. He went on and on about how nice the kitchen was with the new granite countertops and all. Said that he wanted the same kind himself in his home. Well, we got to talking real friendly after awhile. I even offered him some coffee. As he held tight of his coffee mug, he leaned in real close to me and whispered, 'Beth, just pretend we're married, and I can do whatever I want, whenever I want and however I want.'" Beth blushed as she finished her statement, whether in embarrassment or anger, I wasn't sure.

Davis Dunne snatched his glasses from the table and wrapped them back around his ears. He made a few notes on his yellow pad and then stared down Beth, like a mother bear protecting her young from an aggressor.

"Was Butch with you when Ace allegedly made this comment?"

"No. He was outside."

"So no one else overheard Ace allegedly say this to you?"

"Not that I know of. But I know he said it."

"Are you happily married, Mrs. Anderson?"

"Objection. Don't answer that Beth." I stood, leaning across the conference table, and pointed my finger at Davis Dunne.

"Do you want to go off the record?" the court reporter asked.

"No. I want this on the record, thank you," I said. "I will instruct Mrs. Anderson not to answer any questions regarding her marriage. It is none of your business and not part of the litigation and you know it. We haven't sued for any tortuous breaches, loss of consortium or any other cause of action that merits you digging into the Andersons' private matters. You may ask her about the conversation she had with Ace Sanders all you want, but don't you dare try to intimidate her." I sat back down in my chair and took a deep breath. Adrenaline was pumping through my veins like an infection.

"Don't *you* lecture *me* on how to take a deposition, Ms. MacIntosh. I've been in this business a long time. Much longer than you. I can ask whatever question I please. You can object until your voice is hoarse, young lady, but I'm entitled to ask this witness anything that I deem pertinent to the case. So you sit your pretty little self down and take notes. Maybe you'll learn a thing or two from the pro." He turned his shoulders back toward Beth with scheming contempt. "When was the last time you had sex with Everett Fisher?"

Needless to say, the deposition was immediately adjourned.

Chapter 20

I suppose we all have preconceptions about others and often these preconceptions are the result of first impressions. I must admit that I had a preconception about Ace Sanders long before I took his deposition. My preconception proved to be rather accurate.

He showed up an hour late for his deposition without an apology or an explanation. When I asked him about the large bandage below his right ear, he callously explained that he'd had skin cancer removed. I commented on his red hair and freckles, trying to correlate our Irish heritage. He quickly scolded me, informing in a rather condescending fashion that he was of Scottish descent. "Well, we have one thing in common, Mr. Sanders," I said. "We're about the same height."

I suppose this wasn't putting my best foot forward in negotiation tactics, but sometimes it is important to even the score.

In lieu of further small talk, I jumped straight into deposition protocol. Ace Sanders stated that he'd had his deposition taken a number of times previously and that he was fully aware of the protocol. We dispensed with the mantra and proceeded. He told me that he was born and raised in Wisconsin and had a business management degree from the University of Wisconsin at Madison. Sanders met up with Everett Fisher on a jobsite in Montana and they discussed going into business together. Sanders said that he liked Everett's knowledge of the mining business and his demanding nature in general. He wanted a business partner who could fit in with the employees and could tolerate the salty language and lifestyle of the mining community. Everett lacked ties to any one place and was ready, willing and able to move around continuously–a favorable trait for gas players, who never stick around one place too long.

Sanders testified that they had a number of operations going in the Powder River Basin when they heard of the possibilities near the Arvada area, where Butch and Beth owned their ranch. He and Everett snooped around for a bit, then hired Rowdy Rodiger to be their landman, since the kid knew the area better than they did and knew which ranchers would readily "sell the farm" to make a quick buck.

"So, Mr. Sanders, how did you and Everett Fisher decide to purchase the mineral rights on the Anderson ranch?"

"Actually, that was Everett's call. We'd been successful on a number of plays on ranches near there, and he liked the look and feel of the Anderson place. He felt like the topography of the buttes on the ranch screamed of methane gas, so we had Rowdy make the necessary inquiries and we made the necessary deals with the necessary people to buy the rights."

"When you say 'necessary deals with the necessary people,' to whom are you referring?" I asked.

"You know. Local officials. State officials. Higher ups in the energy business. Luckily, our current administration in the White House is pro-energy development so we have connections with the folks–"

"Excuse me," Davis Dunne interrupted. "May I have a minute to confer with my client." When we resumed the deposition, Sanders had the appearance of a man schooled in careful language. He was methodical with his answers–especially to the questions that concerned MethZap's relationships with government entities.

"Mr. Sanders, have you ever used a marriage analogy when describing the relationship between a surface owner and an operator?" I asked.

"Yes, I have. I say that this is a long-term relationship, just like a marriage. There's going to be some give and take on both sides. Not everybody can get along and everything, so, we have to give a little bit and they have to give a little bit and hopefully we can have a union that's going to last for a long time."

"In your mind, Mr. Sanders, Butch and Beth Anderson are only the surface owners of the land, isn't that true?"

"I believe so, correct."

"Okay. Even though they are the people that live on the land?"

"Yes."

"They are the people that raise their children on the land?"

"I assume so, yes."

"And they are the people that make their livelihood from the land, correct?"

"Correct."

"But to you they are only surface owners, correct?"

"They are the surface owners, yes. I don't get your–"

"All right. And when you had that initial meeting with Beth Anderson out on her ranch, Beth kept going on and on about all the things she was upset about, all the things that were getting messed up on the ranch as a result of MethZap being out there, right?"

"Yes."

"She explained there were a lot of issues that she thought you should correct, didn't she?"

"Yes, she did, as a matter of fact."

"And she was upset, wasn't she?"

"It appeared as much."

"And so when you were sitting in this meeting listening to Mrs. Anderson talk about her complaints, you thought she needed to understand that MethZap had the right to develop the minerals under the property, right?"

"That was one of the points I was trying to make, yes."

"And she was probably irritating you a little bit, wasn't she?"

"Well . . . I-I-I don't believe I'd say that, no. No. I wouldn't say she was irritating."

"Well, at some point you decided you needed to make the point to her and you said something like, 'Look, it's like a marriage. We can do whatever we want, whenever we want,' or words to that effect, didn't you?"

"No. No, I didn't say that."

"You don't deny that you've used the marriage analogy before, do you, sir?"

"No, I don't," Sanders said, scratching at his shirt collar like he had fleas.

"So, you have used the marriage analogy, correct?"

"Yes. I mean, correct." Ace Sanders looked like a wolf caught in a trap. But, his calmness told me that he'd swam against this befouled current before. "All's I meant by that is when we are on someone's property, especially in the beginning when all the prep work is being done, we have to be around each other a lot. The owners have to get used to us being out there and there is a certain period when things are a little touchy. Then, after the drilling is going and the wellheads are up, things sort of mellow out. Our rigs aren't on the land as much and the noise simmers down. It's like a marriage. It's all hot and heavy at first, then you settle in and get used to one another. Then after awhile, you don't even notice the little stuff. That's what I meant by my marriage statement."

"But that's not what you *said*, is it?"

Chapter 21

"This is the third time this week them assholes have been out here snooping on my property! Either they get the hell out of here or I'm goin' a shoot 'em. I have several guns to choose from, you know. I may be a woman, but I know how to aim and pull the trigger. You didn't tell me that this kind a crap was going to happen when I signed up for this lawsuit."

It was the third call I'd had so far today from class action members. They were fed up with the lobbing of litigation grenades. The government lawyers were having a field day with their so-called "property inspections" and I didn't have enough legal manpower to fight it. Even with Chance Baker and his legal team as reinforcement, I was understaffed and unprepared for the sheer force of legal bombardment that was being launched on a daily basis. It was completely understandable that the co-plaintiffs were upset. They'd spent a good deal of their autumn in depositions, court appearances or property inspections. I'd already asked for another five thousand dollars from each of them, and the fees and costs were growing exponentially. I would have to ask for more money again soon.

Meanwhile, many of the class action members were complaining that their royalty checks had been sliced in half recently and they suspected that MethZap was screwing them. I had no way of verifying this theory unless I hired yet another expert to go out onto their properties and monitor their wellheads. Of course, this would cost more money, but my hand was almost forced. I couldn't afford a mutiny.

The day started in a peculiar fashion. I awoke abruptly from a bad dream only minutes before my alarm was set to go off. In my dream, a huge flock of Canada geese were flying in formation overhead. I watched them in amazement, noting how perfectly spaced they were. But suddenly, the leader of the formation took a nose-dive toward the earth. Shockingly, every bird followed, smashing headfirst into the salt-laden, sulfurous ground. I ran to the crash site and was horrified to see the carcasses of hundreds of birds with broken necks and bent frames. When I bolted from this nightmare, I sat in bed for a few moments, stroking Ted and thinking about the deeper meaning of my dream. *Did the flock of geese represent the plaintiffs? Was I leading them on a nose-dive into doom?* After fielding a number of telephone calls that morning from disgruntled plaintiffs, I decided to pay Chance Baker a visit.

Chance had two offices—one on the fourth floor of a bank building, and one at the Powder River Basin Resource Council headquarters. Being that he'd been divorced four times and paid child support to several households, it was fair to assume that one could find him at any hour of the day or night in one of the offices. Butch told me that Chance slept on the sofa of whichever office he worked latest into the night.

When I arrived at the office in the bank building, it was early—before eight o'clock in the morning. Chance was not there, but the door was open and the lights were on. I figured that he'd gone to the YMCA for his morning swim and shower. He was slightly overweight and was trying desperately to shed a few pounds.

I walked around the desk of his cluttered office to leave him a note requesting an in-person meeting. I searched under piles of papers and files to find a blank post-it note. I found the post-its that I was looking for—and a whole lot more. Amidst the piles of pleadings and papers and oil and gas leases was a file labeled "Anderson Family Trust." Faced with a parochial schoolgirl decision, I could hear the voice of Sister Agnes Winifred telling me not to open the file. But, a product of the police academy and law school, I couldn't help myself. I opened it.

Exercising poor judgment can quickly create a situation in which only further foolish choices are possible. I knew that snooping in Chance's office was foolish, but it didn't stop me from flipping through pages of standard legal jargon before I found Butch and Beth Anderson's Last Will and Testament. I felt as if I was opening someone's private journal—prying into their belongings and desires. But it was like a car accident in that once you saw it, you couldn't help but gawk as you passed by.

One could learn a lot about another human being by studying their specific bequests. For example, Butch vowed to leave the ranch to Beth, if she survived him. The ranch included the land and the arena and the house. But it didn't include certain horses or equipment or his pickup truck or his dog. Wyatt was entitled to those special things. Didn't Beth like the dog? What about the pickup? Was she opposed to that? Wyatt had his own pickup. It seemed random, yet I was sure that there was a story behind it. The saddles were Wyatt's too. And the guns. And Butch's rodeo trophies. In fact, Wyatt would be the recipient of just about every item special to Butch's heart and soul. I kept on reading.

If Beth died before Butch, her portion of the ranch would go to Butch and Wyatt. Not to Greg! In fact, Greg was barely mentioned in Beth's will, other than some special bequests of photographs and jewelry that had belonged to her mother. I wondered if Greg knew that he'd been virtually disinherited. And then I remembered a comment he made to Butch and Beth when we were at the rodeo. He said something about them giving the ranch to Wyatt. At the time, I thought that I'd misunderstood. *Had there been some kind of family feud? How could Beth agree to such a disparity? Did Greg do something horrible?*

I stood there motionless for a time. *Abandonment.* Greg had known the feeling of being abandoned all his life. His fear of being abandoned caused him to always be on the move. He was hesitant to set roots in any one place–he was always the guy willing to take the far-away assignments in Brazil or China or Mexico. But was there more than the fear of being abandoned that kept him on the move? Was it possible that he had done something terrible that caused him to be ostracized by his family? Had he been in some kind of trouble?

* * *

I turned page after page of living trusts and wills and codicils and thought to myself: we are all simply products of our upbringing. Greg knew about the will and that was why he didn't want me to waste my time fighting for something that he would never be part of. Maybe he was angry that the ranch would never be his and he was inwardly happy that the ranch was being turned into a giant wasteland. Perhaps Greg was angry that I was trying to help Butch and Beth, and inevitably, Wyatt, get a large financial recovery. *Did this all boil down to jealousy?*

Chapter 22

I heard a noise in the hallway outside Chance's office, so I quickly closed the file folder and grabbed the sticky notes, trying to jot something down to make my story legitimate.

"Lucky I don't shoot first and ask questions later," Chance said, pushing the door open. He limped into the office carrying a styrofoam cup of coffee and a bagel. Harry told me that Chance was a paratrooper in Vietnam and suffered an irreparable injury to his right leg while landing near enemy territory, causing him to walk with a permanent limp.

"Oh . . . hi Chance. I was looking for you. Just leaving you a note to call me. I was trying to find a sticky -"

"I was at the YMCA, where I am every morning at this time. No secrets around this town. What are you snooping through?" He kept walking towards me, staring at his desk.

"I–I–I wasn't snooping. I was trying to find something to write on so -"

"Cut the crap. Been around the block more times than I care to count. What are you looking for?" My heart picked up the pace as he stared intently at me. *Paratrooper. Vietman. Been around the block. But quick to back out of a lawsuit after being shot at? It didn't add up.* "If you need to know something, just ask. I'd rather not beat around the bush. It's tiresome." He threw his gym bag down on the sofa next to the window and took a seat. Sipping his coffee with a loud, wholesome slurp, he continued. "Listen, I know that your back is up against the wall. And I know that it is partially my fault. I should have told you more about what was happening on the Anderson ranch, but I needed to get out from under this case. I had conflicts of interest."

"Did you tell Harry about any of this?"

"I told Harry what he needed and wanted to know. This is a good case, Mac. The upside potential is high. Harry wanted to know about those kinds of things. The risk. You know Harry. Risk assessment was his main concern."

"Don't you think that being shot at could be considered a factor in risk assessment?" I asked.

Chance shoved half of the bagel into his mouth. Cream cheese was smeared on both sides of his cheeks. Without swallowing, he said, "Harry's a former football star. He can hold his own. I wasn't too worried about it. And, by the way, that's not why I backed down from the case."

He slurped another gulp of coffee and swallowed hard. "I don't even think the two are related. I think the gunshot was aimed at Butch or Wyatt. Not everyone in town is a fan, you know. Wyatt's a pretty cocky sumbitch. And Butch tried to short a few of the contractors when they built him that arena. I'm sure there are a number of folks that might have aimed a rifle at him. So, to set the record straight, I *had* to find another lawyer to handle this case because I couldn't litigate on behalf of the Andersons and still advise the Council. We might all start off with common goals, but eventually, I knew that fractures would exist. It's the name of the game."

Chance swallowed the rest of the bite of bagel, and then continued. "The Powder River Basin Resource Council exists to protect the environment for the short and long term. We are not helping your firm to get a financial recovery. We are doing it to preserve valuable resources like land and water. As a lawyer, you must understand."

"I understand the conflict, Chance, but I don't understand why you didn't tell Harry about the other stuff. Every day a new can of worms is opened in this lawsuit—and it seems like a lot of it could have been avoided if you would have been honest with us."

"And Greg?" Chance raised his eyebrows as he spoke, as if baiting me. He shoved the rest of the bagel in his mouth and chewed loudly. I could hear the smacking and slushing as he swallowed, chasing the huge mouthful with a slurp of coffee. I hadn't eaten breakfast yet, but somehow my hunger had subsided.

"What about Greg?" I asked. I walked around Chance's desk and stood in front of him. He sidestepped me and made his way to where I had been standing at his desk. He shuffled through a few files, and then picked one up.

"Is this what you were looking for?" He held up the Anderson trust file, waving it in the air like a flag.

"I wasn't looking for it, Chance. But I happened to see it."

"So you rifled through it, looking for something, I presume?"

"No. I was simply curious. Who wouldn't be? Who wouldn't want a look-see into a boyfriend's inheritance? I don't think I was doing something that -"

"Did you find what you were looking for? Did the will answer your questions?"

"I didn't have questions. Like I said, I was just curious."

"Well, now that you know what the deal is—that the ranch goes to Wyatt—does that affect your opinion of him?"

"Of whom? Greg? Why should it? I'm not after his money, Chance. I have no idea what his financial situation is and it really doesn't matter to me. I'm sure he makes a good living at what he does, but we've never discussed inheritance or anything like that." Chance nodded nonchalantly, as if he wasn't buying it. "But what I don't understand is why Beth would agree to write him out of her will. Did something happen that I don't know about?"

"You know I can't answer that, Mac. I'm their lawyer. I drafted this document. The reasons behind their bequests are attorney-client privileged information."

"I *know* that. But come on, Chance. You at least owe me an explanation as to why? Hell, you set me up in this lawsuit without telling me that I might be the subject of target practice."

Chance set the file back down on the desk. He flopped down into the leather wing-backed chair, rubbing the bald spot on the top of his head. He hemmed and hawed, trying to decide what he could say. He pulled his glasses off his nose, reached for a tissue, and swirled it around the lenses methodically, as if he was spinning the tale as he thought. "It's like a cake with many layers, Mac. If we pick at the foundation, the top will topple over."

"If we don't know what the foundation is made of, then it could collapse no matter what," I said.

"It's not that simple."

"You're the one who analogized it to a cake."

"Okay. Okay. But you might as well take a seat on the couch. This is a long story."

"Give me the Cliff Note version. I have a deposition in an hour."

"Greg Fisher's father owns MethZap," Chance started.

Chapter 23

"So, you see, there is a lot of history between the Fishers and the Andersons." I nodded. Chance had been talking for nearly an hour. I would be late for the deposition for sure.

"But what I don't understand is why Butch and Beth would write Greg out of their wills. Why punish Greg for the sins of his father? Hasn't he been punished enough?"

"Let me play this out for you. Say Butch passed away and his share of the ranch went to Wyatt and Beth. Then suppose Beth died and her share of the ranch went to Wyatt and Greg. Greg and Wyatt would own the ranch. They might not like it, being that they don't like each other much, but they'd work it out. But suppose it happened another way. Say that Beth passed first and her share of the ranch went to Butch, Greg and Wyatt. Then say that Greg died accidentally on one of his expeditions somewhere. Suppose Greg died intestate. Meaning without a will."

"I know what intestate means -"

"Greg's share of the ranch would revert to Everett. Now, Everett would own a portion of the ranch with Butch and Wyatt. It would be a downright bloodbath. So, we decided that it would be best to keep Greg out of the picture. Beth has set aside some other money to make up for it to Greg, but she doesn't want it spelled out in her will just in case she predeceases Butch."

"But there are so many ways to work around this kind of thing with modern-day trusts. Why not just spell it out in the documents. Put in a provision regarding Greg's death. Conditional gifts are accomplished every day. It's not like it would violate the Rule of Perpetuities or anything."

"Hold it right there. Don't even bring up the Rule of Perpetuities in my office. That ridiculous notion almost kept me from passing the bar exam some thirty years ago." Chance gave me a fatherly smile, with a quick wink. "But you're right. We could have easily drafted around such a situation. But you have to understand that the Andersons are simple people. They didn't want to get muddled in the mumbo-jumbo of legalese. They wanted to keep it simple. It was all I could do to talk them into setting up a revocable trust. This was the way they wanted to do it, and who am I to argue over inheritance. It's none of my business, really."

"So, does Greg know that he's been disinherited?"

"He hasn't been *disinherited* per se, he's just been provided for on the side."

"I assume he knows, based on a comment he made at the rodeo last summer."

"Yes. Beth told him a few months ago."

"How'd he take it?"

"I don't know for sure, but I'm told that it didn't go over very well."

* * *

I left Chance's office and rushed to the law firm of Wells, Bradley and Thomas. Their office was located in an old Victorian house a few blocks away, across the street from the Catholic grade school. I smiled to myself as I saw the children doing underducks on the swing set and playing kickball in the field—all wearing matching navy uniforms with white shirts. I looked down at my uniform: a navy suit with a cream silk blouse and navy pumps. I could have blended in with the kids on the playground and probably had a much more enjoyable day. Instead, I'd be watching underducks of a different kind in a conference room with a bunch of boring lawyers.

* * *

Chuck Wells, the lawyer for the Bureau of Land Management, was deposing our expert on West Nile virus. Chuck was tall and thin and had an Ichabod Crane-look to him. He was thoroughly annoyed by my tardiness and had started the deposition without me.

"Let the record reflect that Plaintiffs' lawyer has just arrived and it is now forty minutes past nine. We started the deposition of Joseph Archibald at precisely nine fifteen. I'll repeat the question posed to the witness. What is West Nile virus?"

Apparently, I hadn't missed much. I snuck around the conference table and took a seat next to the professorial-looking Mr. Archibald. He glanced at me sideways and made a huffy breath, as if he'd been fed to the wolves in my absence. When I hired him as an expert, he claimed to have given *at least* fifty depositions. He should've been able to handle the laborious admonitions without my help. Given that he was earning a few hundred dollars an hour for his time, I didn't think that the slight delay was much of a penalty as far as he was concerned. He turned toward the stenographer and began his long-winded answer.

"West Nile virus is a mosquito-borne disease that can cause encephalitis or 'brain infection.' Mosquitoes spread the virus after they feed on infected birds and then bite people, other birds, and animals. West Nile encephalitis was previously unknown to Wyoming. These days, three out of fifty-four mosquito species carry the virus and the most prolific carrier is the Culex Tarsalis mosquito."

"How does the methane gas industry play in this?" Wells asked.

"Reservoirs which hold methane water make ideal breeding grounds for mosquitoes. Each year, growing numbers of human deaths in Wyoming are linked to West Nile virus, and the majority of those struck are in the Powder River Basin."

"And why is that, Mr. Archibald?"

"Toxic reservoirs of standing water attract the mosquitoes and serve as fertile breeding grounds. Livestock and humans are attacked at dawn and dusk by the blood-sucking creatures, infecting a growing population at an alarming rate."

"How can you be so sure that this is due to methane operations?"

"Well, in case you haven't heard, we're in the middle of the worst drought in over one hundred years," Mr. Archibald said, as if he was scolding Wells for not paying attention. "Wyoming has few remaining reservoirs, other than the big ones. And even the big ones are very low in water. So, if we follow the logic, Wyoming should be less likely to have mosquito-born illnesses due to the lack of rain and melt-off water. But that's simply not the case because we are seeing thousands of toxic reservoirs all over the Basin—all of which are the result of methane production. The standing water that is spewed all over the place from the methane extraction process attracts the mosquitoes."

"And you blame the Bureau of Land Management for this?" Wells leaned back in his chair, placing his hands behind his head, knowing that the explanation would be long-winded.

"Yes. The Bureau of Land Management is issuing hundreds of permits for methane production without doing proper environmental tests and impact studies." Mr. Archibald asked for a piece of paper and a pen to make a diagram to help explain the process. "See this," Mr. Archibald said, drawing layers of earth with subterranean pockets of water and gas, "these pockets of water under the surface create something we call aquifers. They are essentially natural water wells. In nature, the amount of water in the aquifers vary from time to time, depending on rainfall and weather patterns. When we experience drought and when it is abnormally hot, the aquifers naturally are depleted. But when a good winter rolls our way and we have plenty of snow pack, the aquifers naturally get refilled."

He drew up and down arrows to signify the levels of water rising and falling due to weather patterns. "But the problem with the methane operations is that the water is sucked out of the earth unnaturally, and then re-deposited on the surface. This surface water doesn't replenish the aquifer, resulting in massive amounts of Wyoming water being permanently lost. Discharging methane water into waste pits not only attracts mosquitoes carrying West Nile virus, but also causes the water to evaporate. The Bureau of Land Management has misinformed the public by saying that the water will recharge the aquifers. But—"

"Common sense says that the Bureau is right, is it?" Wells said, smugly.

"No. In fact, the environmental impact studies that the Bureau uses are seriously deficient in describing the existing impacts. The studies don't even address future development. The studies don't even discuss what is happening with our major rivers."

"Won't the discharge of methane-produced water mitigate this reduction in natural groundwater discharge?"

"No, because toxic concentrations of particular elements in the water is also a big scare. For example, barium has been documented at high levels all over the Powder River Basin since the influx of methane gas development. But recently, we've detected increasing quantities of selenium, arsenic and other elements that are deadly to wildlife, crops and livestock. We are confident that some methane-produced water may not meet livestock watering requirements. High levels of magnesium in water may make sodium toxic to livestock. Selenium and arsenic are deadly. And it's only going to get worse. Sage grouse in the Powder River Basin have a survival rate of only fifteen percent. Some experts believe that with the continuation of wastewater from methane development, the sage grouse will be extinct this decade."

"And somehow, in some murky way, this has caused West Nile virus to spread in Wyoming and it is all the fault of the Bureau of Land Management?" Wells had made his point. It was going to very a daunting task to prove causation to the jury, and Mr. Archibald needed to spell it out in simpler terms.

* * *

When we broke for lunch, I grabbed a turkey sandwich at the deli next door and ate it on the way to my office. I wanted to check in with Pamela and see if she was able to track down some information I'd asked her to get earlier.

When I walked in the office, Pamela bounded from her chair, disturbing Ted from his afternoon catnap on the windowsill. "I found what you asked me to," she said, handing me a stack of papers. "Everett Fisher has had a very peculiar past. You won't believe your eyes when you read this stuff!"

Chapter 24

I could barely tear myself away from the stack of research Pamela gave me. She was right about Everett Fisher. I wanted to keep reading the information, but it was time to resume expert depositions in Wells' office.

The Bureau of Land Management's expert testified that sixty thousand new methane wells were approved for drilling in the Powder River Basin over the next ten years, meaning that at least twenty-five thousand wells may be actively producing gas at one time. A single well produces fifteen thousand gallons of water per day—so somewhere in the ballpark of five hundred thousand acre-feet of water could be discharged annually. "Given Wyoming's semi-arid climate and the current drought, this influx of water is a blessing!" Wells had prepared his expert well. He spent two hours testifying as to how great the methane gas business had been to the economy and to the environment.

After the deposition ended, Wells pulled me aside. "What's it going to take to make this thing go away? Because you know that you have absolutely *no* case against my client. The Bureau of Land Management has done everything it is required to do by law. Now, if you're not happy with the laws, you might check in with our local and state and, perhaps, federal lawmakers and lobbyists to see if they can help you change the course of things. But as it stands, my client is abiding by the law. Now, that being said, we understand the nuisance value of these kinds of cases and our insurance carrier is willing to give us some play money to make this disappear. So, what's the nuisance value of this thing? Let's get this over with so you and I don't spend the rest of the ski season in these kind of depositions."

"Two hundred and fifty a plaintiff."

Wells looked pleased. He puffed out his chest before continuing. "Two fifty a plaintiff? That's something I think we can work with, Ms. MacIntosh. Boy, oh boy, I thought you were messing with me for a minute. But I can see that you're really after MethZap and we've been named only as another deep pocket, but I think I can persuade the government -"

"Two hundred and fifty thousand dollars a plaintiff."

I could see the wheels turning quickly in his mind. He scrunched up his already sour face and shook his head quickly at me. "That's roughly twelve million. You're out of your fricking tree." He gathered his yellow notepad and black binder from the conference room table. On his way out the dual glass doors he turned and said, "You'll have a motion for summary judgment on your desk before the end of next week. I was giving you an olive branch. You've just handed me a thorn bush. You'd be wise to learn the ways of litigation in this town. We're pretty hospitable up here. I don't know how they do business in Jackson, but over here in Sheridan we talk straight and act civilized. Twelve million is a slap in the face."

"I don't mean for it to be, Mr. Wells, but there's a lot of reclamation that's going to need to be done. I don't even think twelve million will scratch the surface. We need to ensure adequate regulation of hydraulic fracturing so that the water and toxic fluids are treated before they seep back into the ground. We need sufficient bonding, suitable licensing requirements and–"

"You're preaching to the wrong choir, Ms. MacIntosh. Like I said, this is a legislative issue. You need to get the laws changed if that's what you want. But as far as my client is concerned, we've complied with the letter and spirit of the law."

Chapter 25

The highway toward Ranchester was dry, but the windy road through Dayton and up the mountain was icy and dangerous. My Chevy Equinox had four-wheel drive, which gave me some comfort, but most of the tight, curving road was banked on the right with towering rock walls of mountains and on the left with sheer drop-offs. Silver guardrails gave the curvy road boundaries, but they would freely give way to the crashing, skidding metal of a car out of control.

I passed a road sign that read, "Fallen City." I veered left into the rest area to witness what looked like ancient ruins scattered over the side of the mountain across the way. Boulders and columns, broken from a towering cliff above, had tumbled and come to rest in odd patterns, defying gravity. I looked down the valley below and could see the remains of old cars that had missed the preceding hairpin turn and careened down the ravine.

After fourteen switchbacks, three Dave Matthews CD's and two Diet Cokes, I parked my car in the lot of the Owens Creek Campground and rushed to the port-a-potty before meeting up with the cross-country ski team. It had been years since I had been on cross-country skis, but it was my mode of transportation around the University of Colorado campus during the winter months of my college days. I'd agreed to participate in a cross-country ski race, which gave me a terrific excuse to be out of the office for a day.

The race started at the campground and finished at the Antelope Butte Ski Area. We were assigned into teams of four. The first team to reach the finish line together was the champion. Each team could take whatever route they desired. The only rules were that all members must remain in their respective skis at all times (with the exception of potty breaks) and that no member could use any other mode of transportation or device to supplement their speed.

I was pleased to see that I'd been assigned to an all-women team. We unanimously elected Brenda Rice as our leader (because she said she wanted the job, and she was a big woman with a big attitude), packed our backpacks and headed for the starting line. I looked to the right and left, sizing up the competition. Despite his facemask, yellow goggles and navy ski cap, I immediately recognized one of my competitors. It was Wyatt. He gave me a subtle nod before conferring with his team. His two female teammates clambered close to Wyatt, embracing every word, while his buddies chugged amber liquid from a buckskin flask. I unbuckled my skis and went over to greet him.

"I didn't know you were a cross-country skier," I said. He smiled at me, the way he'd done the first night I'd met him when we'd gone to the Spotted Horse and had a few beers. His dimples were irresistibly charming.

"I told you that I love winter sports. Remember when we were driving back to the ranch last June? I thought I mentioned that I did this race every year." I didn't remember him talking about the race, but it was possible that he had. My nerves had been shattered that night.

"Yes, I remember you telling me something about it," I said, a half-truth slipping through my lips. Wyatt leaned toward me, flicking a snowflake off my nose. His presence was as powerful as a full moon and I could sense his desire.

"You have beautiful eyes," he said. I wanted to thank him in that polite sort of way, but words escaped me. One of the other women on Wyatt's team butted in, whining that it was time for them to huddle up. I quickly excused myself, claiming a need to get better acquainted with my teammates.

As I walked over to my group, I felt a hard tap on my shoulder and I heard a familiar voice call my name. It was Sherman Todd. He had a tag on his jacket that read, "Race Director."

"Glad to see you getting some fresh air," Sherman said. "You've been cooped up in that office of yours for months. Some people around here think you aren't very friendly."

"I don't have time to be social right now," I said. "After this case is over, hopefully my life will settle down. I didn't know that you organized this race."

"One of the many things you don't know about me, but you'll have to excuse me now because I need to make sure that every team has their race bibs and their water." Sherman started to walk away.

"Have you talked to Greg lately?" I said, following behind him.

"Why?" he asked, in an almost accusatory tone.

"I was just wondering. I haven't heard from him and I wanted to know if you had."

"Consider yourself on a 'need-to-know' basis when it comes to Greg. He lets you in on only what he wants you to know. He's secretive." With that snide remark, Sherman gave me the peace sign and walked away.

"I'll see you after the race," I said to him, but he didn't look back.

* * *

The team with the fastest time would win, but the start was staggered, so it didn't matter if you started first or last. Wyatt's team was scheduled to take off first. We started in third position. It didn't take us long to pass the second team. I was thrilled to discover that my team was very good. In fact, I was probably the weakest link as far as skill goes. We gradually gained on Wyatt's team and now had them in view.

We meandered along the trail next to Cedar Creek for hours, trying desperately to catch Wyatt and his teammates. Each time we closed in, he shouted at his teammates and they sprang to life like an antelope in the crosshairs of a rifle. But it was a thirty-three mile race and no team could complete it without at least one pit stop. We needed food and water, but our team captain decided that we would only stop when Wyatt's team stopped, and we would try to take a shorter break than they did.

We'd been skiing on and off through the trees for miles. Every now and then we broke into a meadow–a beautiful blanket of white snow in the middle of the forest. The sky was turquoise and the air was clean and crisp.

When we caught up to Wyatt's team, they were re-gearing from their break. We knew that we were in a time crunch, so we chugged some water and snapped out of our skis for a quick potty break. As we each picked our tree, we could hear Wyatt shouting to his team members to get moving. His intensity was as rough as the edges of an uncut diamond, and I knew that we'd have to quickly gobble our Power Bars and keep the pace.

We'd left our packs near our skis. When we got back, we each finished our water bottles, ate our energy bar and clamped back into our gear. It wasn't long before we had Wyatt's team in view, and we pushed hard to catch them. Mile after mile, the sweat was dripping down my back like a leaky faucet. Vapor rose from us as we generated more heat than a steam engine. Just as we honed in, approximately fifty feet away, Brenda, our captain, yelped in pain. I thought she pulled a muscle from over-exertion. She buckled over at the waist, howling and moaning all at the same time.

"Cramps. Cramps." I made sure that her cramps were abdominal and not the early warning signs of a heart attack. She pushed on her lower stomach and immediately the vomiting began. She fell forward in the snow, convulsing violently with every heave. *Stomach flu*, I thought to myself. The poor thing. Almost to the finish line. Poised to win and she's struck with a bad case of the flu. Or so I thought.

A minute later, Julie started vomiting. Then Robin. Then me. This was *not* the flu. The only logical explanation was food poisoning, but none of us had eaten from a common source of food. Each of us had brought our own energy bars and snacks. If our food hadn't been tampered with, then maybe our water? When we took our potty break, each of us had taken a swig of our water and then placed the plastic bottles together in the snow to stay cold. We'd only been away from the gear for a few minutes. And Wyatt's team was gone before we got back. *Did they tamper with our water?* I thought I was being paranoid. How silly to think someone would tamper with water over a silly little ski race.

But as the cramping and diarrhea set in, and with no port-a-potty in sight, I realized that this was more than poor sportsmanship. Someone had deliberately poisoned us.

Chapter 26

Being rescued off a mountain twice in two months seemed a bit random. Of course, *The Sheridan Press* gave us front-page coverage again, which made Davis Dunne inconsolable.

My suspicions were confirmed when I learned that our water had been poisoned with ricin. I'd never heard of it, but the lab in Cheyenne issued a report describing it as waste that remains after castor beans are processed into oil. In the body, it works this way: ricin gets inside cells and prevents them from making proteins. Without proteins, cells die. If ingested, the symptoms are vomiting and bloody diarrhea, seizures and hallucinations. Death can occur within seventy-two hours, depending on the dose and the method of transmission. As for the treatment, there is no antidote or specific vaccine, but the side effects can be treated with certain blood cleansers and protein stabilizers.

Due to our rapid metabolisms from the cross-country skiing, the ricin had entered our blood streams quickly. The medical staff had to work quickly to pump our stomachs and replenish our fluids intravenously. The Sheriff dropped in on us for an interview while the fluids drilled through our veins. As the Sheriff questioned my other teammates, I thought about the note left on my car earlier in the summer. *Wastewater is not the only poison around here. Watch what you drink lawyer woman.*

"Seems to me that you bring a lot of trouble with you when you move into a town," the Sheriff said. "Threatening notes and poisoned water. What's next up your sleeve?" I didn't answer his question. Instead, feeling defensive, I told him that I thought someone was trying to scare me off. "You know, Ms. MacIntosh, I like horses a lot. But there's one thing about horses that is intriguing to me. In the summer, they stand around and graze most of the day and when they do, their tails are always moving–swatting at flies, mostly. But even when there aren't any flies nearby, the tails keep swatting about. Maybe it's just a habit they have. Keeps the flies from comin' anywhere near them. Well, I'm starting to think that you are like a grazing horse. Your tail seems to always be swatting even when it don't need to be."

The Sheriff continued his interviews with the other three ladies, but left me alone, sitting there, pondering his statement. Although I didn't really understand what he was saying to me, I was irritated at his implication. Did he think that I was making this up? Creating drama? Trying to get attention? The more I thought about it, the more aggravated I became.

After an hour, I grabbed a cotton ball from the nurse's tray next to my bed, and firmly pressed against the needle in my vein. As I jerked the needle out of my arm, I heard a buzzer go off. I quickly grabbed a band-aid, affixed the cotton swab around the dripping blood at my elbow, and bolted from the emergency room.

* * *

Pamela picked me up outside the hospital and together we went to the office to research ricin and its origins. Castor oil had many uses (my Grandmother swore by the stuff as a method of staving off illness), but it was only produced in a few areas of the United States. Savannah, Georgia, was one. New Orleans was another. My mind started racing. *Wasn't Greg just in New Orleans on some assignment?* But he wasn't at the cross-country skiing race, or if he was, I didn't see him. Wyatt and Sherman Todd had been there. Wyatt had been on the ranch the first night–when someone shot through the window of Butch's truck. Then there was the note that was left on the windshield of my car warning me to be careful of what I drank. Ace Sanders certainly wasn't a fan of mine. Neither was Davis Dunne. I was fairly certain that Everett Fisher wasn't particularly happy with me. *Someone didn't want me around. But who?*

Chapter 27

"How did you find out that our ski team captain Brenda Rice served time in prison for attempted murder of her ex-boyfriend?" I asked Pam, who was brewing a fresh pot of coffee early in the morning. Pam was new to computer driven legal research, and I was afraid that she was using our software system to pry into people's personal lives. A lawyer has the right and duty to conduct legal research, but it must be within ethical boundaries. Pulling up rap sheets on friends and family would be considered outside the periphery of the moral code.

"It gets better. She served time in Louisiana."

"Well, that might tie her to ricin, but she certainly doesn't have a motive to kill me. Plus, she would have poisoned herself, which doesn't make any sense." Pam considered this for a moment. She opened up another manila file and pulled out a sheet of paper. "She's not the only one with a rap sheet. I did a little snooping on Lexis and found out that Wyatt's been arrested for disorderly conduct. But it was nine years ago, and he got off with probation." She handed me the piece of paper detailing his arrest record. She opened the file once again and retrieved yet another piece of paper, like she was spoon-feeding me a little bit at a time.

As she was handing me the next sheet, I tried to cut her off at the pass. "I already know that Greg's been arrested, so if that's what this is—it won't be the bomb you might have expected." Greg had participated in many demonstrations and rallies over the years. Most of them were for environmental causes. He'd crossed the police line a few times and had gone to jail for it—once with a broken nose.

"Not Greg. Everett. Greg's dad has served time in a federal prison in Montana." I took the paper from her and read about Everett Fisher's criminal past. He'd been arrested for receiving stolen goods and transporting them across state lines. The rap sheet didn't say what the stolen goods were, but I was certain that we could pull up the case and find out. I kept on reading.

Everett Fisher served a second prison term for armed robbery. Again, the sheet didn't detail what he'd stolen, but there was a notation that his five-year sentence was reduced to one year due to cooperation with the law and good behavior in prison. "He did time in the mid-1970's, so Greg was just a little kid when all of this went down."

"Maybe that's why Beth left him," I said. Pamela agreed. Together, we logged back into the legal research network and started doing a little more digging on Everett Fisher.

* * *

Our research was interrupted by a phone call from the crime lab in Cheyenne. The Sheriff had sent the water bottles from our cross-country skiing misadventure to the lab for analysis. The lab tech that had worked with me to help solve my former legal secretary's murder was great with fingerprint analysis. This time she applied super glue to the water bottles and then put them in a tent filled with a specialized vapor. The vapor affixed the prints to the glue. The prints were then lifted and sent to an expert laboratory in Colorado that specializes in partial and full fingerprint analysis. The prints were then processed through CODIS, the national crime database, and then forwarded to our local Sheriff.

Other than the girls on our cross-country ski team, the water bottles each had three other sets of prints on them. One set belonged to someone unidentifiable because they'd never been entered into CODIS. The other two prints belonged to people I knew fairly well. One set of prints belonged to Greg. The other set belonged to Sherman Todd.

Chapter 28

Everett Fisher was apparently a very rich man. He'd gone from a louse that didn't pay child support to a multi-millionaire. Our research found that he kept a majority of his assets in a real estate investment trust known as KingFisher. KingFisher had recently purchased a five million dollar home on the Powder Horn Golf Community six miles south of Sheridan. I'd dined at the Powder Horn clubhouse last summer with Harry and Chance and it was spectacular. Before we had dinner that evening, Chance took us on a tour of the new golf community. The golf course was manicured beautifully, set in the sweeping vistas of the Big Horn Mountains and Little Goose Valley. Multi-million dollar homes lined the course.

"Check this out," Pamela said, pointing to another page of research on my computer. We'd been sitting side-by-side in my office for a few hours searching Lexis for information about Everett Fisher. "KingFisher also has its own private jet." I looked over her shoulder. "A Learjet. Big money toys."

"Why does a methane gas guy need a Learjet?" I asked out loud. "How could he afford one?"

"He makes a ton of money, doesn't he? Maybe you should hold on to that boyfriend of yours. If his daddy leaves him some of that money, he'll be a rich man someday." I shot Pamela a disdainful look. I had confided in her a bit lately about how I was feeling about Greg. She'd joked with me a few times over the summer that she'd never seen a couple who talk as rarely as Greg and I. When Greg did call the office, both Pam and Megan made a big deal about it. "Sorry. It's just that his dad is loaded. If my ex-husband had a rich dad, I might not have dumped his sorry ass quite so soon."

"You told me that you dumped his sorry ass because he beat you up every time he got drunk," I said.

"Well, we can overlook things, I suppose, if there's a brand new pickup truck parked in the driveway, right?"

I just shook my head. No use continuing that discussion. As Pam and I continued our investigation of KingFisher holdings, the door to my office burst open. It was Greg. He was supposed to be in Louisiana. Pam, sensing the seeds of self-destruction, quickly exited.

"I suppose you've talked with the Sheriff?" Greg leaned over my desk and honed in on the computer screen. It would have been too obvious to toggle to a different screen, so I tried to casually scroll down so that he couldn't see what I was reading.

"I've talked to him a lot lately. Why?"

"Because my fingerprints were on your water bottle. I don't know how they got there or what you must be thinking, but you *have* to know that I didn't have *anything* to do with the poisoning. I'm baffled. You must think I'm a monster. Or that I'm -"

"Protecting your birth father?" The words shot out of my mouth like a cannon. They'd bypassed my brain somehow.

"My father? What does he have to do with this? God. I feel like I'm in the Twilight Zone. Six months ago we were in love and I was planning to ask you to be my wife. Then you took this case. Since then, we've done nothing but fight and *now* I'm a poisoning suspect. I would *never* do anything to hurt you. Never. I love you, Mac. You are everything that I've ever wanted." Greg, disheveled and crying, ambled around my desk and fell to his knees. His face flopped into my lap as the tears streamed over his nose and dripped on my pant leg. I patted him gently on the back and wiped away his new tears. He looked up at me with the gaze of an injured child and slowly pulled his head up. He reached into his jean pocket and pulled out a small white velvet box and handed it to me. My heart skipped a beat as I held this soft yet sturdy object in my hand. "Open it," he said, with a cracking voice, tears rolling down his cheeks.

I pulled at the lid, surprised by my sudden lack of strength. As the box slowly opened, I gazed at a sparkling emerald-cut solitaire set in platinum with three baguettes on each side. I inhaled quickly but did not speak. The silence was deafening. Greg wiped his tears with the back of his left hand and pulled himself up on one knee. He nudged the ring closer to me.

"Will you, my beautiful Mary MacIntosh, grant me the privilege of being your husband?" As if he feared my hesitation, he extracted the ring from its sachet and placed it part way on my ring finger. I touched his hand on mine and slowly helped him slide the ring into place.

I'd been contemplating breaking up with Greg for two months. And now, as he kneeled in front of me asking me to be his wife, those thoughts mysteriously vanished. Pamela's comment about the new pickup truck flashed through my mind. *Was this what she was referring to? Do we overlook mistreatment when there's a flashy new ring on our finger? When there's new furniture in the living room? Is that how it is supposed to be?*

Greg stared up at me, his eyes pleading for an answer. I bent down and tenderly kissed his tear-stained lips and whispered a very faint "yes" into his mouth.

Chapter 29

"KingFisher? What's this?" Greg's tear-stained face sobered up quickly. "Are you investigating my father?" After accepting Greg's proposal, we held each other tightly. His head rested on my shoulder, giving him full view of my computer screen. His mood changed so suddenly that I was virtually unprepared to be economical with the truth. I had no choice but to come clean. I told him about the real estate investment trust and about his father's holdings in MethZap and his rap sheet. Turns out, he already knew most of it. "Why didn't you tell me?" I was angry now. Engaged, in love, elated, but angry.

"You may not feel this way," Greg started, "but I think you got off easy. Your dad left you accidentally. He did not mean to die. He loved you and wanted to be your father. My dad deliberately left me. He chose to leave me behind. Was it that he saw things in me that he hated in himself and couldn't face? Did he hate the responsibility of being a father to me? Did he hate being tied down to a family? I don't know. I don't know why he left. That's one of the reasons that I'm here. I have the right to know. I have the right to confront him. Get to know him. Ask him what happened and why. I have the right to the truth. The lies and the missing parts have burned a hole in me my entire life. Can you blame me for wanting a chance to fill the void? To know my father? Wouldn't you if you could?"

"Is that what you're doing? Filling a void? Is that what this ring is all about?" Once again, the words shot out of my mouth before my mind had a chance to sieve them. I regretted the statement immediately and tried desperately to reel back the unkindness.

"I think you are jealous. Jealous that I have the chance to fill the void. But what you don't get is that I have no choice. For me, if I don't do this–if I don't try to set things straight with my dad, at least in my mind, I'll never be a good husband or a good father. And more than anything else, I want to be those things. I want anniversaries, and birthdays and weddings. I want photo albums and inside jokes. I want sideways glances and deep friendships and little league. I want all of these things for myself. But more importantly, I want them with you. And in order to have all of this, I need to put the last piece in the puzzle. I need to be able to tidy things up so that I don't continue to have these feelings of insecurity and lack of worthiness. Can't you understand?"

I did understand. And I felt horrible for being cruel. Maybe I was jealous. Not only did he have a father in Butch, but also he had a chance of a father in Everett. Maybe deep down I felt envious of his options. When it came to fathers, I had no options. Harry was the closest thing I had to a father, but he was my boss and now my law partner. He had a grown child of his own who would someday give him grandchildren to spoil. I would never be able to give my father a grandchild. But putting that aside, I couldn't help but think about the fact that I was trying to get Greg's birth father to pay millions of dollars to our clients to clean up their land and water. I desperately wanted to succeed. What would this do to my relationship with Greg? My *fiancé*. The word floated through my thoughts like a harped angel in flight.

"But what happens if you fill the void and he makes amends and he is part of your life again, and then I get a huge verdict against him. What will that do to us? To you? I feel like I'm about to cause a terrible car accident and I don't know how to stop it."

"I'm not looking for a new father. I'm looking for some answers. You are my priority, Mac. Believe me. If you get a huge judgment against him, then good for you. You have a job to do and you will do it well. I know that." Greg stood and paced in my office, choosing his words carefully. "I need to let you in on a little secret. I am up here on an assignment. I can't tell you any of the details, but I can tell you that something big is going on around here and it's going to go down soon. It's part of my assignment in South and Central America and it has tentacles that reach as far north as Sheridan. That's as much as I can tell you now. It's why I've been floating in and out of town on a moment's notice. When the story breaks, it'll be one of the biggest scandals this town has ever seen. I have to warn you, though. It's dangerous. There are some dangerous people involved. I have to be very, very careful. And so do you."

I nodded, not fully comprehending what he was saying. "Does it have anything to do with the methane gas lawsuit?"

He shook his head. "I don't think so. But I can't say for sure. I wish I could tell you more, but it would only put you in further danger. I've said too much. I have to go now. I will be out of reach for a few days. Be very careful, Mac. You've had two close calls since you've been here. I know you think that someone's trying to scare you away from the meth gas play, but there are other things going on around here that are much more dangerous. I can't stress enough to you how dangerous it could be. Do you understand? Don't go snooping around on people's ranches without Harry or Chance with you. And I think you should go jogging at the YMCA in the mornings. You shouldn't be out of the roads and trails by yourself. Someone wants you out of the picture, and that scares me to death because I can't be here to protect you. Not that you can't take care of yourself. I know you can. I want to protect you, but right now, I have to leave again. I wish I could stay, but I can't. There is so much that I wish that I could tell you right now, Mac. This assignment I've been on is to me what your trial is to you. I want to share it with you and experience it with you, just like I want to hear about the trial. Unfortunately, our schedules are so out of whack right now. And my boss–"

"It's okay, Greg," I said. "I know that your job is demanding. So is mine. Hopefully, when this trial is over and when your investigation is complete, we can go away together. Get to know each other again."

"I want to take you to Europe for a week or two. Maybe Italy. Drink Chianti late into the night and laugh and talk like we used to. I miss you more than words can express. I love you deeply, Mac. I'm so sorry that I have been pulled away from you. I've made mistakes that I–"

I put my finger over his lips, hushing him from further apologies. I understood. With that, he kissed me on the lips and then quickly slipped out of the office. I watched him leave the building and walk across Main

Street. He turned and waved to me and I waved back from my second story office window. He then slid into the driver's seat of his Jeep Grand Cherokee and drove away. I watched his illuminated license plate disappear into the night.

* * *

In Wyoming, each county is assigned a number for issuing plates. Sheridan was number three. Every license plate issued in the county started with a three, then is followed by a symbol of a cowboy on a bucking bronco. Then, each plate has either a series of four numbers, or is personalized. As the cars crept by at the twenty miles per hour speed limit on Main, I made a mental note of the personalized plates: 3-DDS; 3-BEER; 3-CWBY; 3-METH. Meth. I wondered who drove the truck with "METH" on the plates? A rancher who just struck it rich? An operator who sucked the gas from the bowels of the earth? A crack-head who wasn't afraid to advertise that he was into crystal meth? I didn't know. It didn't matter, I suppose. I was engaged. Engaged.

My daydreaming was interrupted by a phone call from the lab tech in Cheyenne. I stared at the flashing red line on the phone for a minute, thinking about the fact that I'd just agreed to marry a man. He did not have to ask my father for permission for my hand. I hadn't taken time to think it over—to honor my customary rule to never make a major decision for at least twenty-four hours. *Sleep on it*, I always told myself. I hadn't considered this enough. The last few months had been tumultuous. Why rush things? The red light kept flashing. I knew I should pick up the line. Finally, I punched the button and held the receiver loosely to my ear.

"That same sisal fiber was found on the screw cap of the poisoned water bottle," the lab tech said. I could hear her pencil tapping on her desk, as if she was waiting for a response. "I called the Sheriff up there to tell him. I'm no cop, but I'd say that this links the fibers on the threatening note to the poisoning of your water bottle."

* * *

Exactly six hours after Greg asked me to be his wife, the back line to my office rang. Megan and Pamela had left for the day and I hadn't spoke to either of them since Greg's departure. "Do you want me to include you in our 'Engagement' column?" Norma Roberts asked. As chief editor of *The Sheridan Press*, she was working the customary late shift, preparing the headlines for tomorrow's print. I was shocked by her suggestion and stumbled for words. To my credit, I recovered fast.

"Why would you want to do that?" I asked.

"Because rumor has it that Greg Fisher proposed to you today." Small town gossip traveled quickly.

"Norma, you are so kind to call and I appreciate the fact that you thoroughly investigate rumors so that you don't print untruths. No wonder you earned such a high position with the paper. To answer your question, no, please do not include me in the column."

"Does this mean that you are not engaged?"

"It means that I am a private person and this is a private matter and that you'll be one of the first people I call if and when I have information that I want to make public."

"I see. Can you hold a minute?" she said. I heard her cup her hand over the phone and yell to someone, "Stop the presses." She came back on the line. "I need to go."

Chapter 30

Our makeshift conference room wasn't big enough to hold all the lawyers in the case attending Everett Fisher's deposition, so Megan reserved the auditorium of the Elk's Lodge. The room had high beam ceilings that echoed like a gymnasium and windows with rollout cranks. It wasn't state-of-the-art by any means, but it would have to do. Every lawyer from the BLM to the Army Corps of Engineers to MethZap was present and on time. Everett Fisher was not.

"He'll be here," Davis Dunne snapped. "He's always late." The lawyers grumbled about busy schedules and hourly rates. Butch complained of back pain and that the folding chairs were the worst possible thing for a cowboy with a broken-down back. I tried to tune all of them out as I outlined the questions I would ask.

When Everett Fisher sauntered in over an hour late, I was annoyed. I was ready to say something sharp to him about punctuality, but I was overcome by his evil handsomeness. His gray eyes were hollow yet captivating, illuminating the silver in his wavy hair. Greg had Everett's chiseled chin and his sharp nose, but not his air of entitlement. As he whispered with Davis Dunne and settled into his chair, I studied the markings on his flesh–his brandings. He had a deep v-shaped scar just below his right eye and another cris-crossing his chin. His knuckles on both hands had amateur tattoos, something you might see on a prison inmate. He wore a black button-down pressed shirt, new blue jeans and a belt buckle that read "Born to Fly."

Prison had apparently taught Everett Fisher how not to answer a question. He was evasive and short and painfully abrupt with his answers, even to simple questions about where he was raised. His was the last deposition before trial and the lawyers were tired and anxious. We'd put in countless hours sitting through depositions and we wanted this part to be over. Everett was not going to make this easy on us and I could feel resentment intensifying.

"How did you raise enough start-up capital to get MethZap up and running?" I asked.

"What in the hell does that got to do with anything?" Everett shot a look at Davis Dunne.

"Objection. Relevance. Instructing the witness not to answer. Get a discovery referee appointed by the court if you want to continue to delve into his past. He's not going to answer this ridiculous line of questioning. It doesn't matter how he got the money to start the company. It doesn't matter why he was in jail. It doesn't matter if he paid child support. Ms. MacIntosh, ask a pertinent question or we're going to have to move on to a more experienced lawyer, like Chuck Wells, and let him have a shot at my client."

"We're suing your client for punitive damages, Mr. Dunne. The financial stability of your client is pertinent and relevant to the case. I want to know how he raised the capital, whether he has investors, or shareholders or debt. I'm entitled to this information. Judge Laird ruled on this very issue when I prevailed on my motion to compel Mr. Fisher to answer written interrogatories. If you force me to file another motion, I will ask for additional sanctions from both you and your client. Instruct him to answer."

"I saved money workin' the mines. Ace Sanders had money too. Together, we pooled it and leased the equipment we'd need to drill our first well."

"How much money did you pool together?"

"Don't remember exactly. Maybe fifty grand. Maybe more."

"Ace Sanders testified in his deposition that you started out with over one hundred fifty thousand dollars. How much of this was yours?"

"Don't recall. It was a long time ago."

"It was five years ago, Mr. Fisher. How much did you make at the mine at that time?"

"Don't know. Like I said, it was a long time ago."

"I subpoenaed your employment file from Spring Creek Mines and your last pay stub for a two-week wage earning period was thirteen hundred dollars. Does that sound about right to you?"

"Don't remember. You got the records. Why ask me?"

"I'm asking you because your business partner says that you brought over one hundred thousand dollars to the table to start this business and I'm wondering how a man comes up with that kind of money when he's making less than three thousand dollars a month." My temper was flaring like a solar flash, but I had to keep my cool.

As he was about to answer the question, Beth Anderson, dressed in a long red dress and a matching cowgirl hat, sauntered through the door. Everett Fisher stopped short of words, as if his answer had somehow bubbled up in this throat and he couldn't force it out. Her beauty was razor-sharp. His stare was equally cutting. And the tension, as they say, could have been cut with a knife.

Chapter 31

"My finances are in order, Ms. MacIntosh. I have plenty of money in the bank. If your worry is whether MethZap can pay if we lose at trial, then the answer is clearly a 'yes.' We have plenty of reserves and an excellent line of credit. Hell, we have more leases to drill gas than we have machinery and manpower to do the work. I'm a rich man. Don't you worry your pretty little head about collecting money against me if I lose this thing." Everett looked directly at Beth, who'd just taken a seat at the opposite end of the table, and said, " I'm not going to lose, by the way."

"I've subpoenaed your bank records, Mr. Fisher, and you're not as rich as you claim to be. But that wasn't my question. My question was, 'Where did you get the start-up capital'?"

"Maybe I had a rich uncle."

"You didn't have a rich uncle, Ev. Stop screwing around. You're an arrogant, pompous, no-good son-of-a-bitch just sitting here wasting everyone's time. If you had a rich uncle, maybe you could've afforded to pay your child support for all those years."

Everyone at the conference table turned in unison in Beth Anderson's direction. She didn't look apologetic or intrusive. Her emerald-green eyes sparkled, almost as if she'd finally bejeweled him with sentiments left unsaid. I thought that Davis Dunne would object or move to strike, but he was tolerant of her outburst. Almost amused, perhaps. Maybe his ex-wife had said similar things to him. As the exchange between Everett and Beth heated up, we agreed to take a short coffee break.

* * *

I wished I could have been a fly on the wall, because I would love to have eavesdropped on the private conversation taking place over in the corner between Everett Fisher and Beth Anderson. There was plenty of gesticulation and finger pointing–that was for sure. From my vantage point, it seemed like she had the upper edge. But maybe that was because I was rooting for her. I knew I was staring–like one does when passing a terrible accident–but I justified it as a "witness observation." I would have Everett Fisher on the witness stand at trial and I would certainly put his feet to the fire–so it was important to see how he reacted under pressure. At least that was my rationale.

But in all honestly, he looked like an older version of Greg, and I felt almost like a voyeur looking into my own future. Is this what Greg would look like when we were having a fight? Would our marriage last? If not, would we end up never speaking again, like I supposed that Beth and Everett had? I was being selfish–thinking of Greg and me when I should have been focusing on the trial. Harry was right. Never represent family or friends. My judgment was clouded. No matter how I rationalized it.

* * *

The day had started out balmy and warm for November in Wyoming–a Chinook, as they called it. I could feel the warm, dry air blow through my loose hair when I left for the depositions at the Elk's Lodge. The temperature reading on the bank building up the street read sixty-two degrees. But when I stepped outside to get a breath of fresh air after watching Beth and Everett argue, I noticed a sudden chill in the air. As was usually the case following a Chinook in November, a blizzard was on its way over the Rocky Mountains. After wasting the better part of the afternoon trying to get straight answers out of Everett Fisher, I adjourned his deposition and headed back toward the office. I was tired and restless and in need of exercise, so after dumping my briefcase on my desk and feeding Ted a can of cat food, I slipped into my red fleece sweat shirt and black lycra tights and headed out the door.

Jogging in a blizzard was both incredibly exhilarating and frightening at the same time. I headed up old Thurmond Hill and out toward the cemetery, which was one of my favorite places to run when the weather was bad. No one visited gravesites in foul weather, making it peaceful and relaxing to jog around, knowing that I wasn't interrupting anyone, and knowing that I had the pavement to myself. I read the names of loved ones as I passed the headstones, understanding how many generations of a family stayed put in a small town. I thought of the fact that my dad didn't have a headstone because my mother had his remains cremated and scattered near our family cabin in Colorado. I missed not having a special place to honor my father. Thinking about that made me feel juvenile—I could pay homage to him anytime, anywhere. But gravestones were a nice touch, I thought to myself. *Where were they made? Who sat and carved them? Who decided how big they should be or what color or what was inscribed?* My thoughts were random as I jogged in the blowing white snow, feeling the pavement pound against my feet and feeling the kiss of every snowflake brush my cheeks.

I stuck out my tongue and caught a few flakes. They tasted moist and earthy and fresh. I picked up my pace, seeing how many snowflakes I could catch, as if my body thirsted for Mother Nature.

But the snow was tapering off now and the visibility was suddenly lifting. The air grew suddenly colder and I could feel the sting of iciness on the tip of my nose and on my cheeks. I knew that it was time to turn back toward the warmth of my office, but something about the contrast of weather and the freedom of running kept me going.

In the distance I could see a sign across a chain-link fence that read, "Rodiger's Stoneworks." Rodiger? I figured that there were probably a few Rodiger families in town. As I jogged closer, I could now see that there was a large Peterbuilt truck parked in front of the building and there were two men with dollies in hand wheeling large objects down a ramp from the truck and into the cream-colored metal building. The building looked like a small airport hangar. As one of the men came back out of the building, I darted behind a barren maple tree and hid from view. As the fog and snow continued to lift, I could clearly see the skinny, angular face of Rowdy Rodiger. The landman for MethZap. A "good argument for natural selection," as Wyatt had described him. He was off-loading gravestones from the truck. And behind him, taking orders like a soldier, was Sherman Todd.

Chapter 32

After they took the next load into the building, I darted to a closer pine tree. With each load, I inched closer until I was finally within earshot of their conversation.

"When you gonna make your first delivery?" Rowdy asked Sherman.

"I made contact today," Sherman said. "But I think I might need backup on this one. Feels all wrong to me. I told my point man to meet me in the Red Grade parking lot, but he insisted that we make the exchange in town, at the Quick-Shop. Seems too risky. Too many eyes around. And I worry that there could be a hidden camera somewhere."

"Probably safer to do the hand-off in a busy place like a gas station. If you ask me, it's more dangerous to do the deal in a remote area. Hell, for all you know, he has a buddy in the back of the car with a gun pointed in your direction. Shoot you dead, take the booty and that'd be the end of you."

"Never thought of it that way."

"Gotta start thinking like a business man," Rowdy said.

"A business man?" Sherman said in a mocking tone. "You mean a drug dealer."

"Watch what you say, hear me, mother-fucker? You just watch what you say. I've worked real hard to get where I am and I don't need some Greenpeace asshole calling me names. We got a shit-load of headstones to unload. Time for you to shut your big fat mouth and get back to work."

I watched them unload a few more large granite slabs from the truck. When I felt like the coast was clear, I made a mad dash toward the cemetery entrance and ran like a doe being chased by a wolf until I got back to my office. I bolted up the narrow staircase and, as quickly as I could, wrote down the DOT identification number prominently displayed on the outside of the driver's side door of the truck that they were off-loading. I knew from my law enforcement training that the DOT identification number would yield all sorts of useful information. I logged into my legal research engine and typed in the numbers from the door of the Peterbuilt. The truck belonged to Rodiger's Stonework and its last recorded route was from Sheridan to Los Angeles and back. In fact, the truck made this route twice a month, always stopping in Las Vegas for an overnight.

* * *

I called Greg and told him about what I saw. He was furious at me for running alone after he'd warned me to run at the YMCA. "You're just asking for trouble, Mac. I tried to tell you in every nice way I know to be careful. Something very bad is about to go down in Sheridan. You, of all people, shouldn't be sneaking around the cemetery looking for trouble. You're not the most popular girl in town right now. You know that, don't you?"

I knew. The litigation had taken on a life of its own. Half of the class action members wanted out of the mess and the ones who were still willing to stay were starting to have their doubts. Some had received threatening letters, like the one that had been placed on the windshield of my car.

The community had taken an interest in the lawsuit and had taken sides. Surprisingly, many people were against the suit, even though they were unhappy with the threat of contamination. I knew this fact because *The Sheridan Press* had taken a few opinion polls on the issue. Overall, it was about a sixty-forty split opposing the lawsuit. Being the underdog never bothered me before, but this time, it worried me. By the time this case went to trial, which was only a few months away, would the jury pool be convinced that this case was as polluted? It worried me. It worried me a lot.

It had been three days since Greg had asked me to be his wife, but I hadn't told a soul that I was engaged. I realized that this was not normal. I knew that I should have called my mom. My stepsister. My college friends. But somehow, I just couldn't get the words to roll off my tongue. This, too, worried me a lot.

* * *

The roads were slippery with the new-fallen snow, but I felt an overwhelming urge to drive out to the Anderson Ranch and look around a bit. I hadn't been out to the Crazy Woman in months. I'd been to just about every other ranch in town for various property inspections, but I'd left Butch and Beth alone for a bit. I knew I should have called and warned them that I was on my way, but something inside me–some little voice–told me to just show up and have a look around. I wanted to get a few samples of Butch's ropes for my friend at the crime lab to analyze and compare. The crime lab technician explained that each sisal rope has a slightly different weave, and that a particular rope could be identified using forensic science. I didn't have a good excuse to simply ask Butch for the ropes, so I thought that it would be best to just surprise him with a visit. But I was the one who would be surprised.

Chapter 33

When I arrived at the Anderson ranch, no one was around. I passed under the sign reading "Crazy Woman" and, for the first time, noticed a brand beside the name. Every rancher has his or her own brand. It was a sign of ownership–a signal to others to keep their hands off. Like a barbed-wire fence. Or a gun pointed at you. Brands were fascinating symbols–some very plain and indicative of the owner. Some were erratic and demonic. Butch and Beth's brand was an upside-down "A" with ladies' cowboy boots on each "leg" of the letter "A". It almost looked like a woman with her legs up in the air. Maybe it was.

I parked near the arena and poked my head around. No one was there. I knocked on the back door of Butch and Beth's house, but no one answered. I snuck into the barn and clipped a few rope samples before I set out on foot around the ranch. The snow that had fallen made the ground muddy, and my feet felt heavy as the mud caked on the bottom of my running shoes. I looked around for a patch of grass to wipe my feet, but as Butch so adeptly testified during depositions, there was no grass growing on his ranch. I climbed to the top of the hill near the warming hut for one of the wellheads and took a look around the ranch. When Butch took me on a horseback tour, I had only seen a portion of his land. It went on for miles and miles to the south and to the east. I had seen most of the drill sites for the methane gas, but he'd never taken me to the one Wyatt referred to as the "Well from Hell." I had an idea where this well must be, based on deposition testimony and the aerial photographs we'd had taken for the upcoming trial. I headed south down the hill and walked for a few miles.

It wasn't the sound of the generator that alerted me to the fact that I was close to the well. It was the pungent odor of ammonia that nearly burnt my nostrils. I took a few steps back, gasping for air. Pulling my fleece jacket up over my nose, I inched forward toward the hut. The smell was so horrible that I had to step back again. I took a deep breath and held it, while quickly running up to the hut and opening the door. I had previously seen the inside of the huts during property inspections at several ranches, but this particular hut did not look like any other I had seen. The inside of the hut was littered with dozens of plastic containers. I picked one up. It was labeled "ephedrine." Empty plastic bags were stashed in the corner. "Anhydrous ammonia" was printed in big black letters on each sack. That explained the horrible smell. Remnants of other cans littered the floor of this small hut, and a small camp stove stood in the center. I couldn't hold my breath much longer. It was time to get out of there. I tried to memorize the labels on the cans. Hydriodic acid. Red Phosphorus. Stuff that I hadn't heard of since high school chemistry. Whatever it was, I was sure that it had nothing to do with the production of methane gas.

I backed out of the hut, still holding my jacket over my nose, and quickly shut the door.

"What are you doing here?" a voice said from behind me. I was so startled that I gasped, inhaling a huge breath of ammonia-laced air. I coughed and sputtered and threw up on the ground near his feet. Struggling to catch my breath, I stumbled forward, in search of oxygen. Butch grabbed my arm. "People get shot at around these parts for trespassin'. Haven't you learned this lesson already?"

I pulled away and ran a few yards until I could finally ventilate. "I knocked. No one was home."

"Listen here, darlin', it just don't work like that around here. You knock. No one's home. You come back another time. You don't go snoopin' around someone else's property without permission."

"I'm s-s-s-orry. I didn't think you'd mind."

"Well, I do. Damn near shot you. That'd be hard to explain to the judge, now wouldn't it?" Butch eyed me for a long moment, as he pulled down on his mustache. Cody, his sheep-herding dog, sat at his heels. "What are you doing out here anyway?"

"Getting ready for trial. It's only a month or so away, Butch. I was just taking another look at the place. I haven't been out here in a few months and I needed to get another visual of the locations of the well sites. Like I said, I knocked, but you weren't home. I didn't think you would mind. I'm sorry."

He seemed to soften a bit, but he didn't look satisfied with my answer. "What are you doing at *this* well? This one never produced a dang thing. Which gripes me to no end because this was the one I insisted that they *not* put up. Used to be my stud pasture. Now it stinks to holy hell."

"That was my next question to you. What's going on here? There's a ton of strange chemicals in there and the ammonia is so strong that I think it's toxic. Were they doing special testing in there or what?"

"I don't know. They had all kinds of trouble with this well. I don't know why it smells so bad. Can't even let my livestock near this area. I'll take a look."

"Cover your mouth and hold your breath. Literally. It is toxic."

Butch took a red bandana out of his front pocket and held it over his nose. He disappeared into the hut, and stammered out a few seconds later. "Good Lord. What in the world is that crap? It's like a science experiment gone bad. I'm goin' to call that Ace Sanders right now and tell him to get his crew out here immediately and clean this mess up before it blows us to Smitherines."

"Butch, I think we should call the Sheriff. Something's not right here." After we talked about it on the way back to the ranch house, he agreed. We called the Sheriff and told him what we found. He said not to go anywhere near it and that he was on his way out to the ranch. Immediately.

Chapter 34

"Methamphetamine is the biggest drug threat throughout Wyoming. Hell, the arrests for it exceed all other drugs put together. What you got here is *not* the 'Well from Hell.' It is the 'Lab from Hell.' Someone's been operating a methamphetamine lab inside your methane gas hut." The Sheridan County Sheriff made it out to the ranch in less than an hour. Despite his protruding belly, he climbed the hill to the Well from Hell in no time at all. Sweat dripped from his forehead, even though the temperature by this point in the evening had dropped to the high thirties. He carried a large floodlight. Before the Sheriff's arrival, Butch had set up enough lights around the well to make it look like a UFO had landed.

The irony had not escaped me. All along, we'd been pursuing the methane gas folks. All the while, someone had been using the methane gas huts as a disguise for a methamphetamine lab. Meth to hide meth.

"How long has this been here?" Butch asked. "Can I get arrested for this? It ain't mine, you know. Never even heard of the stuff."

"I'm sure it's not yours, and it is doubtful you'd be arrested, but we will certainly have to investigate it. You understand?" Butch nodded.

I knew a lot about methamphetamines. More than I cared to know. My former legal secretary had been murdered because of the stuff. I'd learned more than I wanted to know about its effects. Abuse of the drug caused hyperthermia, convulsions, cardiovascular collapse, kidney disorders, brain and liver damage, and blood clots. Paranoia from meth has led to homicidal and suicidal tendencies.

Meth was widely available in Wyoming. Most of it was Mexico-produced, although some of it was produced in California by Mexican cartels. A small quantity of the drug was produced in-state.

After Lela was murdered, I'd done some research about the profitability of the drug. Distributors in Wyoming made huge profits–more so than neighboring states, due to the remoteness of the area and the high demand. A drug user would pay five thousand dollars for a pound of meth in Arizona. That same user would pay nearly fifteen thousand for the same amount and percent-pure drug in Wyoming. Since the demand was high and the profits were incredible, methamphetamine drug abuse in Wyoming was a chronic problem.

"See this?" the Sheriff asked. He'd crawled inside the hut and pulled out a brown plastic sack that looked like planting soil. "This is dimethylsulfone. It's a nutritional supplement for horses. You probably know that, Butch." Butch nodded. "It's also used as a cutting agent to increase the quantity of meth. It's the same with baby laxatives–drug dealers use it to cut cocaine. Dimethylsulfone decreases the purity of the drug by almost half, so it practically doubles the profits for the distributor."

I told Butch and the Sheriff about my experience with Lela and the drug ring in Jackson Hole. We talked about the powerful nature of the drug and how it caused hallucinations and delusions and violent behavior.

"Heard of the tweaking stage?" the Sheriff asked. Without waiting for a response, he continued. "The user usually hasn't slept for days and is irritable. He craves more meth, which makes him even more frustrated. With little or no provocation, he becomes violent. In fact, a few years back, before I was elected sheriff, a trucker from Cheyenne chased a woman in her car for nearly twenty miles before firing three bullets at her and running her off the road. The woman was a complete stranger to him. He'd never seen her before, but he thought she was mocking him. She died at the scene. He was sentenced to life in prison. An expert at his trial testified that he was 'tweaking' and that his hallucinations were real to him and that was why he shouldn't have been held accountable for his reactions. Can you imagine that?"

I nodded. Butch shook his head.

"So, getting back to our little problem here," Butch said, pointing to the hut, "what are we going to do about this?"

"Well," said the Sheriff, scratching his thinning hairline, "it looks to me that you have a combo here, which I've never seen before. See, normally we see the Birch reduction method of methamphetamine production, which uses agricultural fertilizer. You have some of that in the hut here. But I also see evidence of the hydriodic acid–red phosphorus reduction method. I've never seen both in one lab."

"What's that mean?" I asked.

"It means that whoever has been out here knows how to produce two different grades of drug. I don't know if that means a whole lot to you, but to me, it means that somebody knows how to cook drugs and they've found a perfect hiding spot. A methane gas hut. It's perfect. The sludge produced from methane gas already smells. There's always quite a bit of noise from the generators. The huts have radars on the top, which makes them accessible via satellite, so no one would expect illegal activity from them."

The Sheriff was right. The huts looked like little playhouses for a kid, in the shape of a beehive. They stood about four feet high and had a little door and a radar on the roof for aerial monitoring through some type of satellite technology. The radar at the Well from Hell was inoperable because the well site was defunct. This was a perfect site for a meth lab. It was remote. The smell wasn't inconsistent with fertilizer in high doses. I watched Butch kick at the ground under his feet. He seemed to be thinking something, but he wasn't saying a word. The Sheriff continued talking.

"But it also means that we have a whole lot of contamination sittin' here. Methamphetamine labs produce five to seven pounds of toxic waste for every pound of meth produced. The waste is usually absorbed into the earth or dumped in a local river. I have no idea what's happened here, but I guarantee you one thing. This area is a toxic waste dump."

* * *

I knew that this could mean death to our lawsuit. If Davis Dunne could point to another possibility for contamination, then proving liability would be disastrous. All along, Harry and I had assumed that we could easily prove that MethZap had caused contamination. But if MethZap could suggest that another source had caused the contamination, we were dead in the water. Just like the sage grouse, the cottonwoods and the fish.

Chapter 35

After the Sheriff left, I walked with Butch back to his house. On the way, we talked about the ramifications of another source of contamination on the ranch. Obviously, this was a concern to him, but the bigger concern was how the drug paraphernalia had ended up in the Well from Hell.

"I hate to suggest it, but could Wyatt possibly know something about this?" I asked with the hesitation of a third-grader, afraid to charter murky waters, but also afraid not to.

Butch stopped walking and turned toward me. He pointed his finger toward my chest. "Wyatt? Are you crazy? Wyatt's never done a drug a day in his life. For Christ's sake, Mary. How can you suggest such a thing?" I could see the hurt in his eyes.

"Butch, I'm sorry, I didn't mean to say it that way. I spoke before I thought and I shouldn't have." He turned away and started walking, not wanting to hear what I had to say. I stumbled with my words, trying to set things straight. "Tonight, I came on your ranch without permission and you damn near shot at me. I guess I was thinking that someone has been out here on your ranch cooking up some strange drugs. You and Wyatt keep close tabs on this place. I just figured that one or the other of you would have known if someone was out here, so I made a suggestion. I'm sorry. I reached too far. It's not that I think that Wyatt is–"

"No. No. It's all right. I would do the same thing if I were in your shoes. I'm sorry to jump at you, it's just that I don't understand much these days. Nothing is as it seems. My sons are acting weird. My wife's acting weird. Hell, I don't know if it's day or night half the time. People coming and going. Arguing. I'm a simple guy, Mary, and I like my simple life, and when things get all murked up, I just can't seem to function too well."

It was getting dark out. He held my elbow as we walked down the steep embankment. "My life has always been pretty cut and dry. I've always known what I want and how to get it. It's instinct. That's how I operate. But since this methane gas thing came about, my instincts don't seem to be working right, and I'll tell you what—Beth's instincts are off the charts. I feel like she's floating around the place with her head three feet above her body. She forgets to feed the animals and drives the truck until it runs out of gas. Her head is in the clouds. I don't know if it's the stress of this mess or what, but she is not herself. And, see, she's my soulmate. When she's not herself, I'm not myself. We're connected that way. I can lay next to her at night and listen to her heartbeat and know what her day has been like. And lately, I can feel her heartbeat floating away, as if it's not supporting her body at all. I think about the trial and the stress of having half of the town of Sheridan mad at her for taking on the gas industry and I just feel plain awful. I hate it when she's unhappy. And I know that she's more sensitive than I am. It don't matter a whole lot to me if half the town is not on my side—that's normal. It's like a baseball game. Half of the folks root for one team—half for the other. But that's not how Beth sees things. She thinks that she's been ostracized. Which isn't so. Still, I think she's feeling it. But there's more to it than that. I can't put my finger on it, but something else is bothering her a great deal."

The lights of the ranch house were visible now from the crest of the hill. We were guided by the pull of a full moon, shining brightly with the power of the hope that only a full moon holds. "She's been under a great deal of stress," I said. "Lawsuits are horrible in that way. They are stressful to consider, in the first place. And then they carry with them some sort of sense of entitlement. And then, they take on a burden and eventually the burden seems overwhelming. We are so very close to trial. I'm sure that when the trial is over, she'll come back to earth and things will settle in. I'm sorry that it is so stressful and unpredictable, but there's not much I can do to make it better right now. The pre-trial motions start in three weeks. We are in the eye of the storm. I can't look at you and honestly tell you that's it's going to get better any time soon, but I can tell you that in two months, it will all be over and I hope and pray that you are satisfied with the results."

"I hope you are right. I hope that this is just stress. But it seems more than that. It seems like she's got way bigger things on her mind."

"Like what?"

"Like old times."

"I don't understand."

"You will . . . someday."

Chapter 36

Butch walked me to my car. Before I started the engine I said to him, "Have you heard from Greg this week?" I wanted to know if he'd told Butch and Beth about his marriage proposal.

"He called his mom a few days ago." I looked at Butch, waiting for him to tell me more. He didn't take the bait. Instead, he stood there scratching his right ear with one of his keys.

"What did they talk about?"

"I'm not sure. Beth didn't elaborate and I didn't ask. When he takes these big assignments, his calls are sporadic and usually brief."

"Did he mention that he asked me to marry him?" I asked, jutting my ring finger toward him. I felt awkward breaking the news like this, but the secret of our engagement was sneaking up on me and it was beginning to feel almost clandestine. I wanted to know if he'd told his family. I hadn't told my family yet.

"Beth didn't m-m-mention that to me, so he probably hasn't told her yet. Like I said, our conversations with him lately have been short," Butch said, scrambling for words. "I guess a 'congratulations' is in order." He smiled hesitantly.

I got in my car and started it, waving to him as I jammed my Equinox in reverse. As I crossed the cattle guard on route to the highway, Wyatt stepped out in front of me. I nearly hit him. After I slammed on my brakes and skidded to a stop, he came to the driver's side window and gave a one-knuckled knock.

"What were you doin' up there on the hill?" he asked in a tone reminiscent of my fifth-grade nun—accusatory and flat at the same time.

"Checking up on a lead," I said, staring up into his emerald eyes. The full moon bore down on him, making him look almost demonic. He tugged on the coiled rope that he was holding in his left hand, flattening it with a whipping crack. I studied his gesture, sizing it up. "Are you threatening me, Wyatt? Because I know about the meth lab and I know about the sisal rope. And the Ricin. You know what they say, don't you?"

"Well, since you seem to know it all, why don't you tell me?"

"They say to keep your friends close and your enemies closer. I'm just out here on a little joyride keeping tabs on both."

"Both what? I don't get what you're speaking to."

"Better get on inside, Wyatt. There's a chill in the air." As I pulled away, I heard Wyatt yell my name, but I kept driving.

My heartbeat didn't slow until I was about ten miles away from the Anderson ranch. I felt the rush of adrenaline in my veins and a tingling sensation running through my body. Wyatt was in on something, for sure. He was too suspicious. I just couldn't figure him out. One on hand, he seemed genuine and wholesome. Yet, other times he seemed exasperating and provoking. Above all, he was downright irresistible when it came to good looks. I felt slightly ashamed for my attraction to him. I contemplated these feelings while driving under a dark sky filled with millions of bright starts. The full moon shone down on me, illuminating the dark stretch of highway from the ranch back into town. My mind drifted back toward the cemetery and Rowdy Rodiger.

I drove back toward the cemetery–not sure what I was trying to find or what I'd do if I found it. I wanted to see if anything was going on at Rodiger's Stoneworks. It was late–after ten, and when I pulled up, I expected the place to look dark. In fact, I was hoping it would be dark. I was starving and tired. But I could see a shadow moving through the illuminated window of the upstairs loft. I parked my car a block away, near the junkyard, and quietly circled the building. The light layer of new snow on the ground crunched under each footstep. As I rounded the corner toward the back of the building, a dog started barking. It was hard to tell if the dog was inside the building or nearby–perhaps a neighborhood mutt. I hoped it was inside a fenced-in yard. I'd been bitten as a kid, and held a healthy fear of mean dogs.

I snuck around to the back of the building. Remnant slabs of granite were scattered about in piles. Rusted old machinery and tools cluttered the way, and under the freshly fallen snow, it looked like a miniature fallen city from an ancient world, like the Mayan ruins of Central America.

I pulled my running gloves out of my jacket pocket and slipped them on before reaching to turn the knob of the back door to Rodiger's. It was unlocked. I slowly turned the knob and pulled gently on the door, trying not to make a sound. As the rubber molding around the door gave way with a suction sound, I quietly slipped inside, closing the door quickly behind me.

I could hear voices above me, and movement of what sounded like heavy furniture. I ducked down in between two large, gray headstones and listened. I couldn't make out the words, but the voices sounded familiar. I would have to get closer. I crawled on my hands and knees, past the gravestone of the dearly beloved Beverly Kojesky and Donald Lee Smith. The cold stark carving of the names caught my eye momentarily, but what struck me as odd was that the dates on the headstones indicated that these people died years ago. *Why were their gravestones still here?* As I continued to crawl, I noticed that all of the gravestones in the two rows were for people who'd passed on several years ago. I checked the inscriptions carefully, looking for typographical errors or something that perhaps made these stones rejects, but they all seemed perfectly fine, spelling-wise. Perhaps the beloved changed their minds on the style or the dedication. I had no way of knowing.

As I kept crawling closer to the staircase that led up to the loft, I noticed that I could see light through the lettering on James Felter's gravestone. His gravestone was tilted to the side and leaning up against a pillar. I poked my finger through the hole in the "e" on James. If there was light through the "e," the gravestone must be hollow inside. I reached underneath the titled stone and felt around. Sure enough. There was a fist-sized hole in the bottom of the stone. I carefully slid my hand inside, aware of the notion that one should never stick a hand inside a hole. Rattlesnakes hibernate in holes. So do a number of other creatures that bite. Disregarding my fear of being bitten by some unknown creature, I felt around inside. To my right I could feel something round and soft, wrapped in plastic. I grabbed it and pulled. As my hand exited the gravestone, I noticed that it held a baggie of white powder, ziplocked and labeled "ounce–Birch." *Birch?* I'd heard that name recently. Where was it? I thought for a moment, and then it hit me. The Sheriff. That was it. He said that Birch was one of the reduction methods used for producing methamphetamine.

I wanted to get out of there as quickly as possible to call the Sheriff. In a panic, I stuffed the baggie back into James Felter's headstone. I shoved the baggie through the small hole and, in trying to remove my hand, my wool glove got caught on something. I yanked on it hard, setting my hand free, but my glove remained wedged in the hole. Not wanting to leave any evidence behind, I yanked on the glove, accidentally knocking the gravestone to the floor in a horrible crash. The stone split in two, sending dozens of small baggies in every direction.

"What the *fuck* was that?" A voice from upstairs bellowed. I heard stomping and scraping and yelling about a gun as I scrambled to my feet and bolted towards the back door. I heard my heartbeat pick up speed and felt my legs scramble as the slow motion of fear overwhelmed my senses. The knob slipped through my shaking hand as I slammed my shoulder into the wooden door. It didn't budge. I held tighter on the knob and turned harder, feeling the release of the latch. I smashed my shoulder again against the door, this time successfully breaking free. I could hear the footsteps pounding down the stairs behind me as I escaped past the pile of broken granite and around the side of the building.

"Get him!" a familiar voice yelled. It was Sherman Todd.

I bolted across the street and into the junkyard, dodging in and out of rusted heaps of old cars and piles of old tires. I knew that they would kill me when they found me. No doubt they saw the baggies on the ground at the bottom of the warehouse steps. They would know that I knew they were transporting meth in the gravestones. If Sherman Todd had his way tonight, I would not make it out of the junkyard alive.

Chapter 37

Something sharp gouged my calf as I ran past a seven-foot pile of compressed junked cars. I could feel the pain spurt up my thigh, through my groin, and up my spine. Dampness immediately filtered through my Lycra tights and the sticky weight of blood spread quickly toward my shoe. My leg began to throb with each step.

"Get the dog," a voice yelled. It was Rowdy Rodiger. His high-pitched intonation was etched in my brain after sitting with him and his terrible temperament for days during depositions. He reminded me of a moth flittering too close to a flame—one false move and he would be ablaze. He had no compunction for the value of life and I knew he wouldn't spare mine if given the chance. "Come out, come out wherever you are."

His footsteps crunched loudly and boldly. He was not trying to hide his whereabouts. He probably knew this junkyard like the back of his hand. Probably played there as a kid when he went to work with his dad on Saturdays. Probably took his first girlfriend there in high school for a make-out session. Probably had keg parties there with his buddies who didn't bother to go to college. He would know every good hiding place. Every obstacle. And as I darted in between rows of demolished cars, I saw that he would be able to track me easily. I was wounded prey. He was the predator and he could follow the track of blood seeping from the gash on my calf.

"I know you're in there. Come on out. We can talk. I won't hurt you."

The shadow of the gun in his hand was enlarged by the full moon overhead. I could see the shadow grow—extend toward me with each footstep. I could hear the dog barking wildly in my direction. I needed to move, but my shoe was a puddle of blood and with each step, I left behind a messy trail. I stuffed my glove inside my running tights, trying to get the bleeding to stop and I took a handful of fresh snow and wiped around my shoe the best that I could. The dog was getting closer. So was the shadow of the gun.

I pulled my cell phone out of my pocket and dialed 9-1-1. The operator answered. "Someone is trying to kill me," I whispered into the receiver, cupping it with my hands. She asked me to identify myself and describe my location. I told her who I was and that I was in the junkyard by the cemetery.

"Find him yet?" Sherman Todd's voice boomed. The dog was growling loudly. The fact that they were referring to me as a "him" convinced me that they didn't know who I was. I didn't know whether this was good or bad. I didn't think that Sherman Todd would hurt me, but after what I'd found in Rodiger's Stoneworks, I couldn't be sure.

"Junkyard. By the cemetery. Copy. Over," the 9-1-1 operator said.

"I heard something." Rowdy said. "This way."

I left my cell phone on, but slipped it back in my pocket. I had two choices: I could try to run for it and risk getting shot in the back, or I could lie in wait and hope they wouldn't find me. I knew there was a trail of blood leading right to my feet and that the full moon illuminated the ground well enough to see it. Would he shoot me point blank? Talk to me first? Take me hostage? Could I dart in and out of enough cars and outrun them? I didn't know my way out of the junkyard. Would I have to scale a fence? I'd be target practice if that were the case. *Sherman Todd is a sharp shooter,* I remember Greg telling me when I asked him whether Sherman was a hunter. But Rowdy Rodiger had the gun. Was he a good shot too?

"Here, take this," Rowdy said, shoving a pistol into Sherman's hand. Now they were both armed. Time stood motionless. I could see my breath in front of my face. I could hear Rowdy and Sherman talking. The dog barking. The operator of my 9-1-1 call trying to get me to respond to her questions.

I thought about what was going on around me. Methamphetamines. I thought about the Sheriff and what else he'd told us about the drug.

"It's a powerful stimulant that affects the central nervous system and can induce anxiety, insomnia, paranoia, hallucinations, mood swings, delusions and violent behavior. Distributors are often quite violent defending their territory. The violence poses a direct threat to law enforcement officers."

What if Rowdy Rodiger and Sherman Todd were high on meth? It would be more likely for them to shoot me in cold blood. *Speed. Crank. Go-fast. Zip. Cristy. Could I talk sense to them? Could I outrun them?*

"Ollie, ollie in come free. Come out from wherever you are." It was Sherman Todd this time, and he sounded high as a kite. The sharp shooter. *If the sharp shooter was high on drugs, would his aim be off?* I didn't know. I'd heard that some people who used cocaine or other stimulants were actually more focused. More precise. That is, until they came down from the drugs.

"I know you're out there."

The voice was getting closer. I could hear the sharp, high-pitched whine of the dog barking. I could feel the moon shining down on me, as if it was a spotlight guiding them in my direction. A coffin of fear was closing on me. It was in that instance that I decided to run for my life. They were either going to shoot me or not. Or miss. And my odds were better if I was on the move. I looked up at the full moon, asked for its guidance, saw where she lit the path best and headed in the exact opposite direction. Toward the cemetery.

Chapter 38

The shot that rang out into the night whizzed past my head before I had time to duck. I dodged in and out of trees and gravestones, running as fast as my injured leg would take me. And with every sharp pain I felt, I thought about Greg. My fiancé. The man that I loved. How I had to survive this to get back to his arms–to the safety and love that I was sure he held tight for me. Up until this very moment, I was unsure about getting married to him. But something happened in the split second when I departed the junkyard that assured me that Greg was the right man. He was the man I should marry and the man I should treasure and the man I could look forward to growing old with. Maybe it was the full moon. Or the intense fear. Or the fact that my life might soon be taken from me. Whatever it was–it came to me in the full force of a wave. A tsunami, one might say.

"He went that way," I heard Rowdy Rodiger shout.

"No. There *she* is," Sherman Todd shouted. "It's Mary MacIntosh. Trade me guns, you idiot. You can't shoot worth shit."

* * *

Like many small towns, Sheridan only had one cemetery, so the dearly beloved were all buried in one location. But there was the "old cemetery," which was decrepit and housed only those from the 1800's, and then there was the "new cemetery" that had been the place of rest for Sheridanites since the early 1900's. The "old cemetery" was something one might think of when reading a Stephen King novel–ornate wrought iron gates hung slightly askew. Scraggly old trees barren of leaves. Gravestones knocked over with tree roots growing around them. It was an interesting place to go for a jog in the late afternoon. But it was a scary place to run through when two men were chasing you down at gunpoint.

I dodged behind a large pine tree with limbs sagging from the weight of old age. My heart raced quickly and I could feel the beads of sweat dripping from my forehead. The chill in the air was more noticeable and my breath formed large clouds in front of my face. I took a second to get my bearings. To the right, the cemetery curved down a hill. To the left, it ventured uphill to the "mausoleum"–a Greek-like structure dedicated to a long-time Sheridan family. I knew that if I went right, I'd be forced down into the ravine and since I didn't know my way well, Rowdy Rodiger might be able to outwit me. If I went left and toward the mausoleum, I could possibly circle back around Rodiger's Stoneworks and toward my car. I chose left.

Unfortunately, Sherman Todd also veered left. With the gun pointed straight out at me. My leg was throbbing with each step as I curved in and out of old gravestones. My heartbeat slowed some, as if it was running out of the adrenaline that had kept me moving. I hadn't eaten since noon and my body was starting to fail me. Maybe I could stop and talk reason into Sherman. I could tell him that I was worried about him and that I'd gone to Rodiger's to check on him. I contemplated this idea for only a second when another voice came into my head. It was my father, and his voice told me to run like hell.

Chapter 39

Sherman Todd was, by all accounts, the all-American guy. He had billowing curly blond hair, blue eyes and dimples in his devilish cheeks. He was "Mr. Greenpeace." Mountain biker. Rock climber. Expert skier. Hiker. Backpacker. He was the picture of health. Until he tried meth. It was at a party after the bars in town had closed down for the night. He was starting to feel the pull of being up since five-thirty. The girl that he'd hooked up with at the bar suggested he try a little "ice" to rock him back into the groove. He declined at first, spouting off all the good-boy reasons for never getting mixed up with drugs. But, her wayward glances and swaying breasts convinced him that a little taste of the stuff would do no harm. *Just a little pick-me-up*, he later told Greg. And oh, how it worked. The little pick-me-up sent tingles down his spine as her swaying hips led him to the back bedroom. She made a few moves, convinced him to try another hit, and with a little coaxing, very little, she was naked, on top of him, doing a line on his bare-naked chest. The sex he had that night was grand-slam style. Every move sent her to the moon and she wasn't afraid to prove it. He'd never been rocked like that before and was convinced that her "ice" was the E-ticket. After hooking up with her a few more times, he'd made connections with her dealer. And that was how Mr. Greenpeace met Mr. Rowdy Rodiger.

Meeting Rowdy Rodiger was not a feat in Sheridan. He was a mainstay at the Trails End bar every evening. The Trails End was not a bar frequented by the well-known townsfolk, but was more the style of those just looking for a cold, hard drunk. So, meeting up with Rowdy at the Trails End was as predictable as the sunrise. Greg had no problem figuring out how that all went down. What perplexed him beyond reason was how Rowdy Rodiger convinced Sherman Todd to run drugs.

* * *

Greg had known Sherman Todd since grade school and they'd been fast friends from the very start. From little league to Boy Scouts to fishing trips, they were practically inseparable. They'd made a pact as scouts never to tattle on each other. To stick together through thick and thin. Scouts' Honor was the code. Say No to Drugs was also the code. They led the all-American lifestyle because that's what good Boy Scouts did.

When Greg was assigned his latest undercover investigative reporting assignment on the drug runs from Central and South America across the border and into the United States, he took the job very seriously. He knew that the assignment was dangerous but he also knew that the drugs that were flowing into the United States were destroying people's lives every single day. He wanted to help shut it down.

He'd had a few close calls while tracking down cartels south of the border. He told me that it was scary and invigorating all at the same time. He followed the drug dealers by plane and by boat and by car. When his trail led to a Peterbuilt truck hauling gravestones from Las Vegas to Wyoming and beyond, his interest was piqued. Who dare pollute his home state with drugs? Who dare drive into the picturesque beauty of the Big Horns with a load of methamphetamines? What kind of person would risk getting caught with a truckload of drugs?

When he followed the Peterbuilt to a building near a cemetery in his hometown, he was shocked. He knew people did drugs when he was in high school, but they certainly weren't the kind of people he hung around. They were the loadies. The losers. The flunkies. He and Sherman Todd had no use for those junkies. They were clean cut. So when Greg saw his childhood buddy unloading the Peterbuilt, he fluctuated somewhere between rage, confusion and disappointment. He would have to break his pact. He would have to tattle. He would have to disclose enough information to write a very compelling story, and that compelling story would likely land his childhood buddy in prison.

But this was all still a secret because his investigation wasn't complete. He'd just figured out how they hid the drugs in the headstones and transferred them across state lines. He'd just figured out the identity of the dealers. He'd just put the puzzle together, and was working with local law enforcement to confirm and prove the story before it went to print. It would be a break-through to his career and might put him on track to be a lead anchorman on a major network someday. He had the looks and the smarts to do it. And he was so close. But nothing comes easy and handing over the photographs and documents that would lock away your best friend was excruciating. He had to confirm it, in person, one last time before he sent the article over the wires to his boss. And this final confirmation, this desire to prove that maybe he was wrong and maybe Sherman Todd was not mixed up in this horrible mess, was what led Greg to Rodiger Stoneworks one evening when the moon was full and the snow was freshly sprinkled on the ground.

Chapter 40

When Greg heard the gunshot he knew that Mac was in trouble. He recognized her car parked near the junkyard and realized that she, too, had figured it out and had snuck into Rodiger Stoneworks to confirm her suspicions. She was his soul mate. She thought the same way he did. She got it. And now, she was in trouble.

The gunshot came from the direction of the cemetery, but the grounds were several miles wide and at least a mile long and the reverberation of the sound made its direction unclear. A coyote howled in the distance. Or was it a dog? He sprinted in the direction of the old cemetery, not sure if he was heading the right way. A second gunshot echoed in the coldness of the night, displacing bats from a nearby tree. Greg changed directions slightly—and ran like hell.

He saw her cresting the hill, heading in his direction, weaving in and out of trees and headstones. He knew it was Mac, even in the darkness. He could see the outline of her body and knew her running gait anywhere. More importantly, however, he sensed her presence and knew that she was in terrible danger. He bore down harder, opening up into a sprint. As he closed in on her, he saw the venomous eyes of a stranger cutting across the path. It was Sherman Todd. A stranger now—yet once his best friend. The body belonged to his old friend, but the eyes belonged to someone else. They were wild and distant and dreadfully befouled.

An instant would seem like an eternity when Greg saw Sherman reach out and grab Mac by the back of her jacket. He watched in silent horror as his fiancé, his lover, his friend, went careening down to the earth in a shuddering thud. She bounced once hard before rolling and when her momentum finally gave way to gravity, Sherman was on her instantly.

Greg had no chance–he was simply too far away. By the time he got there, Sherman Todd had the gun to her head.

"Don't take another step, bro, or I'll blow her pretty face to bits. Hear me?" he yelled, yanking back on Mac's hair. Her head jerked back and she made a gurgling sound as if the oxygen in her lungs voluntarily escaped to a safer place. She was panting for breath, wild-eyed and afraid. Sherman was wheezing for air. "Hear me?" he shouted again.

"Hey, buddy, chill," Greg said. "It's going to be okay. It's okay. I'm going to help you. I'm going to get you what you need. Whatever it is you need. Money. More drugs. Help. Whatever you need, I'll get it. Just let her go." Greg lowered himself toward the ground, trying to make himself appear less threatening. Helpful, perhaps. He crept forward a few steps, trying to close the gap between Mac and him. He reached out slowly with his right hand. "It's okay. Just give me the gun, buddy. You've got to give me the gun."

"Don't move or I'll shoot her." Sherman's eyes were bulging and wild.

"You don't want to do that, buddy. You really, really don't," Greg said, catching his breath. "We can help you now. If you do something incredibly stupid, like hurt her, then I can't help you. Please don't do that, Sherman. You're my best friend."

"No. I don't have any friends. I don't need–"

"Do you remember when we were in fifth grade and you dared me to steal that candy bar at Woolworth's?" Sherman shook his head, remembering. "And when I got caught you took the blame. You told the store manager that you stole it and shoved it in my pocket. Do you remember that?" Sherman didn't respond. "And remember when Casey Shelly dumped me the day before Prom and how broken up I was?" Sherman cracked a bit of a grin, nodding again slightly. "You put on your sister's old dress and went with me as a date. You were the hit. You made everyone laugh like hell that night. And when those asshole football players made fun of you, you didn't give a damn. You just flipped 'em off and walked away in your clumsy high heels. Don't you remember?" Sherman closed his eyes a bit, as if he were going back in time to a safer place. "You would have done anything for me then, wouldn't you?" Sherman nodded in agreement. "Then you need to do something for me right now, old pal. You need to let her go. She's going to be my wife, buddy. You don't want to hurt my wife, do you?"

"All that's real touchin' and all," a voice bellowed from the shadow of a grave. "But the problem here is that we can't have no witnesses and your *wife* witnessed some shit that's none of her fuckin' business. So, we've got no choice but to shut her up for good. And this be the perfect place to do it, seeing that there are a few empty graves that need fillin'. It'll be real romantic–I'll see to that. We'll lay you two down, side by side, announce you as man and wife and all that shit and then we'll put matching bullet holes in your heads. A new sort of wedding symbol. Call 'em matching tattoos."

Rowdy Rodiger emerged from the shadow, a cigarette dangling from the corner of his lips. His baggy jeans and scraggly, thin hair flailed in the breeze. He flicked his lighter once and put the flame to his angular face. As his cigarette ignited, he pushed his stringy hair out of his face and inhaled deeply. As the smoke billowed from between his yellowed teeth, he strode in Greg's direction, gun drawn. Without a sound, he motioned for Greg to move toward the deep hole in the ground next to him. The grave was old–as if it were dug one hundred years ago for a long-forgotten soul whose burial had never taken place. Greg didn't move.

"Get on your feet, soldier," Rowdy yelled, raising the gun in Greg's direction. Greg slowly stood and took only one step forward. His warm breath made a cloud in the chill of the evening air. A trickle of sweat rolled off his right eyebrow, glistening in the moonlight, as he peered at Rowdy with a deadly stare. "Get your fuckin' ass over here, I said." Greg looked at Mac and then at Sherman Todd. Sherman looked anxious, as if he feared what might happen next.

"Listen, Rowdy," Greg said, "I know that you–"

"Shut the fuck up. You don't know shit. Lay your sorry ass down right here," Rowdy said, point to the dirt next to the gravesite. "Now!"

Greg calmly walked in Rowdy's direction, his shadow elongating as he closed the gap. "You are making a big mistake. My dad. Your boss. He–"

"What da fuck you talkin' about? *Your dad?* Everett Fisher? He ain't your dad. Butch Anderson is your dad. You're just tryin' to mess with me. Mess with my head. It ain't going to work.

"Everett Fisher is my dad. My *real* dad. He was married to my mom before Butch."

"Are you stupid? Everett Fisher ain't no daddy. Hell, he's the dealer. I run the drugs for *him*."

Mac, who'd been hopelessly silent during this exchange, let out a loud gasp.

"I know," Greg said calmly. "I know all about my dad and his drug running. I figured that one out already. That's how he got the money to start up this methane gas outfit he's running. It's his ruse to hide his drug money. I'm way ahead of you, Rowdy. What my dad doesn't know is that you've been cheating him. You set yourselves up with a 'Well from Hell' on every project and cook up your own little drug lab in there. It's perfect for it. No one notices the smell. Or the chemicals. And you've got yourself a little side business. You're his 'land man' and his drug runner and now you're his competition. And when he finds out that you've been crashing his turf and selling to his local dealers, you'll be dead. His Mexican cartel will wipe you–"

"His Mexican cartel will never know 'cuz you're going to have a bullet in your head," Rowdy said, raising the gun.

Chapter 41

The sound of the gunshot ricocheted through the sky as I watched Greg tuck and fall. Rowdy Rodiger sprang backwards in the same split second. I felt the yell escape my lips but I don't recall hearing it. In fact, I don't recall too much about what happened next. It all seemed to happen slowly yet quickly, and in a thick fog.

Wyatt emerged from the gates to the old cemetery, his pistol–the one I'd used to shoot the mountain lion–smoking. He charged up the hill toward Greg and fell to his side.

The Sheriff charged up behind Greg, his gun out of its holster and pointed toward Sherman Todd. Sherman, wide-eyed and frozen with fear, quickly released his gun to the Sheriff and put his hands in the air as commanded. I crawled toward Greg as quickly as I could and cupped his face in my hands. Conversations flew over me like birds of prey over their kill, but I didn't hear a single word. I heard Greg's heartbeat through his chest and that was the only sound I cared about. It was strong and steady and unwavering, like his love.

Wyatt had been in the Sheriff's office when my 9-1-1 call came through from dispatch. The Sheriff had been questioning Wyatt about his knowledge of the meth lab in the "Well from Hell," and after much discussion, the Sheriff finally understood. Wyatt knew nothing about the drug lab. Neither did Butch. They'd stayed away from that well because it spooked the horses and was dangerous. Half of the ranch was covered in salt from the methane gas nightmare, so white powder around a well site would mean nothing to them. They were simple cowboys living a simple life. Nothing more.

Wyatt told the Sheriff that Greg had come out to the ranch earlier that day and confided in him about the drugs and about Everett Fisher. Greg told Wyatt about his investigation and even told him that he was in fear for his own safety. The threats were real and these people meant what they said. Everett's Mexican cartel was well known as extremely violent and vicious. Greg told Wyatt that I was in danger too. So when my cell call came through, the Sheriff knew it was serious. So did Wyatt.

The dispatcher burst into the Sheriff's office and told him that I'd called from the cemetery and that she heard gunshots from the cell phone call. Despite the Sheriff's pleas, Wyatt sped to the cemetery and did what he had to do to protect his brother. Seeing that his brother had a gun pointed at him, Wyatt yelled "duck" and then shot Rowdy Rodiger square through the heart, killing him instantly.

All things aside, sibling rivalry had never contaminated Wyatt's love for his big brother. I saw that now as I held Greg's face in my hands and listened to his beating heart. Wyatt was right there beside me, holding his brother's hand, tears streaming down his face. It dawned on me that Greg instinctively ducked when Wyatt ordered him to do so. When I asked Greg about this later, how he dropped to his knees without second-guessing or turning around to see who'd said it, Greg told me a story that I'll never forget. It went something like this.

"When we were kids, Wyatt and me, we had a ton of chores to do on the ranch. But when the chores were done, we could fool around. So, one day Wyatt told me to grab our fishing poles and follow him down to the Powder River. I did. He pulled his makeshift canoe from the banks into the water and told me to get in. Well, I'd seen him put this canoe together using old logs and rope, so I didn't really trust the thing. It was a Huck Finn raft, really, and fishing on it while cruising down the river made me nervous. But, he'd worked so hard carving it and making benches and side rails that I just couldn't bear to say no. We pushed off from shore and he handed me a paddle. And then he handed me a bucket—the kind he fed the horses with. A big bucket. He said to me, 'You'll have to paddle and bail and fish at the same time.' Being the older brother, I knew this was crazy and implausible and downright stupid. I would never even try such a foolhardy thing. But Wyatt would. And he would enjoy it. Laugh about it. We had a lot of fun that day. We fished. And paddled. And bailed. The boat sunk a few miles downriver. When it was about to go under, he said one word. 'Duck.' He told me later that it meant that it was time to swim. Like a duck. From that point on, it was our code word for bailing out of something. When I heard someone yell 'duck,' I knew what to do. It was instinct."

* * *

Sherman Todd pled nolo contendere to malicious mischief for the shooting incidents on the Anderson Ranch and for the threatening letter on my car. He denied any involvement with the ricin poisoning. He pled guilty to illegal possession of narcotics in exchange for his testimony against Everett Fisher on federal drug charges. Sherman would spend several years in prison. By all accounts, he was lucky. After release, he would be placed in the witness protection program. Greg would never see his childhood buddy again.

Rowdy Rodiger served the hardest time possible for his involvement in the Well from Hell. He was dead.

SPRING

Chapter 42

We were in day two of the trial. Jury selection had been quite a lesson in theatrics. Davis Dunne was throwing temper tantrums every fifteen minutes over some prospective juror and his or her possible bias against his case. Of course, Harry found Dunne's temper intriguing and, perhaps, tempting. He'd baited him more often than he'd baited his fishing line.

Despite Harry's statement to the contrary, he actually let me give the opening statement. He told me that I'd earned the chance, since I'd worked so hard for the past year getting this case ready for trial. Harry asked Butch's permission and Butch readily agreed, perhaps even encouraged Harry to give me the chance.

I had never been so nervous. In fact, I couldn't sleep for several nights before the first day of trial, so at one o'clock in the morning two days before I was to give the opening, I pulled out my mother's recipe cards and decided to make a chocolate cake from scratch. It was fair to say that I hadn't spent much time baking since we took on this case and it was also fair to say that I was completely exhausted and overwhelmed. So, my cake turned out lopsided and ugly and I was sure that I had used a wrong ingredient along the way. But as I stared at it at three in the morning I decided that it was the perfect metaphor to the case. So I made another cake. I was careful this time. I checked off every ingredient and made sure I followed the recipe to an exact science. My second cake was as masterful as my mother would have made. I took both cakes with me to Casper and used them in my opening. The jury nodded and related to the analogy. Harry loved it. He told me that it was one of the best and most heart-felt opening statements he'd ever heard.

It was March–less than a year since we'd filed the class action lawsuit. We'd hoped that the case would settle after Everett Fisher was arrested for drug charges, but he'd refused to even discuss settlement. His assets held by KingFisher had been frozen by the government and a portion of his MethZap holdings had been placed in trust pending resolution of our case.

As we feared, Davis Dunne used the methamphetamine drug lab based in the "Well from Hell" against us at every turn. He filed a summary judgment motion and a motion on the pleadings trying to get the case thrown out. We'd successfully defended against Dunne thus far because Judge Laird was well prepared and willing to let the case run its natural course, but Harry and I were well aware of the fact that the drug issue made it exceedingly more difficult to prove causation. We'd been forced to hire more experts and the case had become even more expensive than anticipated. This did not sit well with our class of plaintiffs, whom we'd asked to pony up an additional ten thousand dollars each to take the case to trial. Apparently, they gathered for a private meeting–we were not invited guests. After a heated discussion, they had flat-out refused to pitch in more money toward the case. So, Harry and I were forced to finance the rest of the bills. If we lost, I'd be bankrupt and Harry's beautiful home in Jackson would be on the auction block. Nothing like a little pressure to make you work hard.

Chapter 43

"Ladies and Gentlemen of the jury, Butch and Beth Anderson are never, ever going to be satisfied with MethZap until they have forced MethZap off their property and out of business for good. Butch and Beth Anderson, and the other class action plaintiffs, are counting on you not to like MethZap. They are going to paint MethZap as this horrible operator that would do anything to mine the methane under their land." It was Davis Dunne's shot at his opening statement and he presented himself to the jury with a black double-breasted suit and a gold and black striped tie. His chest was puffed out and his dark hair slicked back. He almost looked handsome, if he wasn't such a pompous jerk. Prior to the start of trial, we'd been in the judge's chambers for two days arguing motions in limine and discussing what charts, graphs and demonstrations would be allowed during trial. He fought us tooth and nail on everything, but Harry was very persuasive and had an obvious appeal to the judge. We won most of the major evidence battles and that was good. But there was a big difference between winning a battle and winning the war. Ask the Sioux Indians about that notion.

"You're going to get to meet the president of MethZap. He's here today," Dunne said, pointing to Ace Sanders sitting at the defendants' table. "He's a two-star general in the Army National Guard and he's going to explain to you that on November 2, 2004 the Andersons entered into a Surface Damage Agreement with MethZap allowing us to enter onto and conduct surveys, strat tests, production drilling, pipeline installation, production operations, reworking operations and the like. MethZap did not have to enter into this agreement. In fact, it wasn't their company policy to do so. They had the right to do what they wanted with the minerals under the Anderson ranch, just like they had the right to drill on all of the plaintiffs' land. MethZap entered into the agreement with the Andersons as a token of goodwill–a good neighbor type of thing–a Wyoming peace offering. In return, as you will see during this trial, their goodwill and hard efforts to try to please the Andersons were a waste of time.

"There will be testimony that under the agreement the Andersons accepted a fee for compensation for surface damages. That's right, ladies and gentlemen. They were paid handsomely for the damage that commonly occurs during drilling operations. Handsomely. The Andersons happily accepted those payments. And they were paid for the roads and fences and other improvements made to their land. But MetZap was on the job site a little over a month when they received their first complaints from the Andersons in the form of letters from their previous lawyer, Chance Baker. Did MethZap take those complaints seriously? Yes, they did. MethZap responded to every complaint and fixed everything the Andersons complained about. They had protracted meetings with Beth Anderson, listened to her complaints, appeased her and tried their best to do what she wanted, but it was never enough. Her issues were way deeper than the gas we were drilling.

"See, you must understand that the owner of MethZap is Everett Fisher. And Everett Fisher is Beth Anderson's former husband and the father of her first-born son, Greg Fisher. It's no secret that Everett and Beth had a contentious divorce and that their relations haven't improved a whole lot over the years, so imagine her disdain when she learned that her ex-husband was drilling on her ranch. You look to be a smart group of people. You can put two and two together. Was Beth Anderson really complaining about the ranch? Or was this her way of getting back at Everett Fisher for running out on her?"

Dunne walked over to the defense table and picked up a mayonnaise jar and held it up in the air for the jury to see. The jar was empty. He reached into his double-breasted coat pocket and began filling the jar with golf balls until they brimmed at the top of the jar. "Ladies and gentlemen, like I said, you look like a wise group of folks. But even wise people can be led away from the truth, and this demonstration is a perfect example of the truth about what happened on the Anderson ranch over the last two years.

I ask a question of you. Does this jar look full?" Most of the members of the jury nodded. Davis Dunne walked back over to the defense table and picked up a box of pebbles and poured them into the jar. He shook the jar lightly and the pebbles rolled into the open areas between the golf balls. He then asked the jury if the jar was full. They again nodded. Some even uttered affirmatively. Dunne next picked up a box of sand and poured it into the jar. Of course, the sand filled up the gaps. He asked once more if the jar was full. This time, the jury responded with a unanimous "yes." Dunne then reached over and grabbed a cup of coffee and poured the entire contents into the jar, effectively filling the empty space between the sand. Some members of the jury giggled, as if they knew they'd been fooled. He grabbed another cup of coffee and added it to the mixture.

"Now," said Dunne as the laughter subsided, "I want you to recognize that this jar represents the soil on the Anderson ranch. The golf balls represent the water discharged after the methane gas was extracted. The pebbles represent the salt left behind as a result of the extraction process. MethZap fully acknowledges and accepts responsibility for the salt issue. We've remedied a portion of the problem and intend to rectify it by trucking in thousands of cubic yards of good topsoil to make the ranch pristine again. We understand the problem and have been and continue to be ready, willing and able to fix it. But the real issue, as you will see during the course of this trial, is that the salt is not the only thing contaminating the soil at the Anderson ranch."

Dunne held up the jar and pointed to the sludge inside. "See the sand. The sand represents pseudoephedrine. And the coffee represents hydriodic acid. And as members of the jury, you ask yourself, what are pseudoephedrine and hydriodic acid and what do they have to do with the case? Like I said, you're a smart group. The answer is that these two ingredients don't belong on the ranch, but they are there because there was a methamphetamine lab in one of the huts surrounding a well site. A methamphetamine lab on the Anderson ranch." Dunne paused for a moment, shaking his head. The jury was leaning forward, many of them coaxing a furrowed brow. He shook the contents of the mayonnaise jar up, staring at it for effect. "And the contamination from the methamphetamine lab on the Anderson ranch got all mixed up with the groundwater discharge from our methane gas operation out there, making it darn near impossible to tell what is causing the grass not to grow and the mosquitos to buzz and the sage grouse to die and the trees to fall. The Andersons," he said, pointing to Butch and Beth seated next to Harry and me at the plaintiff table, "the Andersons want you to make MethZap pay for it all. But honestly, ladies and gentlemen, you can't possibly do that. You're smart. You know that it's not our responsibility to pay for other people's messes. And we trust that you will do the smart thing and find in favor of defendant MethZap."

Chapter 44

The opening statements for the Army Corps of Engineers and the BLM were decent too, but not anywhere near as effective as Davis Dunne's. Chuck Wells gave a fairly impressive statement on behalf of the Bureau of Land Management, telling a story about the mouse that sunk the boat. It went something like this.

"There once was this farm, and on this farm there lived a group of animals. Think of Charlotte's Web, if you will. The animals all decided one day that it would be fun to take the boat out for a little afternoon joyride around the lake. So, the cow, horse, pig, goat, sheep, goose, and mouse all ventured down to the lake. The cow got in the boat first, displacing the water a bit, submerging the boat a few inches deeper into the water. Next, the horse got in, again, sinking the boat a little bit more. Then the pig got in, sinking the boat a little more. Then the goat, and the sheep and the goose. By this point, the boat was submerged deeply into the water, and the water was lapping over the edges of the boat. The mouse, not wanting to be left out, quickly jumped aboard and the boat suddenly sunk. The question was, 'Who sunk the boat?' Of course, every other barnyard animal blamed the mouse. 'It was the mouse that sunk the boat.' But the reality is that they all sunk the boat together. There is no way to blame the tiny little mouse, who weighed considerably less than the other animals, for sinking the boat. And, ladies and gentlemen of the jury, the mouse in this lawsuit is the Bureau of Land Management. Yes, we issued permits, but we issued them responsibly and according to the spirit and scope of the law. We didn't sink the boat. We didn't contaminate the Powder River. You certainly can't blame us for what MethZap and the other methane gas operators have done to the land. It's not our fault. We're just the tiny mouse."

* * *

Instead of starting with Butch Anderson as our first witness, we decided to start with a saltier character, Phil Fontana.

"My name is Phil Fontana. My friends call me Philthy," he said with a smirk. The jury laughed in short unison.

"Mr. Fontana," Harry began. "As a member of the class action plaintiffs, please tell us about your experience with methane gas development."

"In 1989, I bought myself a seventy-eight space mobile park about ten miles north of Gillette. The good and the bad of it is that my mobile park is smack dab in the middle of both coal mining and methane development. The good of it is that I'm making quite a nest egg in royalties from the methane gas. The bad of it is that I lost my water well to the de-watering of a coal seam that sucked the aquifer dry and I've been forced to drill a new well at my own expense. I joined in the class action to get my money back. The laws are queer in these parts. See, the government officials told me that the coal mining company would have to reimburse me 'cuz there's laws that say they must replace depleted water wells, whether they caused the harm or not. And I guess in the past they've been willin' to do it. But now that the methane gas plays are interferin' with the coal mining operations, there's a little war goin' on and my mobile home park is stuck in the middle of it. The Wyoming Department of Environmental Quality determined that my well was lost due to a combination of the coal mine and the methane de-watering, so now those two outfits are fighting over who should pay, and the Bureau of Land Management, who done issued the permits for both operations, says that it is out of their jurisdiction to force either to cough up the money for my new well. Hell, I'm stuck in spring mud with this one 'cuz I have to supply water to my tenants. You should hear them ladies scream and yell when the well went dry. Good God, you've never heard so much complainin' in your whole entire life. It's been quite an education, I tell you what. When there ain't no water to make a baby's bottle or to wash dishes or do laundry, you'd think the world had come to an end. I was threatened with my life several times, and a few of the broads looked like they were damn serious about it. They'd done shot me if I didn't pay for a new well.

"Anyway, I know I'm ramblin'. Wife says I do it 'til the cows come home. We don't even own cows—"

* * *

Phil Fontana was a good witness in that he painted on canvas the reality of how the methane business affected the middle to low class people. Unfortunately, Davis Dunne was good at evoking one's temper, and he got Phil good and pissed off quickly during cross-examination. As a result, Phil showed his less-than-flattering side early and often. Harry quickly did a change in line-up and called one of our expert witnesses to bolster Phil's testimony.

"Shallow alluvial sands on Phil's property were being flooded by the discharge of water," our expert witness explained to the jury following Philthy's testimony.

"What was causing the flooding on Phil's land?" Harry asked.

"Between 2000 and 2003, MethZap discharged two hundred million gallons of methane water into Little Rawhide Creek, a tributary of the Powder River. The water superabsorbed and began traveling laterally down gradiant to Phil's property."

"Then what happened?"

"When Phil wrote a letter to complain, the Wyoming Department of Environmental Quality declined to take action because they said that the discharge was considered a beneficial use of the water."

Harry handed the expert a copy of a letter written by the DEQ to Phil. "I hand you a copy of Plaintiff's Exhibit 12. Tell us about this letter."

"Objection!" Dunne was on his feet, angrily tapping his index finger on the Defendants' table. "Hearsay. Best evidence—"

"Your Honor, may we approach for a sidebar?" Harry asked. The judge nodded. Dunne, Harry and I crossed the courtroom in a hurry and met the judge on the side of his large wooden platform of a desk. Judge Laird put his hand over the microphone so that the jury wouldn't hear the conversation. Laird, in his mid-sixties, had a mustache similar to Butch. In fact, I thought they resembled each other in distinction and mannerism. Laird listened patiently to us argue over the evidence and then made his ruling loud enough for the court reporter to copy it down in stenography. Harry would be allowed to continue his line of questioning.

Our expert continued testifying. "The letter states that the 'DEQ only deals with water quality problems, not water quantity problems.' So, Phil had to replace his leach field and has had to fix or replace several mobile homes due to heavy cracking and water damage. Most of the trees, shrubs and grass have been killed by this contaminated water and the white mineral deposits permanently cover his land. When the attorneys called and asked me to come out and take a look at the water, I measured as high as eleven inches of excess water on the land. That's almost a foot of water in some parts. I know it's hard to imagine how much this is."

I motioned for Pamela to drag in the blue plastic swimming pool that was out in the hallway. I followed her with a garden hose that had been hooked up to a faucet in the courthouse bathroom. Before trial commenced, I asked Judge Laird's permission to demonstrate the quantity of water on many of the plaintiffs' land. Dunne went ballistic over it, but Judge Laird agreed, so long as it didn't take up too much time. While the swimming pool was filling up with water, the jury was adjourned for a fifteen-minute break. When they returned, the pool was filled with a foot of water. After the courtroom reassembled, I handed the expert a yardstick.

"How much water did you say was on Phil's land when you were asked to go out there?" Harry asked.

"Like I said, I went there a few times and it was as high as eleven inches. Sometimes it was considerably lower–maybe five or six inches."

"Could you take that yardstick that I just handed to you and measure the amount of water in the wading pool in front of you, please?" The expert came from the witness box and stuck the yardstick in the pool. The yardstick sunk to the twelve-inch line. I watched the jurors' reaction to this experiment. Even the "Missouri–prove it to me" men in the back row of the jury uncrossed their arms and gave the "lean to." We'd caught their attention, for the time being.

"And you testified earlier about the salt content of the water, correct?"

"Yes, sir, I did," Mr. Donaldson continued. "I said that salinity refers to the mineral content of water, but it is much simpler to use the electrical conductivity of the water as a measure of its salt load. The more salt a water sample contains, the more readily it conducts electricity and the higher the electrical conductivity, or EC, value. Typically, the conductivity is reported in units of micro-mhos per centimeter. The norm in these parts is somewhere around five hundred micro-mhos. Phil's EC value ranged from three to four thousand micro-mhos per centimeter."

"How much salt would you need to add to the water in the wading pool here in the courtroom to make it reach the electrical conductivity value of Phil's property?" Harry asked. Again, we'd asked Judge Laird's permission to demonstrate the amount of salt in front of the jury. Again, Dunne had screamed and shouted words like "inflammatory" and "unduly prejudicial," but Judge Laird allowed the demonstration. I motioned for Pamela to roll in the wheelbarrows stacked with ten-pound bags of commercial grade salt. Pamela, a large woman who often bragged about the size of her arm muscles, was dripping wet with sweat when she was finished bringing in the sixth wheelbarrow.

"If we added these gunny sacks full of salt to this little pool," the expert continued, "it would amount to four thousand micro-mhos per centimeter. Of course, I'm not going to add the salt, because it would be a waste of salt. Not to mention the fact that we'd have to dispose of this later, and we don't need any more contamination around here, I think."

Chapter 45

"Mac, highly effective trial lawyers teach the jurors not only what they need to know, but also what facts the jurors need to persuade and build a consensus. Consensus is the key here. We need consensus to win."

The first day of testimony was over, and Harry and I were in our adjoining hotel rooms in Casper, pacing back and forth, going over the evidence and trying to formulate a strategy for day two. I wanted to call Butch to the stand—let the jury get to know what a great guy he is. Harry wanted to call Beth. He felt that Davis Dunne had blown a hole in her—making her out to look like a scorned lover seeking revenge. He felt that rehabilitating her would help build his consensus faster.

Harry was the consummate professional. He looked like a Saville Row model with his navy pinstriped wool suit and his crisp, finely-woven, cotton white dress shirt and his red silk tie. And now, at ten o'clock at night in a Holiday Inn in Casper, he wore maroon silk pajamas and a paisley robe. He paced back and forth, spouting out ideas about how to approach Beth and make her more motherly and wifely and less of a steward of the land, as she commonly referred to herself. We'd devoured four entrees of Chinese food and had shared a bottle of crisp wine. Harry, a self-proclaimed gourmand and wine snob, had a wine cellar in the basement of his Jackson Hole home that was second to none. He never traveled without a small war chest of fine vintage. I liked that about Harry. Sharing good wine with him had become a pleasant pastime.

"A good lawyer must absorb the details, be fascinated by them, but not be overwhelmed by them." He sipped on his plastic hotel room cup, complaining that he'd forgotten to pack wine glasses in his carrier. He'd send Pamela out tomorrow to Wal-Mart to buy wine glasses, he noted.

Although he liked Pamela for her work ethic, I noticed that Harry took a real liking to Megan. Her spunky personality caught his attention. I joked with him about it. He lightheartedly responded that he'd been married to Jane for thirty-five years, had never cheated, and happily and zealously enjoyed the beauty and zest of youth. "Nothing wrong with chiseled beauty," he'd say.

"What details are we absorbing tonight?" I asked, half-heartedly. I wasn't ready to buckle down yet.

"We have to hammer on our case theme. Which is?" He turned my way, catching me in the middle of an email to Greg.

"Respect. Our case theme is respect." I looked up at him, seeing my reflection in the cheap hotel mirror. My curly auburn hair was piled on top of my head in a haphazard fashion. I'd taken out my contacts hours earlier because my eyes were tired from trial, so I wore my tortoise shell glasses halfway down the bridge of my nose as I wrote to Greg. I had on a black tank pajama top with a rhinestone butterfly on the front and leopard print pajama bottoms. My leopard print slippers remained askew on the floor at the foot of my bed, which was covered with papers and trial binders and law books. I was full from too much Chinese food and half drunk from too much wine. I needed to go to sleep more than anything, but Harry was pontificating trial strategy, so I was stuck for the time being. He'd eventually tire of hearing himself talk and I was confident that we'd put Beth on first, rehabilitate her, and then move on to other plaintiffs.

I was ready. I knew the theme. I knew the intricate facts of the case. I knew the law. But what I didn't know was that our clients were engaging in World War III a few doors down the hall. We would learn this tomorrow when Butch steadfastly and apologetically informed us that Beth would not be testifying in our case. In fact, the argument was so severe that he doubted that she would attend the trial at all.

Chapter 46

"What is 'chronic wasting disease'?" Harry asked our expert, who had refused to remove his cowboy hat before testifying. Judge Laird was more persuasive than Harry, apparently, because the expert was hatless and on the witness stand. Due to Beth's sudden disappearance, and Butch's mental state, we were forced to put on witnesses that didn't carry a lot of pizzazz, to say the very least. But the information was necessary for the jury to understand what was happening to the plaintiffs' land and their livestock.

"Outward symptoms in animals with chronic wasting disease and 'mad cow disease' are loss of body condition, which is commonly referred to as wasting, behavioral changes, excessive drinking and urinating, salivation, uncoordination, and tremors. The cause of this is copper deficiency. The alfalfa hay fed to the cows in the Powder River Basin is laced with coalbed methane salt, which wipes out the copper, magnesium and other minerals in the alfalfa, and the cows are literally poisoned from the lack of copper in their diets. So, many farmers, realizing that their livestock is suffering from a chronic wasting disease, boost them up with animal protein feed to fatten them up. This meat-bone meal is high is sulfur contents and can cause polioencephalopathy. The use of animal protein, which increases nitrogen in the feed, leads to a deficiency of essential fatty acids in the cell membranes, reducing membrane integrity, and making the animal more susceptible to encephalomalacia.

"What is fescue toxicosis in horses?" Harry continued on with the technical information that was necessary to make the record. But he showed no sign of interest in the case. I'd never seen Harry so despondent, and it worried me a great deal. Greg was on assignment again, somewhere in Central America. And Wyatt, who'd agreed to be present in trial every day, was nowhere to be seen. Butch sat alone at the plaintiffs' table, idly twirling a pencil between his index finger and thumb.

"Is this what happened on the Anderson ranch last year?"

"Yes, it did." The expert's answer continued on indefinitely, it seemed, and by noon, the jury appeared to be sleeping. Judge Laird, bless his soul, recessed for an early lunch, giving us the chance to recuperate from a dreadfully boring morning of testimony. There were plenty of other plaintiffs that we could have called to the stand, but, unfortunately, I'd told them that we wouldn't need them until the third day of trial. All of them lived at least two hours away and were unable to get to the federal courthouse in Casper at a moment's notice. We were forced to put on experts. We needed a more lively set of witnesses for the afternoon. Or we faced losing the jury forever.

* * *

"Please state and spell your name for the record," I said to Joyce Browvonski, one of our class of plaintiffs who was able to make the drive to Casper in record time to save the jury from napping through the afternoon. Joyce, an attractive fifty something ex-station nurse, nervously answered. After the preliminary questions about her background were set out, we charged forward into her medical problems.

"It's been almost four years since I've set foot out of my climate-controlled house. That's a slight exaggeration, I admit, but that's about how it feels. Now, I'm not sayin' that I never leave, but if I go anywhere, my husband has to have the air conditioning already running in the car before I dash out of the house. If I get even a whiff of the outdoors air, I begin to wheeze. My husband takes me to the air-conditioned mall. That's about all I can handle."

"Why are you a prisoner in your home?" I asked.

"Well, I have a heart condition. Have for years, but I was able to man the third floor nurse's station at Campbell County Memorial Hospital. I didn't have to move around too much and I loved my job."

"Did you quit your job because of your heart condition?"

"No. I quit my job because I got asthma. See, since the methane gas development started, there is a layer of pollution so dark overhead that if you drive up the mountain a bit and look out, it looks like someone smeared peanut butter over the horizon. The air is smelly and brown and painful to breathe. I never had a breathing problem in my life. And even with my heart condition, I used to walk everywhere. I used to get off work at three in the afternoon and walk two miles, rain or shine. It was helping my heart. But the air quality has deteriorated so much that I can't be outside for a minute. And my husband, he has a case of dust pneumonia from breathing all that junk in the air. I'm telling you, I'm glad I worked in the health care industry all those years and learned the value of good health insurance, because boy, you need it living here in the Powder River Basin."

After her long-winded answer, Joyce pulled out her inhaler and took a squirt in her mouth. She took three deep breaths, decided she needed more, and sprayed again. "Are you okay?" I asked.

"Will be. Takes a few moments for the meds to kick in." After the lunch break and a more intriguing witness, I could see that the jury was back listening to our case. They weren't on the edge of their seats like they were during the opening statements, but at least their eyes were open. I finished by asking her questions about her future and whether she would remain living in the area due to health concerns. Campbell County was her home. Her kids and grandkids lived there, she said. She didn't want to leave, but it might be inevitable.

It was Davis Dunne's turn to cross-examine Joyce. She looked like a deer staring into headlights as he approached the wood-paneled witness stand. Federal courtrooms were much fancier than state courts. Most federal courtrooms were spacious and clean, with marble floors and mahogany desks. Judge Laird's courtroom was perhaps a step above any federal courtroom I'd seen. He had a beautiful display of artwork on the walls. Most of the art was wildlife photography, and the one immediately above Joyce's head was a picture of a pheasant in flight. I imagined that Joyce would have liked to have been that pheasant at this point and fly sky high away from the beady-eyed lawyer staring her down.

"Define asthma for me, Mrs. Browvonski," Dunne started.

"Well … asthma is a breathing disorder."

"According to Webster's, isn't it 'a condition often of allergic origin that is marked by continuous or paroxysmal labored breathing accompanied by wheezing, by a sense of constriction in the chest, and often by attacks of coughing or gasping'?" Dunne wasn't reading from notes. He'd memorized the definition.

"That sounds like a better answer," Joyce said, smiling with the grin of an assassin.

"You received a bachelor of science degree as a registered nurse, correct?"

"No. I have an associate degree from Sheridan College."

"I see. So, you're not qualified to make medical diagnoses, are you?"

"I *am* a nurse and have been for nearly thirty years. I think I'm qualified to make certain medical diagnoses." She straightened herself in her chair. He took two steps closer to her and she immediately shrunk down again, like a turtle slipping back into its shell.

"Did a medical doctor diagnose you with asthma?"

"Yes. Dr. Wender did. I told him what I thought he had and he agreed with me."

"Did you pay this Dr. Wender for the medical opinion?"

"Pay? Well, not exactly but–"

"Do you have medical insurance, Mrs. Browvonski?"

Joyce shot a look at me, her eyes wide. She shook her head sideways, not wanting to answer.

"You must answer audibly in court, Mrs. Browvonski. Our good court reporter here," Dunne said, pointing to the stenographer who was busy punching keys, "she needs to be able to transcribe what you're saying. So is your answer 'no'? You do not have medical insurance?"

"Yes. I mean no. I mean I don't have medical insurance. See, it's because of my heart condition. I'm uninsurable and–"

"How do you get your 'asthma' medication then?" Dunne asked, using imaginary quotation marks with his fingers in the air as he said the word "asthma."

"Objection," Harry said. "This line of questioning is irrelevant to the lawsuit. He's badgering the witness."

"Overruled, Mr. Harrison. She's suing for all damages related to the toxic pollution on her land. He's entitled to determine how much she pays for her medications as they relate to toxic tort illness. Go ahead and answer the question, Mrs. Browvinski," Judge Laird said.

"F-f-from my friend."

"Speak up, Mrs. Browvonski," Dunne said tersely. "Did you say that you get your prescription asthma medication from your friend? Is this friend a fellow nurse at the hospital?"

Joyce, who was now on the verge of tears, nodded affirmatively. Quickly realizing that Dunne was about to admonish her to audibly speak her answer, she blurted out, "Yes."

"So, you diagnosed yourself with asthma, claim it's from the methane gas industry and medicate yourself by asking a nurse friend to steal meds for you from the hospital, is that correct, Mrs. Browvinski?"

"Objection, your Honor. He's badgering her." Harry was on his feet, hands held out like he was her savior.

"Withdrawn," Dunne said, smirking like a schoolyard bully. "I have nothing further for *this* witness."

Chapter 47

Apparently Beth had calmed down and come to her senses. After Mrs. Browvinski left the courtroom, Beth slipped in and joined Butch at the plaintiffs' table. She wore a long, tan, ultra-suede skirt with a white blouse and ornate turquoise jewelry. Butch gave her a sideways smile and patted her hand in a reassuring manner where words couldn't do justice. Whatever was said was forgiven and whatever was done, forgotten, probably. The timing was perfect because after Mrs. Browvinski had been shredded on the stand, we knew we had to put Butch on. Beth needed to be there for the jury to understand his story. We started with his childhood and how he became interested in horses.

"Well, I've been riding horses since I was a kid," Butch said, "going back to when my foster brother and I used to sneak into the pasture at night and ride the ponies bareback." Butch told the jury about his foster family and how his dad taught him to shoe a horse and how to ride a colt. Harry leaned over the podium of the witness stand toward Butch, like they were just two old buddies at a local bar having a drink and a chat. It was informal and conversational. With Harry in a dashing suit and tie and Butch in nice new blue jeans and a button-down shirt, they looked like they could be old pals that had taken a different path in life but ended up in nearly the same place.

"Some of the folks here on the jury mentioned in their questionnaire that they knew of you from your rodeo days. But other members of the jury don't know of you, and that's why we're going to take a moment to let them get to know you a little better. To understand where you've come from and what you do today for a living. It's important, you see, because they're going to be asked to evaluate how much damage you've suffered as a result of MethZap's debauchery. So, as uncomfortable as it might be to tell us your life story and to tell us about how much money you made when you first started out as compared to now, we have to do it. You good with that?" Butch nodded. "Once you moved away from your foster parents as a young man, did you start right off the bat on the rodeo circuit?"

Butch told the jury about Hunter Ray and how he'd learn to talk to horses.

"What's the difference between the things that you do today from the old west ways of dealing with a horse?"

"Well, I don't mean to brag, but it's really quite a phenomenon," Butch said. He'd brought his glass of water with him to the witness stand and he took a quick sip. After he set the glass back down on the narrow shelf in front of him, the ice that was stuck at the bottom of the glass suddenly floated to the top. "Twenty years ago, cowboys would have called me crazy. In fact, they did. But bein' a foster kid and all, I knew what it was like to be talked down to and made fun of and beaten up a little. And I saw that many of the folks out there did that kind of thing to the horse to train it. They'd whip it and yell at it and chase it around. All that bothered me. I guess I have one of them bleeding hearts or something. Call it what you want. I just plain didn't like it. I really like horses. A lot. Sometimes I like 'em better than people. I feel straight with them–like they understand me and I understand them. We communicate. So, I guess you can say that my approach to working with horses is really a willing communication. Instead of punishing them, I set them up." Butch explained his methods of positive reinforcement, and the jury seemed intrigued.

"Sounds a little new wave." Harry wanted to prepare Butch for the line of questioning that Davis Dunne might throw at him.

"I know you must think I'm a bighead or boaster, but, you oughta see it sometime. Come on out to the ranch. It works. It's been working for decades. All living beings respond better to praise then criticism. Here's a case in point. Miss Mary, over there, is your associate lawyer. From what she tells me, she's been begging to give the opening line, or whatever you call it, at trial for years. You let her do it at this trial and she done quite swell. I loved the way she talked about the cakes. It made good sense to me. She did a good job describing the mess MethZap has made of our ranch." Butch looked at the jury when he said it, and they all nodded in unison. "Well," he continued, "horses are just like that. They do you right when you give them positive accolades."

I could tell that Davis Dunne was chomping at the bit as a result of Butch's testimony. It was plain and neat and compelling and the jury was falling into line with him. They trusted him. Which is just what Dunne did not want. From his body language, which included twisting and turning and tapping, he wanted to interrupt the flow, but as a seasoned lawyer, he knew that if he acted like a jerk, the jury would dislike him. Harry, being astutely aware of Dunne's discomfort, along with being theatric and cunning at the same time, sauntered over to the defense table and leaned against it, nodding in Butch's direction. Butch took the cue and continued telling his tale about his lean years, before he made much money. Butch took a breath and grabbed another gulp of water. After he'd drained his glass, I quietly grabbed some bottled water and re-filled his glass, conscious of my attention to the plastic bottle in my hand. I nodded at Butch as I turned and headed back toward the plaintiffs' table. I wanted to make sure that the jury understood that thirst must be quenched. Stories must be told. And the two of them together made up Butch's life.

Chapter 48

"It slowly grew into something where I was busy. I was finally getting some work doing clinics for the rodeo circuit. But that meant that I was on the road most of the year following the circuit, and if I wasn't on the road, I was hanging out at a ranch somewhere, with somebody that I knew, kind of riding the grub line."

"Did your personal life change at some point?" Harry was still hanging out over by Davis Dunne. Harry looked comfortable as he leaned back on the table with his legs crossed over one another. Dunne, however, looked as cross as could be.

"Yes. I got married. To my beautiful wife, Beth, over there," he said, nodding in Beth's direction. "After that, I hated being gone. I couldn't stand being away from her. She changed my life in every way." Butch looked squarely at Beth, as if a silent reckoning was taking place.

"So the jury understands the chronology, let's back it up a bit, before you got married to Beth. Did you rent or own a house?"

"I had bought me a house up in the Bozeman area. I paid next to nothing for it. The bank owned it, really. It was a teeny tiny little house. Maybe four hundred square feet. I guess it was more like a hut." The jury laughed. Butch told the jury about finding the ranch and saving their money and making the offer to buy the place. He laughed with the jury over the name of the ranch–the Crazy Woman. He even told them about the brand that came with the ranch and how much Beth despised it. But folks around knew the ranch and knew the brand and Butch and Beth felt that it was best to keep it. People in Wyoming liked things as they were.

"Was the ranch in good shape when you bought it?"

"The Crazy Woman? Heck no. The place was a dump when we bought it. That's why we could afford it." The jury laughed again.

"What made your clinics unique?" Butch explained how they worked on basic skills in the arena in the morning and how they implemented the skills that the horses had learned by taking them out to the pastures in the afternoon. He explained that although people came from all over, some of them wanted to vacation in Wyoming while training their horse, so Beth set them up with travel plans and itineraries for a fun-filled "Ranch Camp."

"Let's explore how MethZap interfered with your business. That's what the jury is here to do. I'm sure they are wondering why you couldn't have done your clinics in the arena? Mr. Dunne, here," as Harry leaned back and gave a sideways glance to Davis, "Mr. Dunne is going to try to convince this jury that your business wasn't going well and that you're blaming MethZap for what was really poor business planning on your part. Did the condition of the ranch really matter to your livelihood as far as the clinics went?"

Butch explained how he worked the horses with fresh cows and how he needed plenty of pastureland for the process to run smoothly. "But you just got to understand something about cows. Cows are smarter than they look. And they look pretty darn dumb." The jury laughed in unison. Butch continued to explain his formula for fresh cattle at his clinics and how MethZap's drilling affected his work.

"Where did you keep your horses?

"Well, that was another problem. Can't keep 'em with the cows. And you must keep the stud alone. Away from the mares, if you catch my drift." Butch smirked at the jury with his "birds and bees" reference. They smiled back. Butch continued his explanation of where he needed to keep the horses and the cows and how MethZap had messed up his system of whole range management. "I know this sounds complicated, but what I'm trying to get at is that I needed a lot of pasture to run the clinics right. That's why I bought the Crazy Woman. The ranch was run down, but it had a lot of pastureland, and that's what I needed."

"I'm setting up an aerial shot of the ranch so that you can help the jury better understand the layout," Harry said, putting an aerial blowup of the Crazy Woman on an easel in between Butch and the jury box. Butch used a pointer and told them which pasture was used for what purpose. Harry put labels on each pasture as they went along. The aerial photo had all the wellheads on it, as well as the piping and warming huts and other paraphernalia that MethZap dumped on the ranch. Butch walked the jury through each well site and road and fence as Harry continued labeling. By the time they were done, the aerial poster looked like a jigsaw puzzle that didn't quite fit together. Harry admitted into evidence about forty eight-by-ten photographs of the wells, the orange sludge, and the reservoirs of salty water. The jury passed the photos along, one by one, studying the filth as Butch spoke.

"MethZap was using up half of my ranch with their drilling, and messing up the other half with their pipes and filthy dams and salty soil, to the point where my horses couldn't pasture properly and my clinics couldn't run smoothly and it was just a big stinking mess. And I mean that literally. The place smelled like hell. I don't know how else to explain it. Other than it was screwing up my dream."

"Couldn't you have avoided the areas where MethZap was operating?" Butch explained to the jury that he tried to avoid the MethZap operations, but it was impossible. "Part of what you're asking this jury to do is award you damages for the losses you incurred as a result of MethZap's destruction of your property. We're going to have to go through the numbers so that the jury can make a proper determination," Harry said. I grabbed another poster from behind the plaintiffs' table and put it up on a second easel next to the aerial of the ranch. This poster contained a blow-up of a profit and loss sheet and a detailed analysis of Butch's damages. "Very shortly, Butch, we're going to be putting on evidence through an expert witness regarding the damage done to the soil on the ranch, but they need to hear it from you, too." Butch went through the numbers with the jury.

"Based on your analysis, and your discussions with your soils engineers and accountants, you believe that MethZap should pay you seven hundred fifty thousand dollars?" Harry acted as though Butch was reaching a bit too far.

Butch looked guilty and remorseful for such a high number. "Really, Harry, all I want is I want my home back the way–maybe it can't be the way it was, but I want it restored as close as I can. I bought this ranch for a reason, or I'd have stayed on my measly little five acres in Montana. I want a place to be able to carry on my business, and it's–it seems like it's asking quite a bit now this late in the game. But this is my home; and this, this ranch–and it may not mean anything to the MethZap folks or to the BLM or the Army Corps of Engineers issuing permits willy-nilly, anyone else, but this ranch represents everything to me. This is everything. It's what I have to leave to my boys. This is my entire working life wrapped up in this piece of property. Hell, it's all that my youngest son thinks about. Wyatt–Wyatt loves this ranch as much or more than I do. It's all he's ever known. It's all he wants. And twenty years ago, it didn't even look like I'd get this far, so this ranch, and all it represents, is something I'm real proud of. I want it back. That's it. That's all. And I'm told that it's going to take that huge wad of money to truck in enough topsoil to give the ranch a chance at life again. And they can't guarantee that it will work. The topsoil is tricky. In a rainy season, it could all run off back into the Powder River, creating an even bigger mess. The plants might not grow back, I'm told. Listen, I know it seems like I'm asking a lot, but all I'm asking for is my life back."

Chapter 49

Dear Mac,

I'm writing this letter from the Wyoming State Penitentiary, where I will be serving time for the next two years. It's not as bad as I imagined it to be, as far as the other guys who are prisoners here. The food is terrible and the cells are cramped and dirty, but we get plenty of time to read and watch TV and workout. So, I've decided to treat it as an extended vacation and use it as a time to reflect and get my act together. I am in a detox program for meth and it's going ok. I feel like I'm slowly re-entering my body. I still don't know how I got mixed up in this mess. I don't know if I'll ever unravel it.

The real reason I'm writing is to clear things up between us. I feel terrible about what's happened, now that I'm understanding it. You need to know a few things before you move forward with your commitment with Greg. First, it was him that asked me to shoot at you at the Crazy Woman ranch. I'm a good shot. I was supposed to miss and I did. It was just a warning shot, meant to scare you away from the ranch. Second, it was his idea to write the letter and leave it on your car. I did it to scare you away from the case. I didn't mean the words. I hope you know that. I like you and I think you probably saved my life. Third, it was Greg who gave me the idea to put ricin in the water bottles during the cross-country race. He helped me load the water bottles into my car before the race and he handed me a sample of the ricin, telling me how it worked. It was meant to be a small dose, just enough to make you sick. I wanted to keep you away from the ranch and the meth lab.

Greg's motives were different. He wanted to scare you off the case. But there's more to it. So, you'll have to ask him what his reasons were. That's between you and him. All I can say is that I don't think you should marry him, but you are a smart lady and I know you can think for yourself. I just hope you can at least understand that I did not intend to hurt you and I am truly sorry for my actions.

Sincerely,

Sherman Todd

The letter was sent to my office in Sheridan and forwarded to me by Megan. I was doubtful at first as to its veracity, but after mulling it over while jogging after court was adjourned for the day, I realized that Sherman might have been telling the truth. I knew it was too good to be true: that a man who was smart and handsome and outgoing could be honest, respectful and trustworthy. I had a history of falling in love with men who were unavailable or commitment-phobic or extremely selfish. Apparently, I'd struck out again. I was deflated. As I added another link in the long chain of disappointments, Harry walked into our hotel room, elated and excited from a good day in court. The dichotomy of our collective emotions was paradoxical. He was up and I was down, like a seesaw. It didn't take him long to catch on. When he asked what was wrong, I handed him the letter. He read it by the plate-glass window, and then quietly folded it back into a rectangle.

"You should talk to Greg before jumping to conclusions. There could be a number of explanations for this," Harry said.

"Like why he asked me to marry him after trying to poison me? That'd be a good place to start, don't you think?"

"Think about the source. Sherman Todd is serving time for being a drug dealer. Greg and you put him there. Maybe this is his way at getting back at you for turning him in. Revenge is sweet, as they say. Hell, Mac, don't forget that this guy is hooked on drugs. Maybe detox is taking its toll. Maybe they're giving him other meds to help with detox. There are a lot of possibilities. Give Greg the benefit of the doubt and talk to him before you make a judgment. He's a good guy. And I can tell that he loves you very much."

I thought about Harry's words. It was possible that Sherman was angry and bitter and trying to drive a wedge between us. But in the back of my mind, I couldn't help but think of the coincidences that had taken place. Greg knew all along about the methamphetamine drug ring, but never told me about it. He tried to keep me off the case. He certainly wasn't happy when he learned that I was representing Butch and Beth. He was in town during that time, dropping in at odd moments. Wyatt even claimed to have seen him around town when Greg denied even being in the country. Things didn't add up. Even the marriage proposal seemed rushed, like he felt like I was getting too close and he needed to pull me back, own me, control me. I told Harry all of this and he listened for a bit, but when the tears started pouring down my cheeks, he walked back into his hotel room, stripping off his silk tie on the way.

I loved Greg very much. I wanted to believe that he would never do anything to hurt me. He'd saved my life a few years ago when I was investigating my legal secretary's murder, and he saved me from Rowdy Rodiger and Sherman Todd. He'd been there with me through good times and bad. Greg was going through a rough time. His work was incredibly demanding and he'd been dealing with some major personal issues with Everett Fisher. How many people can say that their fathers are cartel-connected drug dealers? And I knew that he was deeply hurt by the fact that Butch and Beth had essentially written him out of their wills, at least as far as the ranch was concerned. Would this man allow his best friend to shoot at me? Poison me? It didn't make sense. I would have to hear it from Greg's mouth to sort it through.

Harry poked his head back into my hotel room, yelling out food choices for dinner. "What do you think?" Harry asked, referring to a steak dinner.

"What I think," I muttered to myself, "is that sometimes, love isn't enough."

Chapter 50

The next couple of days of trial washed over me like a tidal wave. Harry gave me the lead on two of our expert witnesses, so I was busy preparing deposition indexes and outlining testimony at night, which was good, I suppose, because it kept me from thinking about Greg. He was out of the country again on assignment, so I had Pamela scan Sherman Todd's letter and download it onto my laptop. I sent a copy of it to Greg via email and I hadn't heard back.

"It'd be a hell of a lot easier if you'd stop picking that scab," Harry said to me on the fourth night of trial. He was referring to my incessant habit of checking emails, awaiting Greg's response. I decided to change the subject.

"How'd you think it went today with Dr. Roderick? Do you think the jury understood the electrical conductivity of the soil and the sodium absorption ratios?" Harry looked at me as if I had two heads.

"Mac, the jury rarely understands this stuff. We put on this evidence for appellate courts. The biggest issue with experts is whether the jury likes the guy. Dr. Roderick is handsome and well spoken and humble, so to answer your question, I think the jury had a good day looking at his kind face and your nice legs. And don't even think of suing me for sexual harassment because I'll deny ever saying it and I'm only offering an opinion as to the status of the trial." He winked as he grabbed his glass of pinot noir and went into his room to change into his pajamas and robe.

Pamela, who was staying a few doors down, knocked at my door. She tucked her stout body into a brand-new pair of Wrangler jeans and a tight knit top. "I'm in the mood for pool tables, beer and sorry ballads of love gone bad. Wanna join me down the street for a drink?"

Normally, I would have declined. But since I hadn't received a response from Greg and I was feeling a little sorry for myself, I agreed. I slipped on my faded 501's and a low-cut chocolate-colored v-neck and followed her down to a good-old-fashioned country western bar.

"Shouldn't you be preparing for trial tomorrow?" a voice asked from behind. I quickly spun around. Davis Dunne, wearing black cowboy boots and a hat, squared me up. "You seem to like to keep those experts on the stand for a very long time. Maybe you could learn a lesson or two from the pro. Shorten it up a bit. Keep the jury interested. Entice them a bit. Maybe you could drop your notebook in front of the jury box and take your sweet time bending over to pick it up. I'd like that. So would those seven men on the jury."

I fumbled for a response, but it was lost to the twang of loud music. He walked away confidently and ordered two beers at the bar. I assumed he was getting me a drink, but he walked right by me and handed the second beer to Pamela, who readily accepted with the glee of a schoolgirl. I thought to myself, this guy is good. He really knows how to get under a person's skin.

Not to be outdone, I grabbed a cute cowboy who was very tall, and pulled him out on the dance floor. After twisting and twirling to a few songs, I sauntered back with him toward the bar. As I passed Dunne, I leaned in and said, "Thank goodness for tall men." I winked and smiled and wandered back to my hotel room, alone, for a good night's sleep before the fifth day of trial.

I awoke early and checked my email. Still no message from Greg. I slapped on my running shoes and hit the pavement before showering and heading to the federal courthouse. On my short walk to court, I saw Judge Laird through the window of a greasy spoon restaurant eating biscuits and gravy. He waved as I passed by. I waved back, almost too enthusiastically, still hovering from my runner's high. Ten minutes later we were all settled in the courtroom, ready to get the day underway. Pamela, who was as punctual as the sunrise, dashed in fifteen minutes late, disheveled and full of apologies. I didn't ask for an explanation—the look on Davis Dunne's face said it all.

Chapter 51

Harry and I decided not to call Beth Anderson as a witness in our case in chief. The jury would have loved her poise and beauty, but we were concerned that Dunne would slice her like sashimi on the witness stand regarding her relationship with Everett Fisher. Plus, Butch had testified as to everything we needed on the Crazy Woman. So, we decided to call a few more of the other plaintiffs to the stand. One of these plaintiffs was a smart and sassy woman by the name of Jacqueline Bontierre. She was French and opinionated and sure of herself. And we knew that she'd take the jury on a wild ride into the depths of her anger with the methane gas industry. Jacqueline did not disappoint us. She practically called herself as a witness and marched up to the stand with the confidence and drive of a wolf honing in on prey. Without need for introduction or questioning, she began.

"My name is Jackqueline Bontierre and my husband and I own a sizeable ranch on Spotted Horse Creek in the Powder River Basin. Primarily, our ranch is geared for raising cattle. We've lived there nearly thirty years, and my husband's parents lived there another fifty years prior to that. The ranch was originally homesteaded by my husband's great-grandfather and has been expanded by the family over the generations. The Bontierre family has survived a hundred years of drought and locust invasions and beef pricing wars, but it looks like we're going to lose the ranching battle to the methane gas industry. The last five years have been horrible. We've suffered the deceit of landmen who shake our hand one minute and lie behind our backs the next. The Bureau of Land Management and the Army Corps of Engineers continue to permit activities that are in violation of their own rules and regulations."

"What damages have you suffered as a result of methane development on your land," I asked, trying to hone her in.

"We've lost all three of our artesian wells that feed our cattle. So, we must truck in industrial-grade water every day so that our cows can drink. We've also lost our domestic water well because the methane developer, MethZap, sucked all of the groundwater out from our property. I guess the experts call this 'dewatering.' As you might imagine, this is a long-term problem for us. For now, we are getting by with trucking in industrial grade water for the cows and residential grade for us. But it is extremely expensive. Sometimes, if the methane water tests okay, meaning that it isn't too high in arsenic or other deadly chemicals, we can use it to water the cows. But those days seem to be fewer and farther between. MethZap refuses to agree to provide long-term water for us. They say that they are done developing on our property and the water was our problem to begin with. They also make snide remarks like, 'Your royalty checks should cover your water expenses.' And sure, we have received some good checks. We've made a profit beyond our wildest imagination from this operation. But, money doesn't replace land or groundwater or our kids' future on the ranch. So, that's why we are here. So that some changes are made in how methane development takes place in this state. We need better regulations so that these turkeys can't run amok bribing and paying off people in order to get whatever permit they want."

I followed up with her on a few points regarding her damages, and then it was Dunne's turn at cross-examination. He looked like what the cat dragged in, with tousled hair, a crumpled suit and swollen eyes the color of lava.

"Didn't MethZap drill you a fourteen hundred foot domestic water well, Miss Bontierre?"

She gave him a disgusted look. "We could not drink this water without getting diarrhea, and I could not wash clothes without having them turn orange from the high iron content. So, to answer your question, yes. They did drill us a new well, but no, it wasn't suitable for human consumption."

"Didn't MethZap provide two water treatment systems for you? It says here in my log of costs from MethZap that they paid over ten thousand dollars to the Bontierre ranch for reverse osmosis and iron treatment systems."

"Yes," Mrs. Bontierre said, "They did install a reverse osmosis system for the drinking water and an iron treatment system for the daily use water system, but our electrical costs for pumping the deep well have doubled and the first time we had the treatment system serviced we were charged six hundred dollars. Imagine the cost of that over a lifetime? And why should we have to bear these costs?"

"MethZap was more than agreeable to pay for the service charges for these systems. I have a letter here from Ace Sanders, marked as Defendant's Exhibit BB-1 that says that they would pay it. Why haven't you submitted your bills for payment?"

"I submitted the bills two or three times and they didn't get paid. The service company threatened to turn us over to a collection agency if we didn't pay, so I paid them. I guess it will be my lucky–"

"Let's just stick to the facts, shall we, Miss Bontierre?"

"Mrs."

"Mrs. Bontierre."

"And it says here that MethZap trucked in twenty thousand cubic yards of topsoil and spread it on your property. Is that so?"

"I'm sure they did. But the problem–"

"So, your answer is 'yes'?"

"Yes, but they–"

"So MethZap dug a new well, has agreed to pay for the service of the well and has spread new topsoil on your property and continues to pay you, let's see," Dunne said, looking at a spreadsheet in his hand, "An average of sixty thousand dollars a month in royalty checks, is that correct?"

The jury sucked in air in unison. Sixty thousand dollars a month. On average. Immediately, I could feel a change in attitude in the courtroom. The jurors looked disdainfully at her, as if she were a rich, greedy lady with nothing to do but complain about what's not right. A "glass half empty" sort. Dunne knew that he had them so he did the right thing. He rested and asked no further questions.

Chapter 52

"What happened to the twenty-some cubic yards of topsoil that MethZap spread on your ranch, Mrs. Bontierre?" I asked, hoping to bolster her testimony a bit on re-direct. My cell phone, which was on the silent tone, was vibrating in my suit jacket. The call would have to wait. Cell phones were obviously forbidden in court, and it would be a major faux paux to even glance at the display to see who was calling.

"For the past two years another energy company has been discharging methane water upstream of us into the Spotted Horse Creek, which despite the drought, overflowed its banks and washed a majority of our new topsoil away. Now we have even more water with a high salt content and this new mess has killed off more native grass and has even drowned and killed hundreds of our century-old cottonwood trees that used to line the banks of the river."

"Have you incurred legal fees as a result of MethZap's operations on your property?"

"Seventeen thousand and climbing," Mrs. Bontierre said with a large exasperating breath. "We've spent thousands of dollars on legal fees tying to get MethZap to honor the agreements they entered into with us. And we've spent oodles more trying to get the governmental agencies to follow the long-term policy of the law. Some of the laws are pretty open to interpretation, apparently. It's been a real education for us. A real education. We are luckier than a lot of the other plaintiffs in this action because we are getting a good return from royalties. But our lives have been turned upside down. My husband and I have been chronically sick and I'm sure that most of it is related to the stress we've been under dealing with this methane gas mess. We went from being ranchers—enjoying the fruits of our hard labor—to advocates and warriors and environmentalists. We would like nothing better than to go back to the time before we ever heard of MethZap or any other methane operator, and live the simple life of a ranching family. We were happy then. We are not happy now. I truly wish that all of you could come out to our ranch—our home—and see what sacrifices we've been forced to endure as a result of the methane drilling on our land. We have no water. And without water, land is useless. Ask the Indians. They'll tell you all about that."

* * *

Megan called my cell phone while we were on our morning recess from court. She was bored at the office with very little to do, so she decided to walk down Main Street in Sheridan and check out King's Saddlery. Despite the fact that she'd been raised in this small town, and despite the fact that King's and their famous ropes were a local sensation, she'd never stepped foot in the ranch supply and western wear store. She loved the wafting smell of leather when she walked in the door. Being cute and perky and full of life, she had no trouble getting the grand tour of the place. In fact, when she started asking general questions about sisal ropes, the proprietor couldn't wait to tell her everything he knew. He told her that they came from special grasslands in Africa and that some local ranching families used them exclusively on their ranches for cattle roping. When Megan asked for specific names of these ranching families, he was eager to prove to her that he knew what he was talking about.

"See here? We done computerized this place about five years back. Was a pain in the seat at first. But I've grown to like it now." He clicked on a few buttons and pulled up the information he was searching for. Megan scooted herself up on the counter near the computer and watched as he scrolled down.

"Stop there," she said, as she pulled a notebook out of her purse and jotted down some information. She continued to look on with interest, despite the fact that she had all the material she needed. After making more small talk and meeting all the staff, she found a convenient excuse to leave. She bolted back to the office and placed a call to my cell phone when I was in the middle of re-direct examination of Mrs. Bontierre.

"Greg bought sisal rope at King's Saddlery last spring. Quite a bit of it, actually." I thought about the implications of this fact, but didn't really have time to process it. What was Greg doing with sisal rope? Was he using it on his expeditions to South America? Maybe Sherman Todd was telling the truth. Maybe Greg helped Sherman load the water bottles for the ski race and that's how the sisal fibers and both of their fingerprints were on the poisoned water bottles? My mind was racing, but Judge Laird was calling the court back to order and we were about to put on our last witnesses in our case in chief. I had to keep my head in the game.

Chapter 53

"The defense calls Mrs. Beth Anderson to the stand," Davis Dunne said with theatrical poise. Harry had called the last few experts to discuss the ramifications of West Nile virus and Mad Cow Disease. Although we hadn't called many of the fifty-some class action plaintiffs, he figured that we'd hit the jury enough with the gist of the methane gas disasters on the land in the Powder River Basin. More is not always better, as Harry always said. So, keeping the case as simple as possible, and hammering the jury one last time with the amount of damages suffered by each plaintiff, we rested. It was Davis Dunne's turn to take center stage. And by calling Beth as his first witness, he was off to a rip-roaring start.

Beth, wearing a denim skirt and a red blouse and red cowboy boots, walked with confidence to the witness stand. An observant person would have noticed that her hands were shaking, but to the oblivious, she looked like she would rather be doing nothing else.

"Who is Everett Fisher?" Davis Dunne started out. Butch shot a glance my way, silently begging for me to object or do something to save his wife from this. There wasn't much we could do. The question wasn't objectionable, based on their history. The jury already knew that she'd been married to him before she met Butch, so objecting to it would make it a bigger deal than it was worth. Harry and I did nothing, for the time being, and watched to see how Beth responded to the question.

"Well, Mr. Dunne, I'm sorry that you have to ask me that question, since he is the President of MethZap, your client. But what I really think you're getting at is who he was to me. And it's no secret that I was once married to Everett Fisher and he is the father of my first-born son, Greg.

But I use the word 'father' quite loosely because your client was never a father to my son. The only father my son ever knew–"

"Thank you, Mrs. Anderson, you've more than answered my question. Your honor, I move to treat this witness as hostile."

"You've made her that way!" Judge Laird said. "But under the circumstances, your motion is granted."

"When you learned that your ex-husband, the man that you claim was no father to your first-born son, was the owner of MethZap, how did that make you feel?"

"It made me feel confused, like it would make anyone feel, I suppose. I hadn't heard from this man in years. He never made his child support payments. Let me struggle on my own to raise a boy as a single mother. Those were tough days, Mr. Dunne. So, when I learned that it was his company digging holes all over my ranch, I had a whole rainbow of emotions charging through me. I'm not going to sit in front of this jury and pretend that I wasn't angry and bitter, because I was. He was getting rich off my land and all of my neighbors' land. I hadn't seen a dime in royalty checks. And my husband's business was suffering greatly as a result of the methane gas business. So, to answer your question, I was angry and upset and confused."

"After you learned that Everett Fisher owned MethZap, how long was it before you consulted a lawyer?"

Beth looked sideways, away from the jury and slowly gnawed on her lower lip, partially removing a trace of her red lipstick. "The next day, probably. I remember calling Chance Baker and asking him what I should do. He recommended that Butch and I come together to his office to have a discussion about it."

"So, right away after you learned that your ex-husband was drilling on your land, you contacted a lawyer to try to derail the deal?"

"Objection, your Honor. He's misstating her testimony," Harry said. Judge Laird was about to make a ruling on the objection when Beth continued to speak.

"To be honest with you," Beth said, looking very composed still, "I wish that I had the foresight at the time to have been able to 'derail the deal,' as you say. I wasn't savvy enough in the methane gas business to do such a thing. My goal at that time was to find out what the 'deal' was and whether there was anything we could do to stop it, or at least modify it enough so that Butch could still do his clinics out on the ranch."

"But you would have derailed it if you could?"

"That's like asking a horse if it would have jumped the barbed-wire fence if it could. Of course I would if I could. That's just nature. I would have loved to have found a way to stop Ev from drilling on my ranch. But I soon learned that I couldn't stop him. I thought that I might be able to tone it down a bit."

"And that's when you got in touch with Ev, as you call him, right?"

Beth looked at Butch and then she looked down, in shame. Harry gave me a slight kick under the plaintiffs' table. We'd asked Beth this question one hundred different ways and she'd always denied contacting him in any way.

"I gave him a call, yes."

"On his cell phone, right?"

"Right."

"From your cell phone, right?"

"Right."

"How did you get his cell number?"

"I asked Ace Sanders for it and he gave it to me."

"Did you tell Butch that you were going to call him?"

"No."

"Did you tell Butch that Everett owned MethZap at that point?"

"No. I needed to think things through–"

"Just answer the question, Mrs. Anderson."

"No."

"No, you didn't tell your husband that your ex-husband owned the business that was setting up rigs on his ranch?"

"Objection, your Honor. Asked and answered."

"Sustained. Move along, Mr. Dunne."

"Did you pay Everett Fisher a visit around that time?"

Beth shook her head sideways, tears welling up in her eyes. Secrets that had been kept were slowly coming alive. Promises made were being broken. She'd worked too hard to protect everyone from her past, and now it was inching up on her. "I went to visit him at the Powder Horn."

"And this was about a year and a half ago, right. Last winter?"

"I suppose. I don't know for sure."

"Where did you meet?"

"At his new house that he was building out there on hole number seventeen. He was there supervising some part of the job and I pulled up. He didn't know that I was coming. I hadn't called and set up some clandestine meeting, if that's what you're implying. I was driving out towards Big Horn to deliver a horse and I saw the sign for the Powder Horn. I'd learned that he was building a huge house out there, so I went in and found him."

"What did you say when you first saw him? It'd been a number of years since you'd seen him, right?"

"I don't recall what I said exactly."

"Was it friendly?"

"I suppose not," Beth said, as she slowly settled back in the witness chair. Her face grew more serious, her gestures more rigid.

"You were yelling at him, weren't you?" Dunne put both of his hands on the witness stand, staring her directly in the eye.

"I was confronting him, much like you're doing to me right now." Dunne pulled back, sensing that he was within striking distance of a coiled snake.

"Did you threaten him?"

"Did I threaten him? You obviously don't know your client very well, Mr. Dunne. Ev spent years threatening–"

"Just answer the question, Mrs. Anderson. Did you threaten him?"

Beth looked at a woman on the jury for an instant and then quickly dropped her gaze to the floor. Her silence was long and deliberate as if she was choosing her words rather carefully. Just as Dunne was about to press her for an answer, she said, "I believe that I told him that I wanted him off my property and out of my life for good. There may have been a few expletives included. I can't say for sure. I try to be a lady most of the time, Mr. Dunne, but there are times when a lady has to speak her mind. This could have been one of those times for me. You probably don't know what's it's like to raise a son on your—"

"Your Honor, could you please instruct the witness to just answer the question?"

"Mrs. Anderson, if it is humanly possible, you need to try to answer Mr. Dunne's questions with a 'yes' or a 'no.' Mr. Dunne, you might try not asking such vague and open-ended questions. That way, your witness might be able to give you more direct answers." Judge Laird was rather enjoying himself, it seemed. I could tell that he liked Beth. He hadn't taken his eyes off her since she took the stand.

"When was the last time you had sex with Everett Fisher?" Dunne asked.

"Objection! Your Honor, I request a sidebar!" Harry shouted, as he bolted out of his chair and headed toward the judge's bench. I had no choice but to accompany him. I didn't want to miss out on this one.

"Your Honor, you said to ask more direct questions. So I did," Dunne said.

"Oh, please, your Honor. He's only trying to incite her and make her look bad on the stand. The question is highly prejudicial, not to mention irrelevant and inflammatory and every other evidentiary and ethical violation I can think of."

"What if I have evidence of them having sex that day at his new home on hole number seventeen?"

"Offer of proof, your Honor, outside the ambit of the jury. And even if he does have that kind of evidence, which I truly doubt, I adamantly object to the introduction of it. It is inflammatory and has absolutely nothing to do with the case."

Judge Laird, seemingly intrigued by this development, excused the jury and cleared out the courtroom for a fifteen-minute break. Dunne, thrilled with the opportunity to turn the lawsuit into a circus, scurried over to the defense table and grabbed a manila file. He pulled out eight-by-ten glossies and held them up for the judge to see. Judge Laird thumbed through them, one by one, flipping some of them sideways and turning his head right or left, then moving on to the next shot. There were ten photos in all. When Judge Laird was through looking at them, he handed the photos to Harry with a raised brow. "Looks like we have a dilemma here, Harry," Judge Laird said.

After looking at the pictures, Harry agreed. "Whatever happened between Beth and Everett Fisher that day, or any other day for that matter, is irrelevant to the case. Not to mention that the probative value of this is highly outweighed by its prejudicial effect. Even if she had an affair with him, it has nothing to do with whether his company contaminated her ranch. This case is about–"

"What if she bribed him? What if she had sex with him in exchange for an agreement that he pay her off? What if–"

"That's ridiculous, your Honor," I said, cutting in. "This case is about respect. Respecting other people's land and property. Maybe Beth wasn't showing Butch much respect in those photos, but that is an issue between husband and wife and has absolutely nothing to do with this case. Nothing. And if you allow that kind of inflammatory evidence to be admitted, this trial will take on a whole new life. One that has nothing to do with a class action lawsuit for the clean up of the Powder River Basin. Let's not turn this case into tabloid fare."

"But it is relevant to–"

"Hold it right there. All of you," Judge Laird said. "The photos are out. The entire line of questioning will be stricken from the record. Ms.

MacIntosh is right. We are not turning this case into a spectacle. What Mrs. Anderson does is her business."

"But, your Honnnnnnooooor," Dunne whined.

"I've made my ruling. Take me up on appeal if you don't like it. Otherwise, get on with your case."

Chapter 54

Beth Anderson looked as white as a ghost walking back into the courtroom. She knew what was being discussed, apparently. Her eyes were red, as were Butch's. Her hands were shaking as she approached the witness stand. "May I speak," she said to Judge Laird.

"No. I've ruled that Mr. Dunne must strike the last question posed to you. He will likely ask you a different question, at which time you may speak."

"I want to answer the question he asked."

"No, you don't. And I've already ruled that his line of questioning won't take place."

"But I need to set things straight."

"Maybe you do, Mrs. Anderson, but my courtroom is not the place for that."

"Please, your Honor. Please." Beth's eyes welled with tears. Judge Laird looked quizzically at Harry, as if he was silently saying, "What do I do with this?" Harry shook his head, not knowing what to do. He leaned into Butch and whispered in his ear. Butch answered. Harry nodded to the judge to let her answer if she wanted. Of course, Dunne couldn't wait to pursue this line of questioning. So Judge Laird let her speak.

"Like I said, I went to Everett's house to give him twenty years' worth of pent-up anger, and I did yell at him. And he yelled back. And we got carried away yelling at each other and he suddenly grabbed me and kissed me hard on the mouth. And I'm ashamed to admit this, but I kissed him back. I guess you could say that we always had sort of a love-hate relationship. We had passion and then fury. Well, the passion rose up in

"

me a bit and things got a little carried away. But I finally got a hold of my senses and I stopped it from going all the way. I knew that what I was doing was wrong and that I would be very, very angry with myself if I let him get the better of me again. Not to mention the fact that I love my husband very much and I didn't want to do that to him. So, I stopped it and left. And nothing like that has ever happened again. I'm so sorry Butch. I'm really sorry." Her face, now flooded with tears, somehow looked relieved. Butch nodded at her—a gentleman's nod, closing his eyes slowly, allowing his tears to trickle down. The moment was priceless. The jury was shocked, but very interested. Perhaps concerned. A connection happened. Atonement? Forgiveness? Understanding?

Dunne sprung to his feet, ready to pounce on this subject, but Judge Laird stopped him before the first word escaped Dunne's lips. "You will now move on to another topic, Mr. Dunne. We will not be pursuing this line of questioning any further."

"But, your Honor, she opened the door—"

"You heard my ruling! Now move on or sit down."

* * *

Dunne tidied up with Beth, but the wind was out of his sails. He proceeded to call one expert witness after another to testify about the overall health of the environment surrounding most of the methane gas wells and the long-term remedial efforts that were underway to make sure that the land wouldn't suffer irreparable harm. He put on professors who regarded the West Nile virus to be a typical plague of nature—not the result of contaminated cesspools sitting on barren ranchland. He refuted Mad Cow as a few isolated incidents of poorly stored meat. Contamination—sure, but not due to the environment or gas plays. And after he rested his case, the Bureau of Land Management and the Army Corps of Engineers put on their cases, in which they contended, of course, that they followed the spirit of the law in issuing permits and making inspections. It wasn't their fault that the federal government didn't have stricter standards for air and water quality. They'd obtained the requisite Environmental Impact Reports and applied them to the National Environmental Policy Act. They were in compliance. Or so their experts said. Harry got one expert to admit that perhaps they could have more thoroughly considered the quantity of permitted wells in the Draft Environmental Impact Statement, but nevertheless, they followed the spirit of the law.

It would be a tough call for the jury. Their experts were compelling and well seasoned in the art of testifying in court.

"How is groundwater going to be monitored in the future? Does your Draft Environmental Impact Statement address that?" Harry asked Don Allen, head of the Bureau of Land Management office in Sheridan. "Where is the water in containment pits going to go? Is the methane water going to come back up on the surface again to cause bogs and salt fields? Where are the studies of subsurface geology that prove that this water can be safely allowed to infiltrate? Why doesn't the environmental impact statement require numerical standards for sodium absorption ratios and electrical conductivity? What will be done to protect our air quality from diesel generators, dust, new roads, compressor stations, and general degradation of the land due to traffic? Who will enforce air quality standards? What is being done about leaking reservoirs?"

All great questions. No good answers. The jury would have to decide.

Chapter 55

"Ladies and Gentlemen," I said, at the beginning of my closing statement to the jury, "I'd like to thank you for your patience and time in considering the issues at this trial. You have a big responsibility on your shoulders in deciding the future of the environment in the Powder River Basin. You very well could be setting the foundation for the future of Wyoming's water quality. You have my respect. This is not an easy assignment.

Let's talk about respect for a moment, because it really is the underpinning of this case. The Andersons, and the other forty-eight plaintiffs would not be here before you today if their land had been treated with respect. Respect is the cornerstone of all relationships, whether it be the relationship of husband-wife, parent-child, boss-employee, or rancher-methane gas developer. If we treat one another with respect, good things follow. If we are rude or dishonest or insincere, the relationship fails. That is precisely what happened to the Andersons. MethZap was rude and dishonest and insincere, and the Andersons now have a ranch that is polluted with sludge water and salt and contaminated water."

I continued to go back through the evidence with the jurors, discussing what the experts had testified about. I reminded the jurors of the cake and how salty the bad cake tasted. Then I picked up the black box that had been sitting on a windowsill in the judge's chambers throughout the course of the trial. I reached in and pulled out the two potted plants that I'd shown the jurors during my opening statement. The plant with the perfect amount of water and fertilizer was green and in full bloom. The plant with the same soil mixture as the contaminated dirt on the Anderson ranch was dried up and dead. I held both plants in my hand and examined them carefully. "Ladies and Gentlemen, I'm taking a dropper full of diluted hydrochloric acid and I want you to watch what happens when I placed three drops on the soil of these two plants."

The jurors watched as I put three drops of the acid on the healthy soil. The liquid absorbed into the healthy soil, just as water would. When I put the three drops of the acid into the contaminated soil, the soil immediately formed white bubbles on the surface and fizzed up like a soda bottle does when opened after being shaken. The comparison was effective. The jurors' eyes widened as they saw the contaminated soil react to the acid. I held both plants up in the air and continued.

"When you go back into deliberation room, you need to ask yourself a few questions. 'How would you feel if this happened to you?' 'How would you feel if someone stole your livelihood and your land?' 'How would you feel if someone treated you and your land with such disrespect?' Would you boil up, like this contaminated soil does? Would you want them to pay for what they'd done? If your answer is 'yes,' which I expect that it is, then please do the right thing and give the plaintiffs enough money to do what they must to make their land and lives healthy again. Thank you."

* * *

"I don't know what to say," Greg said, standing on the courthouse steps. He'd flown all night from the dredges of Columbia, South America, to talk about Sherman Todd's letter. Greg was unshaven and disheveled, wearing frayed cut-off shorts, hiking boots, filthy socks and a green cotton shirt with large sweat rings under his armpits. His eyes were red and encased with large black circles. Still, he was gorgeous. I felt my heart grow heavy and my knees grow weak as my stomach started churning with nervousness. So many feelings were fluttering inside me that I felt like an aviary in spring. But my inner aviary had been befouled with deception and in the split second that these feelings twirled around, I found myself falling deep within the pit of anger. And, naturally, that is when my mouth began to function.

"You'd better think of what to say because our relationship is a time bomb and there are landmines every step you take." The words didn't even sound like mine. Greg sunk his face into his hands and remained two steps below me. He didn't speak for at least one minute. I stood there, looking at the scuffmarks on my black heels, wondering how long they'd looked so tattered and why I hadn't noticed. I heard Harry's voice approaching from behind. He was talking with Butch and Beth.

"Greg! You're here!" Beth went running to her first-born's side. She stopped short a few inches, sensing his pain. She turned to look at me, as if I was the one holding the smoking gun and then turned back to him. "What's wrong? Is everything okay?" He pulled his hands away from his face, revealing his tears, which were streaking through the dirt on his face. His tears reminded me of how the ranch looked–sludge sliding through salty earth until reaching a sulfuric river. "What is going on here?" she demanded now. She turned to me. "What have you done to him?"

I was about to defend myself when Harry came to my rescue. "Beth, let's go to lunch. They need to work some things out. Alone." Harry reached for her elbow, to guide her along, but she swung free.

"Beth," Butch said, reaching for her with both hands, "They need to be alone. They're adults–they'll figure it out. Their way. Now come along, honey." Butch gently guided Beth in Harry's direction.

"Take your time," Harry said over his shoulder as he led Butch and Beth down the street. "I'll page your cell if the jury comes back in, but I doubt it will be for at least a few hours. Probably much longer." I stood there, frozen in time, staring at Greg. Cars passed, birds flew and people talked. The camera crew from the local news snapped shots. I didn't care. I reached with my right hand to my left and slowly pulled the ring from my finger. It hurt as it scraped my knuckle, but I didn't notice much. I held the ring in between my index finger and thumb and shoved it in Greg's direction.

"Don't do that, Mac. You don't mean it. I can explain everything. This was all a big misunderstanding. A mistake. A big mistake. You just need to hear me out. Please, please put that back on your finger. At least until you've heard my side of the story. Please?" I shook my head and pushed the ring closer to him. He crossed his arms over his chest.

"Take it. It doesn't belong to me." He refused to grab it, so I let it drop. It made a high-pitched "ping" as it hit the ground and bounced.

It wobbled back and forth a few times before coming to a stop on the courthouse steps between us. We both just stared at the ring for a while. Greg finally reached down and picked it up.

"It's scratched," he said, examining the setting.

"How fitting," I said, "Because so is my heart."

"I'm so sorry. I'm so sorry I've hurt you like this. Take a walk with me, please?" He reached out with his left hand. I didn't take it, but I did follow him across the street to a local park. He led me to a wrought iron bench under a giant elm tree. The bench had a dedication on which it read:

"'Tis the gift to be simple, 'Tis the gift to be free, 'Tis the gift to

Come down where we ought to be. And when we find ourselves

In the place just right, 'Twill be in the valley of love and delight."

He gestured for me to sit. He sat next to me, and leaned forward, resting his elbows on his knees and cupping his hands over his head. He looked like he was taking cover from artillery. His silence was annoying. But even silence has a sound. And a temperature. I felt cold and numb, yet he had sweat breaking through the back of his shirt.

I pictured what he must have looked like as a boy out on the ranch. Running around on the day of branding, making sure that the calves were lined up and ready. I saw him dangling by a rope from the loft of the barn, swinging with freedom and smelling like hay. I pictured him helping Butch fix barbed-wire fences–doing it just right. Following directions closely. I thought of him careening down the Powder River in his makeshift canoe with Wyatt–laughing and trusting that his brother would steer them back to the banks. I thought of him busting through snow banks with his snowmobile. And flying down runs on his skis. And climbing to the highest peak in the wilderness. And catching the biggest fish. My mind took me on his life tour and somehow this journey softened me. His silence was helping his cause. But I was still mad as hell.

"It all started when my mom told me about the will," he said, slowly pulling his head up as he spoke. "I was incredibly angry and felt abandoned and betrayed. It was as if my dad still had the power to take things away from me. So, when I learned that he was the owner of MethZap and that he was drilling out on my parents' ranch, I decided to have a little fun. The first few gunshots I fired were pranks, really. Meant to screw up Rowdy Rodiger's day. When I got called out to South America to track this drug smuggling cartel, I asked Sherman if he'd do me a favor and do a little target practice in my absence. He was supposed to scare off Ace Sanders or anyone else from MethZap that got near the ranch. That's how this how mess started. Simple little game of revenge.

"But after a few weeks of eating nothing but dehydrated food in the jungles of Colombia and crawling on my belly to track down low-life scumbags, the anger took over and I started hating my mom and Butch for not standing by me. They were more worried about losing their ranch to Everett than they were providing for and protecting me. That ate away at me like a maggot on a corpse. So, when I got back to Bogota, I emailed Sherman Todd to pipe it up a notch. Start shooting at my no-good brother who stood to inherit it all. He was the prized son anyway. Their real son. Apparently, my sharp-shooting friend's aim was closer to Chance Baker than to Wyatt, and Chance decided that he wanted nothing to do with the issues my parents had with MethZap.

"When Sherman called me in New Orleans and told me that you were with my dad at the Powder River Basin Resource Council meeting, I snapped. I have no other plausible explanation. I simply snapped. Now they had you too. I told him to take the shot. Just to scare you off. I should've known that it wouldn't work. You don't scare off easily."

He sat up a bit and looked over my way, revealing a very slight but warm smile. "Instead of coming to my senses and realizing that you were following your dream–setting up your own firm and taking on your own first really big case–I sunk down to the level of Everett's debauchery. I guess the apple doesn't fall far from the tree, does it?" The wind had started to pick up and a few leaves from the elm tree floated sideways in the breeze. I watched one leaf slowly traverse its way to the ground, landing softly and silently.

"In the middle of the drug cartel story that I was covering, my boss called me back to New Orleans to edit the final version of my story there. While doing so, I wandered into a witchcraft museum in the French Quarter and read about different ways of poisoning people. It was interesting. I thought it might make for a good story some day. I took some notes.

"Then my boss caught wind of a huge shakedown near Sheridan–one that would blow the pants off most investigative reporters. We'd learned that the cartel from South America had temporarily teamed up with a Mexican cartel, which was using gravestones to smuggle drugs across interstate lines. The cartels got into a war with each other, naturally, over which cartel was entitled to what territory. But what I thought was fascinating about the deal was how the drugs were being smuggled. This was new. And I was snooping it out. But so were you. I was so close to blowing this story out of the water. It would be the career boost I needed to get me the network job. But you were getting in the way."

"How was I getting in the way?"

"You were figuring it out. You found out about Everett Fisher and I figured that you'd thread the needle quickly. You figured out who killed your secretary so fast–and I know how tenacious you are once you get your mind stuck on something."

"So you tried to poison me? Because I might blow your chance at the network job?"

"No. No! Mac, no. That is not how it went down. I just needed you to stay away from it for a few more days. I told Sherman to distract you for a few more days, just so that I could put the finishing touches on my story."

"So you told him to spike my water with poison?"

"No. I told him to leave another note on your car or to hire some protesters or something. I didn't tell him to poison your water."

"Then how did he know how to do it? It's not like ricin is for sale at the local pharmacy."

Greg shuffled his feet in the grass beneath the bench. He took a deep breath and continued. "I might have told him about how just a little bit of the ricin in water might make a person sick for a few days . . . but I didn't tell him to do it to you. I was at his place, helping him load stuff in his car for the cross-country race and we were just shooting the bull. I told him about ricin and gave him a sample. I had no idea he'd spike the race water with the stuff."

"But that doesn't even make sense because Sherman was the story. Why would he agree to shoot at me or threaten me, or whatever other devious plan you had in mind so that you could catch him smuggling drugs? You're not telling me the–"

"I didn't tell Sherman what my case was about. I'm sworn to a confidentiality clause. I just told him that I was about to crack a story wide open. I didn't even know at the time that he was involved in it. I learned about his role that night in the cemetery. I had no idea. I knew about my dad and Rowdy Rodiger. That's all. I was shocked–no stunned–stupefied when I found out that Sherman was involved. But it all made sense later. He agreed to do all this crazy stuff for me without question. Probably because he was high on drugs and he needed the cash that I paid him. Anyway, I'm so sorry. I screwed up, big time. I'm a selfish fool and it's cost me everything. You are my everything."

I sat there on that bench with the breeze in my hair and the sun at my back feeling total isolation. None of it made sense. He paid his best friend cash to scare me away from a story he was covering?

"What I don't get is why you didn't just tell me about the story and tell me to stay away from Rowdy Rodiger. You could have told me something without breaching your confidentiality clause, I'm sure. Instead, you sunk to extreme and ridiculously dangerous measures to keep me away."

"To protect you!"

"Protect me? By shooting at me? Poisoning me? You're more screwed up than I thought." My heart was racing and my anger on the rise. The more I heard him talk, the more offended I became.

"You don't listen to reason, Mac. You're stubborn and bull-headed and you would have tracked down Rowdy Rodiger no matter what I said. I know you. I know your fierce determination. I couldn't risk having you killed by a member of the cartel for being in the wrong place at the wrong time, so I–"

"So you poisoned me." The words hung in the air like a kite with a runaway string.

"No! Please, Mac, you've got to believe me. I didn't poison you. Sherman did. I would never hurt you. Never. I know it's going to take time and I know that I have a lot of ground to make up, but please, tell me you'll work with me. Please tell me that you love me. Please tell me that we can work this through. I want you to be my wife. I want to travel with you and share the dreams that we talked about. I want to have children —"

At that moment, my cell phone vibrated. I flipped it open and read the text message from Harry. It read, "Jury has a question. All counsel are to report back to court." I stood and looked at Greg, still slumped over on the bench. He pulled his wet eyes up to me.

"Please. Don't go. I need to hear you say that we can work this out. I love you more than anything in the world."

I turned and started walking and I didn't look back.

Chapter 56

As I crossed the street to the federal courthouse, I spotted Wyatt on the steps. He held his cowboy hat over his heart and smiled at me. I stopped a step below him. "Howdy, Mac. Don't you look lovely." I thanked him demurely and started to walk toward the entrance. He gently grabbed my arm as I passed him. "What I mean to say is that you are beautiful. And since rumor has it that you and Greg are on the outs, I was wonderin' whether you might be interested in seein' me sometime." I watched him shift the chewing tobacco from one side of his lower lip to the other, awaiting my reply.

"The judge has ordered me back into the courtroom. I need to go," I said.

"Poaching season still open?" I heard Greg yell from across the street. I quickly ran into the courtroom, welcoming the sound of the door closing behind me.

Judge Laird presented us with the jury's questions regarding the damages the plaintiffs might have suffered. The questions were posed in such a way that Harry and I were very hopeful that the jury would find in our favor. But, as class action jury trials often go, it would be a long wait until we got our answer.

Chapter 57

"All rise," the bailiff announced as Judge Bruce Laird entered the courtroom, cloaked in the authority a black robe provides. Butch and Beth clasped their hands together tightly. Harry put his right hand on my shoulder. I was too overwhelmed to fully comprehend the moment. I was still consumed with what had transpired with Greg. I kept mulling over the theme of the lawsuit: Respect. Did Greg respect me? Since he'd chosen his career over my safety–himself over me–I knew that the only thing I should concentrate on now was whether I'd be bankrupt within the next few minutes. I should have been thinking of Butch and Beth and the other forty-eight plaintiffs we represented, but if I told you that is what I was thinking about, it would be a lie. I was thinking of myself and what would happen if we lost this case. "We're back in session. You may be seated. For the record, Ladies and Gentlemen of the Jury, I need to ask you a question. Have you reached your verdict?"

Madam Foreperson stood, her voice shaky. "Yes, we have, your Honor."

"The Clerk of Court is going to do a roll call so that your presence will be reflected on the record. So when you hear your name, please respond with a 'here' or 'present.'" The Clerk called all twelve jurors' names and one by one, they answered. I tried to figure out how each one voted simply by the tone or strength of their voice. It was a pointless exercise, but at least it gave me something to do while my stomach did flip-flops. "Ladies and Gentlemen, if you would pass the verdict form down to the bailiff, he'll bring it up to the court." The jurors passed their special verdict forms to the foreperson who collected them and handed them to the bailiff. I could hear whispers in the gallery. I could hear myself breathing and Harry tapping the table with his fingers. It all happened in slow motion.

"Before I read the special verdict form, I will make my rulings. The class action plaintiffs have sued MethZap for a variety of causes of action, which I will address in due course. They have also sued the Bureau of Land Management and the Army Corps of Engineers for the unlawful issuance of permits for methane operations in violation of the Clean Water Act. The cause of action against both the Bureau of Land Management and the Army Corps of Engineers is a judge question, meaning that I make the ruling on the question of law.

"After careful consideration, I hereby find that the Clean Water Act permit for methane operations in Wyoming is illegal. The unlawful permit has allowed methane operators to dump millions of gallons of polluted water into the Powder River and its tributaries. Quite frankly, I am amazed and saddened that the Army Corps of Engineers has issued these rather expansive permits without considering their respective impact on landowners, ranchers and Wyoming's natural environment. Due to these permits, ranchers have had their lands flooded, their water rights eliminated and their fields poisoned. The Corps and the Bureau of Land Management have failed to consider cumulative impacts that multiple reservoirs have had on non-wetland resources. Furthermore, both the BLM and the Corps have failed to consider the impacts to private ranchers. Mineral resources should be developed responsibly, keeping in mind those other values that are so important to the people of Wyoming, such as preservation of Wyoming's unique natural heritage and lifestyle. This Court will not rubberstamp an agency determination that fails to consider cumulative impacts, fails to realistically assess impacts to ranchlands, and relies on unsupported, unmonitored mitigation measures. As a result of this ruling, operators cannot build new dams and reservoirs until the Corps corrects its permit approval process.

Therefore, on behalf of the class of plaintiffs herein represented by the law firm of Harrison and MacIntosh, I hereby find that the BLM and the Corps each compensate each plaintiff twenty-five thousand dollars, for a total of fifty thousand dollars to each plaintiff."

Harry patted me hard on the back and leaned in, "Two point five million. Not bad."

"With respect to the special verdict forms, they will have to be read into the record one by one. There is a special verdict for each individual plaintiff."

We'd won. By that statement, I knew that we'd won. I didn't know how much and for some reason it didn't really matter for the moment. The fact that I'd dedicated over a year to this lawsuit made me feel like it was worthwhile. I stopped thinking so much about myself in that moment, and felt proud for Butch and Beth. They deserved to win.

Judge Laird continued to read the verdict into the record. "The special verdict form in the case of William "Butch" Anderson and Beth Anderson versus MethZap submitted by this federal district court in Casper reads as follows:

> "We, the jury duly impaneled in the above-captioned cause, hereby find the following answers to the questions presented to the Court: Did MethZap breach the Surface Damage Agreement with Plaintiffs Butch and Beth Anderson? Answer, yes. Did any breach of contract found directly cause damage to the Andersons or their property? Answer, yes. Did MethZap engage in conduct breaching the implied covenant of good faith and fair dealing contained in the Surface Damage Agreement? Answer, yes. Did any breach of the implied covenant of good faith and fair dealing directly cause damage to the Andersons or their property? Answer, yes. Did MethZap commit fraud in the inducement with regard to the Surface Damage Agreement? Answer, yes. Did any fraud directly cause damage to the Andersons or their property? Answer, yes.
>
> "Determination of Damages: What amount of money do you find would fairly compensate the Andersons for the following elements of damage relating to any breach of contract or breach of the implied covenant of good faith and fair-dealing or fraud? Answer, One million four hundred eighty-nine thousand dollars. What amount of money do you find would fairly punish MethZap for its

reprehensible behavior towards the Andersons? Answer,
Seven hundred twenty-five thousand dollars."

The verdicts for the rest of the plaintiffs were read into the record. MethZap would owe the class of plaintiffs a combined sum of over thirty million dollars. The sum was mind-boggling.

"Ladies and Gentlemen of the Jury, thank you very much for your attentiveness during the course of this trial. Any system of justice is only as good as the people that support it. And America has the greatest legal system in the world. I really appreciate your efforts. I hope you've learned something about the court system. It's not like you see on TV, is it? Let me also explain something to you. You need not answer to anyone as to your verdict or your reasons for it. Whether you talk to the attorneys or anyone about the case at this point is your own decision. It's not necessarily improper for an attorney, for example, to call you up and say, hey, you know, would you mind talking with me about what went on, because sometimes that's how they learn about their craft. But you're not required to discuss it. If someone persists in trying to discuss the case with you over your objection, I would like you to report it to my office or the sheriff's office immediately so we can find out what's going on, because it's a hard enough job without having to take any guff.

"I should also instruct you that due to your service on this case you are discharged from further jury service during this term of court as a matter of law." The jurors gave a collective applause.

Harry and I gave Butch and Beth each a big hug. They looked so relieved and proud that they'd accomplished their goal. As we gathered our graphs and charts and trial notebooks, they spoke of how important it was to ensure that the money was used to protect the land.

Dunne was collecting his trial exhibits, shoving them haphazardly into boxes. I went over to the defendants' table and extended my right hand. "You are a good lawyer, Mr. Dunne. It has been a real pleasure—"

"Get over yourself. It has not been a pleasure, Ms. MacIntosh. And you can wipe that shitty grin off your smug face, because the pleasure is going to be all mine when I take this case up on appeal."

Amused by this comment, Harry sauntered over and gave me a "high five." "She's one hell of a lawyer, isn't she?" Harry said to Dunne. "I'm giving her a little vacation time next week, so I'll have my secretary send you instructions as to how your client can pay us."

With that, Harry shoved a box of documents in my hands and nudged me toward the door. Dunne's response was drowned out by the shouts of reporters throwing questions at us from all angles as we left the courthouse.

Butch and Beth were beside themselves as they exited the courtroom into a flashing mob scene of reporters thrusting microphones in their faces. They were polite, as always, in giving interviews. I kept hearing the phrases, "We are stewards of the land," and "It's not about the money, but we'll take it to clean up the ranch." I was very happy for them.

Chapter 58

Harry and Pamela helped me clean out our hotel rooms. There were notepads and diagrams and papers everywhere. It would take a week just to sort through the junk. As I glanced out the window of my hotel room, I could see Greg waiting by my car.

"Now that you can afford a nice vacation, do you have any plans?" Harry asked me as I balanced a box on one knee while pushing the elevator button with my elbow.

"Paris, perhaps. Or London. They sound inviting."

"They sound romantic. Will you be taking anyone along?"

I thought about the question for a few seconds. I didn't know. I'd need some time to think things over and put them back on the shelves from which they'd fallen. "Probably not, Harry. Maybe I'll get lucky and meet someone new while visiting art galleries and sipping wine near the Seine. Hopefully, the French haven't polluted their rivers."

"They're all polluted some, Mac. You just have to find one that's clean enough and that ebbs and flows in the same direction you're heading. Have you found one like that?" Harry asked as the elevator door opened.

I looked at Greg, who was holding the hotel lobby door open for me. "No, I don't think I've found one yet. Guess it's time to throw my line back in."

"You'll have to bait your own hook this time."

"I'm well aware of that, Harry. Sorry to say, but I'm well aware."

Greg followed me to my car and tried to convince me to join him for a drink–to talk things over. I refused. I told him that I needed time and space. Greg didn't want to give me either, but he reluctantly agreed and left.

As I shoved the last box in the back hatch to my Equinox, I noticed that Wyatt was standing three feet away from my car. "Mind if I hitch a ride?" he asked.

I threw him my keys. "I'm exhausted. You drive."

Books by Maureen Anne Meehan

Dying to Ski, a Mary MacIntosh novel
Snake River Secret, a Mary MacIntosh novel
Powder River Poison, a Mary MacIntosh novel
Pandemic Predator, a Mary MacIntosh novel
Poisoned by Proxy, a Mary MacIntosh novel
The Five, a Mary MacIntosh novel
Rodeo, a Mary MacIntosh novel
60 Dates in Six Months (with a Broken Neck)
Push You Away
Let Me Be

ABOUT THE AUTHOR

Maureen Anne Meehan received her bachelor's and master's degrees in education before becoming a lawyer. She lives with her family in Southern California, where she is a mental health judge and crafts legal thrillers, as well as nonfiction dating satire.